MW01674616

WOLF HUNT

Wolf Hunt Book One

RJ BLAIN

WOLF HUNT

WOLF HUNT BOOK ONE

BY RJ BLAIN

What should have been a preliminary scouting job for a future art heist turns into Declan McGrady's worst nightmare when he discovers the gallery's owner has exotic—and live—tastes. Breaking a group of werewolf women out of a hostage situation is above his pay grade, but he's left with no choice.

Worse, what he doesn't know might kill him—and dump him back into the world of black ops at the cost of his freedom or his life.

Copyright © 2018 by RJ Blain

All rights reserved.

No part of this book may be reproduced in any form or by any electronic or mechanical means, including information storage and retrieval systems, without written permission from the author, except for the use of brief quotations in a book review.

Cover Art by Rebecca Frank (Bewitching Book Covers)

To Elric,

Rest well.

~StabbyStabby

Chapter One

I'D SOLD my dignity for half a million dollars, and I regretted it.

At least I'd been smart enough to insist my client pay in advance for the preparations required to storm the castle, including the arrangements for the yacht and its captain, and I believed the captain had ulterior motives.

Benjamin Scully's offers to handle all of my transportation to and from his property stirred my suspicions. Unfortunately, old habits died hard, and I refused to drop my guard, aware anyone might be an enemy waiting to backstab me.

Scully's castle perched on a cliff somewhere along the coast of France but belonged in Transylvania. All I needed to creep me right out of my skin was a good shake of thunder and a flash of lightning.

Fortunately for me, the skies were clear, the day was young, and the ocean was calm.

Swimming back to America sounded like a better and better idea. But no, instead of turning around and heading home like a smart man, I straightened my back, lifted my chin, and stepped over the ledge of the yacht, lifting my skirts and showing off my ankles and three-inch heels so I wouldn't trip over the hem.

"Mademoiselle." The man wearing a black suit at the end of the dock greeted me with a smile and held out his arm for me.

I had a mile-long list of things a lady didn't do, which was partnered with the substantially shorter and a lot less entertaining list of things ladies did do. Going over my mental checklist, I flashed the man a smile, accepted his help, and stepped with care so I wouldn't fall into the ocean.

"Thank you," I murmured. I longed to call him a cantankerous spotted liver, but cursing at the servant of the obnoxiously wealthy American playing a French lord was on the list of things a lady didn't do.

If I wanted my half a million, I needed to play my role perfectly, and that meant no one could learn who I really was or why I was scoping out a French castle.

"His Lordship is waiting for you, Mademoiselle Lenore. I trust you had a pleasant journey?"

Engaging in polite conversation was on the list of things a lady did do and sighing wasn't, which left me with the option to smile until my jaw ached. I'd spent a month practicing pitching my voice and sounding as feminine as possible.

It was a good thing I was a tenor.

"It was lovely, thank you."

Lovely wasn't the word I'd use for the transatlantic cruise from New York City to Hamburg, Germany. Who could've predicted that a late-season hurricane would unexpectedly wander into the North Atlantic and cause trouble?

Reenacting the sinking of the Titanic topped my list of things never to do again. At least the cruise ship had waited until *after* the storm had blown over to give up the ghost and sink to the bottom of the Atlantic.

Instead of having a week to prepare, I had had a day to perform and execute a modern-day blitzkrieg through Hamburg and transform into Cinderella. At least my heels weren't glass, though I would've given anything to have a pair of my preferred boots instead.

What had I been thinking when I had accepted the job to gain access to a French castle and take notes and pictures of the owner's collection? Why had I thought it was a good idea to do it in a *dress*?

Why hadn't I talked myself out of the plan in the two months I'd spent earning my mark's favor?

I'd sold my dignity for far too little, and if I wasn't careful, I'd sacrifice my reputation right along with the remnants of my morals. It'd been difficult enough to smile while other men tried to take me to bed, and I hoped I never heard another catcall aimed at me. As it was, the leering stares of the marina workers were permanently seared into my memories.

I really needed a new plan. I needed a new life, too. Half a million dollars would go a long way towards accomplishing that, at least. I had five hundred thousand reasons to smile, pretend my name was Lenore Faraday instead of Declan McGrady, and act like I admired and respected Lord Benjamin Scully, businessman and collector of unusual art.

"Please call me Barnet, mademoiselle." The man's soft voice dragged me back to my miserable reality. I'd somehow navigated the dock on autopilot without tripping over the uneven planks or breaking an ankle.

One thing was certain: I had a whole new appreciation for the effort women went through to dress up. It took me an hour to prepare for a black-tie event, but it had taken me almost five hours to become Lenore—five hours I never wanted to repeat.

"Of course, Barnet. I'm quite grateful Lord Scully had the time to see me."

"He is always eager to meet another lover of the arts. Please, come this way. The lift is waiting."

The lift was the sort of thing I expected to crumble into the sea right along with the rest of the cliff and the castle. If I'd been offered the option of steps, I would've taken them in a heartbeat. At least that way, if I fell to my death, I'd only have myself to blame.

"Do not worry. The lift is quite safe."

Barnet's scent soured from his lie, but I didn't call him on it. I had bigger problems to worry about, including my first face-to-face meeting with Benjamin Scully.

The game was on, and it had been far too long since my last hunt.

LORD BENJAMIN SCULLY, an American businessman with a crooked nose, met me at the top, opened the curved door of the lift, and gestured for me to step out onto the deck stretching out over the cliff. "Miss Lenore, it's a pleasure to meet you at long last."

"The pleasure is mine," I assured him, hoping my perfume masked the annoyance in my scent should he also be some form of supernatural. He didn't smell like a werewolf. My mother had been a witch, and it was only a matter of time before I ran into someone with a better-than-human sense of smell. I fought the urge to bare my teeth, growl, and ram my fist into the earth-vexing coxcomb's face.

Instead, I smiled and met his gaze. The photographs I'd been given of my mark matched the man, right down to the streaks of gray in his hair, his black suit with white shirt and black tie, and his frown. He looked me over head to toe before his gaze settled on my fake breasts.

Was I the only one who noticed the uncomfortable silence? Scully seemed enthralled by my breasts, blissfully unaware I was one hundred percent man underneath my sky blue, puffy, and frilly dress.

My breasts were a work of art; the artificial silicon insets attached to the bra digging into my shoulders, which pushed them up and gave them the right amount of jiggle to look and feel real enough to give me a solid case of the creeps.

Fortunately, my dubious non-quite-human heritage put me on the lean and almost feminine side. Lazing about had trimmed my muscle to something a little closer to a lady's build, although my two months of planning and preparation hadn't been enough.

The puffy sleeves on my gown, a monstrosity straight out of the Elizabethan era, hid the evidence of my masculinity well enough while offering a certain measure of protection from the fall chill.

It had seemed like a good idea at the time. A French Castle with an American playing at being nobility called for appropriate attire. I wanted to blame alcohol for my poor decision, but I didn't drink.

Alcohol made me do really stupid things. I did enough stupid things without any help.

Two months of planning had led to meeting the businessman and collector in his castle where he kept his prized collection. I shifted the straps of my purse on my shoulder, wondering how women dealt with the annoyance of carrying one day in and day out.

I was never going to take a woman's preparations for granted ever again. I wouldn't dress up as a woman again, either, especially not after experiencing the horrors of having my beard and mustache waxed off to make certain they didn't make an untimely appearance at five o'clock.

While my mark's quiet scrutiny annoyed me, I passed the time studying the grounds in front of the castle; a hundred yards of lush lawn separated the building from the cliff. The main structure rose seven stories, although the spires decorating each corner towered twice as high.

"Like what you see?" Lord Scully linked his elbow with mine and gave a gentle pull in the direction of the castle. "Please, let me give you a tour. You have no idea how honored I am that you would travel all of this way to see my art collection."

"No, Lord Scully, I'm the one honored." It took all of my will to keep my voice as high-pitched and feminine as possible. "Yours is a collection any true lover of the arts would wish to see in their lifetime. Thank you so much for your invitation."

I smiled. Under the guise of slipping his hand to my back, Lord Benjamin Scully copped a feel of my ass, and it took every bit of my willpower to keep my wolf in check. I'd make the human pay for it somehow.

My client never said I couldn't pocket something from the slug's collection. He'd get their half a million worth of photographs. If I took a little extra on the side that didn't show up in the pictures, well, what he didn't know wouldn't hurt him.

THE MONET PAINTING HANGING in the foyer drew my eye, and I stared at it, my mouth gaping open as I took in every inch of its splendor. The vivid colors and distinctive strokes drew me to it, and Lord Benjamin Scully made a pleased noise in his throat when I stepped to it, my heels clicking on the marble floors.

I knew every public Monet like the back of my hand; rare pieces of art made me forget myself, filling me with a fidgeting excitement and desire to possess one of my own.

The style was distinctly Monet, and I got as close to the painting as I could without breathing on the canvas and potentially ruining it. I narrowed my eyes, drew in a deep breath, and focused my attention on the scents in my nose.

An unpleasant heat tainted Scully's scent;

lust and arousal coming from him were the last things I wanted to face, ever. I had a feeling the man-harpy scoped out my ass since he could no longer enjoy my breasts.

My wolf whined in my head, voicing his desire to come out and rip the human's face off for daring to admire my human body in such a way. He wanted to find us a proper mate, a woman who would remain with us for the rest of our life.

The businessman wasn't even on my wolf's radar, for which I was eternally grateful.

I filtered out the man's scent and focused on the painting, searching for the non-visual cues it was a fake, and I found it in the fresh bite of oil paints. Over time, the scent of the paints changed as time did its work. Sometimes paintings were restored, renewed to their original glory, but the thought of anyone diluting the splendor of an original Monet made me shiver.

I examined the brush strokes, appreciating the care the impersonator had taken mimicking Monet's style. Close, but not quite his. Drawing closer, I took another sniff.

New paint and thinner taunted my nose, further adding to my disappointment.

I stepped back, narrowed my eyes, and examined the forest and stream scene, the vivid colors, and the wistfulness I always associated with a real Monet. Sighing my regret, I canted my head in Lord Benjamin

Scully's direction and said, "Someone studied Monet's style and created a piece worthy of him. It is such a shame it's not a true Monet."

Instead of the anger I expected from the man, he laughed. The sound grated on my nerves, and my wolf growled his discontent in my head. "I remembered your love of Monet. Forgive an old man's testing. It is rare to find a true collector of the arts."

"You're hardly old."

He chuckled again. "You are charming, my dear, but I am fifty to your twenty-three."

I blamed my werewolf heritage for my ability to trick people into believing I was so young. I clasped my hands in front of me, fiddling with the band circling my right ring finger. Six different cameras sewn into my gown, set to photograph images in twenty second intervals, gave me complete coverage of my surroundings. Another camera, embedded in a hair clip near my ear, recorded everything, although due to data limitations, I'd have to pull the intel off its internal memory chip after the job. My ring also hid a camera, and I aimed it in the direction of the fake Monet before tapping the sensor at the bottom of the band.

"It's a really good fake, I'll give you that, Lord Scully."

"Please, call me Benjamin, Lenore. You do not mind me calling you Lenore, do you?"

I minded in more ways than one, but I

smiled so I wouldn't growl at the man. "I don't mind."

It was a damned good thing my perfume reeked and Lord Benjamin Scully smelled like a regular human, else he might've detected the sourness of my lies in the air.

I would need to squirt myself with more of the wretched perfume in my purse to get through the rest of day at the rate things were going. I didn't need another werewolf coming along and figuring out I was poking my nose in places it didn't belong.

Lesson learned: half a million dollars was not worth the job I had to do at the French version of Castle Dracula. I turned in a slow circle to take in the rest of the art hanging from the wood-paneled walls. Most of the pieces seemed modern with a focus on spring landscapes, each boasting a bronze placard declaring its artist and origin.

Once again, I was left to my devices while the castle's owner watched me with an unnerving amount of lust stinking up the air. I hadn't even made it out of the castle's foyer, and I wanted to heed my wolf's instincts to run for another country.

I didn't recognize any of the artists in the foyer, although I liked a few of them. I took pictures, careful to make sure my ring's gem would capture painting and placard.

Hopefully the chandeliers would offer enough light for the paintings to show in the digital images.

"What do you think of them, Lenore?"

"The spring theme is welcoming; cool yet warm. These are modern pieces. A choice to showcase the blend of antiquity and modern interests?"

With half a million dollars, I could retire and become an interior decorator. Interior decorating could be lucrative, couldn't it? It sounded substantially safer than being stalked around a castle by a perverted marmot.

Killing my mark wasn't an option. My wolf wasn't too happy with me over that, but he didn't fight me, either. We'd come to a few agreements on things over the years, including who—and what—we hunted. Humans weren't on the allowed list of edibles.

He wasn't too happy with me about that, either, and his growls filled my head.

Lord Benjamin Scully sighed, came to my side, and placed his hand on the middle of my back. "I have more exotic tastes, but such things are expected of a man of my position."

I wondered if a high heel could pierce through a man's dress shoe if I stomped hard enough. "Of course. There are always expectations. Perhaps they don't have the exotic allure of a Monet, but they are still lovely pieces."

"Paris is full of amateurs capable of decent pieces. I am looking for something more."

"Like an original Monet?"

"Exactly. I intend to fill these halls with an original of all of the masters."

The man had expensive tastes, I had to give him that. "An ambitious goal, and a very expensive one. Have you had any success yet?"

"I've acquired a few pieces," he evaded, and the lust in his scent faded under new odors.

Wariness. Anxiety. Something else lingered in the air, too, something my wolf couldn't identify.

The foyer opened to a large room featuring two staircases sweeping up to the next floor. Statues lined the walls, and my eyes widened. Busts and full-figured women, likely Roman in origin, lined the walls to my left and right. Deeper within the room, the pieces became more modern, right up until the staircase landings, which showcased metal abstract art.

Iron ore littered the floor, forming a mountain at the base of an eruption of steel and other pale metals.

A shudder ran through me. Pure, unrefined iron never failed to chill me to the bone, the scent of it singeing my nose and deadening my senses. My wolf whined. With so much of the metal in close proximity, I couldn't transform into my wolf even if I wanted to.

Silver hurt worse, but the presence of pure iron sapped me of strength, leaving me shaking as its influence reached across the marble floors and seeped into my skin.

"Vesuvius," Scully murmured, gesturing to the sculpture at the base of the staircase. "I have always been intrigued by the fall of Pompeii and Herculaneum. The rusting iron represents the fires of the eruption."

Someone had put a lot of thought into the piece; the red of iron oxidation would streak the ore in time, turning the clean and new piece into true art as it decayed. "Its true beauty will be exposed over the years."

I appreciated brilliant art. I regretted the iron, its size, and the fact it wouldn't fit under my skirts, because I wanted to steal the entire sculpture and watch it decay over the years, the decades, and the centuries until the iron bled away to dust.

"You like it?" Surprise in the man's voice drew my attention back to him.

For the first time since my arrival, my smile made way for a grin. "I appreciate history as well as art, and this is both."

I wanted to steal it so much my fingers itched. Instead, I spun to face the first of the ancient statues. "Is everything in this room of Roman origin, then?"

"I had no idea you were so interested in the origin of things, Lenore."

Snorting wasn't on my allowed list, and neither was snapping my teeth, growling, or punching. I sighed. "I enjoy reading."

"An appropriate pursuit for a lady."

"I'm a traditional lady in a modern world," I murmured, turning my back to him so I could restrain my wolf's growing desire for bloodshed. Taking my time, I captured pictures of every statue, although I didn't linger long in front of any of them.

I gave Vesuvius a wide berth. All it would do was burn me.

Chapter Two

I LUSTED for the authentic Van Gogh painting in the same way its owner lusted for me. *Girl in the Woods* went from private collection to private collection, and now that it was within my grasp, there was absolutely nothing I could do about it.

I hated my life.

The painting enthralled me with the same dark spell as the full moon, and its spirit sang to me and my wolf. The gentle strokes, transforming the scene into something both ethereal and real, reminded me—and my wolf—of what we lacked.

Somewhere in the world was a girl in the woods, one who would become our mate, and the painting captured our solitude through the years. Over a decade ago, my wolf and I had written off finding a mate, retreating to a secluded cabin for the winter months until it was safe to emerge in the spring. We roamed the world in search of something more substantial than a wolf's mating rut.

I sighed, took a picture of the painting, and stepped back, shaking my head to clear it of my regrets. "This is a true jewel of your collection. An authentic Van Gogh. I'm impressed."

"I have another Van Gogh."

"Another?" I turned to face him, careful of my heels, which were killing my toes and ankles. "Which one?"

A predatory edge marred the man's smile. "Guess. One guess. Should you get it correct, I will give you that painting—the original *Girl in the Woods.* If you fail to guess correctly, you will remain here for two weeks as my guest to spend time getting to know me."

I narrowed my eyes, the challenge riling my wolf. "Van Gogh had approximately two thousand paintings. I don't have two weeks to spend here at the current time."

"Make the two weeks," he demanded. "An original Van Gogh is worth the risk. Surely you do not have anything of importance to do, Lenore? You are young and wealthy."

"I have a business to run," I hissed through clenched teeth, burning my mental checklist of things ladies didn't do.

My wolf approved.

Lord Benjamin Scully smirked. "Do you? Do not think you can trick me. You are not a business woman. You are an heiress with a love of art. Two weeks to explore and examine everything in this castle is your dream come true."

If I spent two weeks in the same castle with the illiterate fribble pretending he had the cunning of a wolf, there would be bodies. If I indulged in my desire to rip out the businessman's throat, my life would be the second to end as predator became prey.

Other monsters lurked in the dark places of the world, and I had lived for so long by slipping beneath their radar. I didn't know the name of the organization, but I knew enough. If I killed a regular human, they'd hunt me. They'd discover my existence, and I would die.

My mother's warnings had been clear, branded into me with her dying breath.

They'd killed her for killing a human, and as her life had bled out of her, she'd confessed her crimes as a witch. Then she'd told me to run, and I had, leaving her body to rot in the woods.

I had returned twenty years after her death. No one had found her, and no one else had cared. The moss had covered her bones, but it hadn't taken much to dislodge the little covering her skull.

Lord Benjamin Scully cleared his throat, demanding an answer.

"Tomorrow, I have a conference call with a client in Rome. Friday, I have an investment meeting with a bank in Switzerland. I'm already booked for my return trip to the

United States." My voice took on a toneless neutrality, the voice I reserved for business transactions. "Upon my return to New York, I'll begin negotiations for a new property."

I had spent too long at the cabin deep in the mountains of West Virginia. I needed a new place, somewhere farther away from people, somewhere with more plentiful prey.

Five winters of hunting had thinned my woods, and I needed a new territory.

"You're seriously invested?"

I fiddled with my ring and took another photograph of the Van Gogh before turning to admire the rest of the paintings in the room. The Van Gogh was the only famous painting in the lot, and most dated within the past forty years.

Counterfeiters and frauds topped my list of annoyances as someone who relocated pieces of fine art out from under the noses of their custodians. However, the castle filled with false promises and lies made its way towards the number one spot. Instead of snarling my frustration, I kept on smiling, moving away from Van Gogh's *Girl in the Woods* to photograph the remaining pictures in the room.

"There is a reason it took me so long to come to your castle. It takes time to step away from business affairs, as you are well aware. Tomorrow, I work. I don't have two weeks to spare for you, Lord Scully. The painting is beautiful, but it is a gamble I can't afford."

Tomorrow, not only would I go through every picture I took, I'd create a catalog for my buyer in preparation for the conference call meant to secure my half a million dollars.

The Van Gogh would be my primary bargaining chip to ensure my client paid up in full for the job, although I didn't expect any problems.

I'd worked for the client before, and he had paid without issue. While the catalog would streamline things, I earned an extra fifty thousand on the deal by allowing them instant access to the files.

They likely looked over them as I wandered the gallery, assuming I had cellular signal in the castle.

Scully cleared his throat again to catch my attention away from the paintings. "I see. Humor me, then. Guess what my second Van Gogh painting is, without reward or consequence."

"What else would partner with *Girl in the Woods* than *Girl in White in the Woods*? They were painted in the same year. If you were a true collector, you would have three, reuniting them with *Edge of a Wood*." I shrugged, masking the taps of my finger against my ring by holding my hands together in front of me. Step by step, photo by photo, I explored the gallery.

"You're exquisite."

"Your collection is impressive. One of the more comprehensive collections of modern art I've seen in a long time, with a few special older works to add spice and flavor to your gallery." My wolf growled at me for daring to compliment the jolt-head, but I ignored him. "Do you have works other than paintings and sculptures?"

"Of course. Do you want to see them?"

"Please." I took the opportunity to dig my hand into my purse and pull out my phone, checking the time. "I have three hours before I need to leave. I'd truly like to see the entirety of your collection before I must go."

"I was hoping you'd reconsider and stay for dinner."

"I can't, but your invitation is appreciated. Perhaps another time. It was difficult arranging my schedule as it is."

"It wouldn't do for anyone to miss you. I was unaware of your…business engagements."

"I lead a very private life."

"A private and non-existent one, Lenore." Snorting, Scully stepped between me and the painting I'd been examining. "Why is it I can't find you or any of your business associates on the internet?"

I arched a brow. I'd expected the man to search into my background; any wise and wealthy man checked before inviting someone to a place holding a fortune of fine art. "I work in acquisitions, Mr. Scully. Advertising my role in business activities would be the equivalent to shooting myself in the foot. I work on behalf of certain companies to handle negotiations they don't want made public. Exposing myself on the internet would be foolish."

"And when you make these acquisitions, you do not introduce yourself as Lenore Faraday, do you?"

I made a show of checking through my messages, making thoughtful noises. All of the photographs I'd taken had already uploaded while the remainder were queued for uploading. Pleased with the castle's signal strength and speed, I stowed my cell into my purse. For such a quick connection, Scully had a cell tower installed specifically for his use. "You're a quick study. I like my life private, the same way I like my art collections."

"Is that so?"

The man's audacity to coo in my ear ignited my fury. I tensed. Killing the lord of the castle wasn't an option. I dredged up my charred mental list of things ladies didn't do. Slapping him was out, although feminine enough for a replacement to driving my fist into his gut. Kneeing him in the groin wasn't completely off my list; if he even thought about touching me, I'd crunch his family jewels and find out if a werewolf could actually survive a swan dive off a cliff into the ocean.

"I'm a traditional lady in a modern world," I said again, the habit of neutrality saving me from deepening my voice or growling at the man I wanted to murder.

THE SO-CALLED artifacts collection was so small I was torn between mocking laughter and groaning at the torment of dealing with a private collection belonging to someone convinced counterfeit arrowheads classified as *artifacts.* While ignorant about Native American pieces, I believed every piece in the glass case was a fake.

I took pictures anyway.

My wolf growled his hatred of me in my head, and I swore to a good run as soon as I finalized the purchase of the most remote cabin in the woods I could find.

My bribe shut him up for a while.

"Is Native American not to your taste, Miss Faraday?"

"I prefer Egyptian," I murmured. I preferred anything that got me through the rest of the castle without its owner copping another feel.

Did all women feel like meat? I was tempted to check my ass for a price tag, wondering just how cheap of a slattern he thought I was.

"I have a couple of Egyptian pieces, but not much. They're, unfortunately, in the storage gallery."

Hello, bait. "Storage gallery?"

"It's where I keep my unsorted pieces, much like a museum curating new exhibits or retiring old pieces."

Hello, hook, line, and sinker. I needed just a tiny taste. It couldn't hurt me too much, could it? What art collector wouldn't go into a lustful frenzy over the idea of going into the unsorted, unpolished collection?

I didn't need to feign excitement. Unsorted, dusty places with hidden treasures got me in trouble each and every time. "I'd really like to see the Egyptian pieces, even if they're in storage. The good Egyptian pieces are never close enough to truly appreciate."

Or steal.

I'd stolen things from all across the world, but I'd never stolen something from Egypt, not even a single copper *deben*. With my luck, he'd have a silver *deben,* ensuring I couldn't get within ten feet of it without breaking into a rash, one that would stain my dress the black of tarnish.

"If we have time."

If I wanted to maintain my stance and get all of the pictures I could, I'd have to speed up my pace without being obvious about it. I grinned at the aspect of a challenge, kept my hands clasped in front of me, and went from piece to piece, tapping my ring in front of each one.

I asked questions about the pieces, dodged him groping me more times than I wanted to think about, and counted down the minutes to freedom and my payout.

HUNDREDS OF PHOTOGRAPHS LATER, Lord Benjamin Scully led me into paradise. His storage gallery held a wealth of wrapped paintings, curio cabinets loaded with antiques, and crates upon crates covered in dust. The collector in me wanted to turn on the man and defenestrate him for neglecting so many fine pieces.

"This is amazing." How could anyone put all of the best pieces in a filthy room and leave the truly spectacular things to rot away, hidden from those who might appreciate it?

The castle was owned by a lunatic. That was the only explanation.

The source of my anger and disgust made a show of checking his watch. "Twenty minutes isn't a long time, but please feel free to explore if that suits you. I wouldn't want to make you late for your business engagements."

"I appreciate you showing me your gallery, Mr. Scully. It's been fascinating." I turned to the curio cabinets, half of which were open, leaving the pieces within exposed to dust and other contaminants. I wanted to steal everything I could get my hands on just to free them from the man's abuse, but I ignored my itching fingers and went to work.

A phone rang, but the ring tone wasn't mine. Scully frowned, dug into his pocket, and pulled out a slender cell. Sighing, he excused himself and headed into the other room.

Learning to identify valuable pieces at a glance was part of my job as a thief, and while I listened to the man talk in the hallway, I took advantage of the time to look over his goods, take photographs, and satisfy the urge to make off with something on the side.

Anyone who treated antiques and art with such disregard didn't deserve any of it, and if I could have run off with the entire store room, I would have. The dust made my nose itch, which suited me just fine. With one strong sneeze, I could stir up enough dust to cover the fact I'd made off with something from the collection.

While most of the curio cabinets were located near the door, I found one hidden away near the back wall of the room. Unlike the others, it lacked a door, leaving the items within to the mercy of the room's dust collection. My curiosity got the better of me, and I squeezed through the gaps in the crates, pausing to photograph everything except the cabinet that had captured my attention.

A glint of gold caught my eye, pulling my attention to a black and silver urn of Anubis. The gleam of metal drew me closer, and I leaned to peek behind the urn. Lapis lazuli partnered with turquoise, carnelian, and amethyst formed the shape of a scarab beetle set into a golden bracelet, which was more of a hinged cuff designed to be worn by a prominent man of Egyptian society. Unlike most of the other things in the storage, it was free of dust, reflecting the room's dim illumination.

The scarab held a high standing in ancient Egyptian society, the representation of Khepri, the morning aspect of Ra, the Sun God. Historians and artisans could spend a lifetime wondering about the meanings of the colors and choices of the stones for the bracelet, but I liked the simple meaning the best.

Lapis lazuli, blue speckled with flakes of gold, represented the starry sky lightening under the influence of the rising sun while the amethyst and carnelian edging the scarab spoke of the promise of a vibrant sunrise. The gold of a new sun bound it all together.

"Yellow-bellied titmouse," I breathed, torn between horror and shock anyone could abandon something so spectacular. The urn of Anubis it hid behind was no slacker in the ancient relic department, either.

Werewolves had a certain association with the Egyptian god of death; once, Anubis had been linked to the golden jackal, but scientists had undermined the mythos with genetic testing.

I shared similarities with the African golden wolf, Anubis's new animal avatar, except they were prettier and a lot more normal than I could ever hope to be.

To reach the bracelet, I needed to move the urn, which contained enough silver inlaid on its black surface to singe my nose. I sighed, contemplating how I'd thieve away the bracelet before the creepy lord of the castle finished his phone call and stole away my chance to make off with a grab of a lifetime.

If I wanted the bracelet, I'd risk getting burned. Sighing my resignation, I pushed up the sleeves of my dress and reached for my prize.

The scarab had ideas of its own, and fluttering its lapis lazuli wings, it sprung at me, flying into my face and driving me back. I bumped into a crate, and yipping my astonishment, I crashed into the wall.

The wall also had ideas of its own. Instead of holding my weight and giving me something to brace against so I could make my escape, it opened. I staggered back several steps, falling through a doorway. The scarab fluttered in front of my eyes, blinding me with flashes of blue and gold.

Its glow intensified to a shimmering radiance, and the bracelet clicked, its hinges opening. I lifted my right arm to deflect, hopping back another step to avoid touching the animated, ancient jewelry.

My heel caught on a step, and with a startled cry, my foot slipped out from under me. I pinwheeled my arms for balance, my left hand slapping against a smooth stone wall without finding purchase.

The way back into the storage room slid closed in silence, leaving me alone with the shining scarab. It latched onto my right wrist, and the golden bands snapped closed over my skin before its light winked out.

I fell down the curving stone steps into darkness.

Chapter Three

THE BEEP of an incoming message roused me, and I batted at the annoying device in the hopes of silencing the damned thing forever. Its proximity to my ear hurt, painful enough to penetrate through the pounding in my head.

My phone pinged again.

Stifling a groan, I grabbed for the device, and my fingers closed over the leather of my handbag. Every muscle in my body tensed, and a split second later, my nerves reported there was absolutely nothing right about anything.

My yip echoed around me and was answered by silence. Shuddering, I cracked open an eye to enjoy a close up view of a dusty stone floor. The blood rushed to my head, and I inhaled my alarm, resulting in a nose full of dust and dirt. Sneezes tore through me, and pain zapped through my back all the way up to my toes.

I forced open my second eye. Tumbling headfirst down a staircase was a good way to get killed, and I marveled I still lived while my arms and legs twitched and spasmed.

"Fly bitten bilge rat," I hissed through clenched teeth, squirming on the staircase to make a grab for my phone, which had miraculously remained in my bag where it belonged. The scent of dried blood—mine—warned me the staircase had likely won more battles than it had lost.

Once I had my phone in my hand, I braced for the pain of my stupidity, and rolled onto my back. My hips, legs, and feet were above me on the staircase. One of the high heels was missing, and while the other one was still on my foot, the heel had snapped in half. In the darkness, my eyes didn't perceive color quite as well, but my dress's days were over, stained and ripped in more places than I cared to think about.

Declan: 0, Staircase: 1.

To delay inspecting the damage I'd done to myself, I unlocked my phone with my thumbprint and blinked at the message and missed call tally. Over a hundred messages waited for my attention, and the twenty-three calls startled me. I checked the messages first, groaning at the repeated string of incomprehensible gibberish.

To execute a job, I had used a relay to work with my clients, a younger man I'd helped get on his feet a few years back. In exchange for helping him with the funding to set up a computer security business, he'd agreed to help me as my go-to techie.

Adding software to the camera to take pictures when my phone received a certain text string had been his brain child, allowing him to control the cameras hidden in my clothing and accessories. Most of the missed calls were from him.

He was also one of the few who knew I had dressed up as a woman for my hit on the castle, making all of the necessary arrangements to pull off my transformation from man to woman. Groaning, I checked the battery icon, which warned me my phone was about to go into its death throes.

Anthony had planned for that, too, forcing me to carry two spare battery cases for my phone. My hands shook as I peeled the device out of its first case and dug through the purse for a replacement, wiggling it into place. Blood had long since dried on my fingers, pulling at my skin with my every movement.

My phone rang in my hands before I had a chance to dial, and I didn't recognize the number. I stared at it, wondering who had my contact information and would call me from a restricted number.

Missing the call staring dumbly at the screen wasn't one of my finer moments, and I groaned again, flopping limp onto the stone landing. I closed my eyes, swallowed, and willed the pounding in my head to ease.

Declan: 0, Staircase: 2.

My phone beeped at me again, and I lifted my arm so I could see the glowing display. The gleam of gold captured my attention to the scarab cuff. I winced at the pain of rotating my arm. The cuff wrapped firmly around my wrist, and while I could make out the seam of the hinges, I couldn't locate its clasp.

My phone reminded me I had just missed a message, and I forced my gaze back to the notification. I unlocked the device again and tapped to access the message, which informed me Anthony wanted me to answer my phone.

"What a load of poppycock," I muttered. I kept hold of my cell so I could answer it if it rang again and began the tedious process of testing for any breaks. My back throbbed when I moved, but I doubted I'd broken anything on the way down. I thanked my wolf for my ongoing survival, doubting a human could've lived through such a fall.

Declan: 1, Staircase: 2.

My phone rang again, and after swiping my finger to answer, I put it in the general vicinity of my ear. "Hello?"

"Jesus Christ, Declan. I thought you were dead," Anthony bellowed in my ear.

"At current tally, the staircase won." I groaned, used my feet to push the rest of the way onto the landing, and hissed at the new reports of aching, sore muscles. "Not dead yet."

"What happened?"

I sat up, grimacing at the fire consuming my spine. Leaning against the wall, I took several moments to catch my breath. "I don't even know." Had Scully somehow managed to drug me? Drugs made sense. Flying, face-assaulting scarabs didn't. Under the influence of some drug, Scully could have easily opened a secret door in the wall and shoved me down it. "I fell down a staircase."

"I guessed that from the camera feed. Pretty damned glad I installed a night-vision camera in one of the pieces right now. Take it from the top and keep talking. I'm pinging for your location now."

"I'm at Castle Transylvania, the French edition. I think I missed the boat."

"That was about twelve hours ago, Declan."

Declan: 1, Staircase: 3.

"Why are you calling me from a restricted number?"

"My phone is charging. Your client traced me, is sitting about ten feet away, looks grumpy as hell, and might just shove his Beretta up my ass if I don't get a successful ping on your phone with the exact location of Castle Transylvania. I'm on his cell. The yacht captain's out; he left without you and went to shore, and even if I find him, I doubt he'd give the location. Fucker's on Scallywag's payroll."

"Of course he is, he wanted to make the arrangements for the yacht from the beginning, Tony. Why do you even sound surprised? How did the client trace us?" I also made a note to steal my friend's name for the yeasty gibbet.

"Hell if I know. He showed up about six hours ago with a check for two hundred thousand if I pinpointed your exact location."

"If he even thinks about groping my ass, I'm ripping his hand off and feeding it to him."

In the background, someone barked a laugh and said, "I have no interest in your ass, Mr. McGrady."

"I'm on speaker, aren't I?"

"Sorry, Declan. The gentleman with the Beretta makes the rules. The two hundred thou doesn't hurt much, either."

"Yeasty giglet," I grumbled.

Anthony snickered. "You can't be hurt too badly if you're digging through your antiquated insult grimoire."

While I could have left my friend and conspirator hanging, I got down to business. "Concussion is almost a guarantee, but I think I escaped without a major break. Jury is out on fractures," I reported. "As for what the hell happened, I don't know. I was in Scallywag's storage room poking around while he was on a call in the hallway. Found a secret door in the wall, tripped over my heels, and ended up taking a plunge down the staircase."

"He didn't push you?"

"I can't confirm I wasn't drugged and hallucinating things."

"You didn't eat or drink anything, did you?"

"Of course not," I snapped. "The guy's a lecherous piece of pond sludge. He had plenty of chances when I was doing my job while he was copping feels."

"Jesus Christ. You're serious?"

I sighed.

"Pardon my intrusion, but that behavior from Benjamin Scully is not unprecedented. He is a suspect in the disappearance of seven young women. When you pitched your plan to infiltrate his castle for the photographs disguised as an heiress, I thought it would be an excellent opportunity to confirm whether or not he may be the one behind their disappearances. More importantly, I was seeking evidence to prove I am not the one behind their kidnappings."

"He wanted to play 'Guess the Van Gogh,' so I buy into the theory," I replied, the man's bet immediately coming to mind. "If I guessed the title of his second Van Gogh, he was going to give me *Girl in the Woods*. If I failed to guess it, he wanted me to extend my trip by two weeks."

"I knew I should've installed a wire," Anthony grumbled.

"Too much data," I reminded him.

"Did you take this bet?" my client asked,

his voice deepening, probably from annoyance or anger.

"Do I look like a nitwit to you? Of course I didn't take that bet. Van—"

"Forgive Declan, sir. He's a right surly bastard when he has a headache."

"Your British is showing, Anthony," I complained.

"I'll stop showing my British when you use a curse that wasn't dated a hundred years ago. In *Britain,* thank you very much."

"You're using logic on me. Don't use logic right now, Tony."

"How hard did you hit your head?"

With my left hand, I began the tedious process of checking my scalp for injuries. I found three bumps, and the second one resulted in fresh blood staining my fingers. "At least three times, and one's a bleeder. No idea how bad."

"Can you walk?"

"Give me a few minutes. Sitting up wasn't a cakewalk." My stomach chose that moment to gurgle, reminding me it had been far too long since I had anything to eat or drink. "I'll manage."

"You sound like you drank a bottle of my rye, Declan."

Was I slurring? I couldn't tell, which probably wasn't a good sign. "Why is the client there, and why is he armed with a Beretta?"

"He likes your work, apparently, and felt I

needed some additional motivation to locate you."

"Should I ask how a computer security specialist got located?"

"Fuck you, Declan. I already fixed the hole. It won't happen again."

"You can't fix a hole in your head if gun-happy over there decides to take a shot," I snapped back.

"I have no intentions of hurting your accomplice, Mr. McGrady. I do, however, have every intention of working with him to ensure your recovery. It wouldn't serve my purposes to lose such a talented asset," my client replied.

"I can get myself out of the castle on my own, thank you very much."

Professional Pride: 1, Common Sense: 0.

Anthony sighed. "Declan, the job's botched. Let me arrange an extraction before you kick the bucket in some jackass's dungeon."

"Like hell the job's botched. I got the photos, and I'll get myself out. There's gotta be a Declan-sized window down in this dusty hell-hole somewhere."

"Why are you talking about yourself in the third person?"

"Anthony, have I ever, ever questioned you when you decide to do something extraordinarily stupid?"

"Yes, every time I do it."

"Poppycock." I grumbled curses under my

breath. "You worry about getting me a ride out of this joint, and I'll worry about getting out so I can get a ride out of this joint. Deal?" I clenched my teeth, gathered every last bit of my willpower, kicked off my broken shoe, and staggered to my feet. "I'm on my feet. Let me get my bearings. You got my coords? You're giving me a headache."

"I got your coords, Declan. I'll make arrangements for the extraction team."

"Check my honey traps for any contact from Scallywag. If he's out to make me disappear, he probably took the bait I left him. Details are in her email."

"You set up new honey traps without telling me?" Anthony hissed.

"Do I look like a fly-bitten giglet to you? Of course I set up new honey traps. I trust Scallywag about as far as I could toss him right now. *He groped my ass.*" I hung up before my flaring temper could get the better of me.

It was official. This was the worst job I'd ever taken, and I had a feeling it would get a lot worse before it got any better.

DUST SWIRLED around me with each and every step, and I needed the castle's cold stone walls to keep on my feet. My wolf was quiet in my head, probably exhausted from the strain of keeping me alive after my tumble down the staircase. I had no idea how far I had plummeted, but it had been more than a couple of stories.

The spiral, containing a small gap in the center of the staircase, continued into darkness far above.

Instead of trying to climb more stone steps than I wanted to count, I explored a maze of narrow corridors. Arrow slits in the stone reassured me I was on the ground level.

If I could find a window large enough for me to slip through, escape would be easy. The arrow slits were only four inches wide, which eliminated them as an option. They also let in the cool autumn air, and I shivered as my skin chilled. I wondered if Scallywag knew about the passages. Unlike in his main galleries, there was no evidence of security. If the blankets of dust covering the floor were any indication, no one had been in the place for years.

I lost track of how long I spent wandering around the castle, but when I finally found a stone wall with a lever, I hesitated, sniffing at the air.

The sweet scent of cinnamon lingered, and I recognized it as the signature of another werewolf. My wolf roused, and his attention fixated on another marker.

Female. My eyes widened, and I sniffed again. No, *females.* I couldn't tell how many, but there were at least three different undertones, and my wolf whined in my head, as eager as any puppy.

We'd never met a female of our kind before, and while it wasn't yet winter, his enthusiasm bled into me. The phone call with Anthony and our nameless client set me on guard.

Could the missing women be missing *werewolf* women?

My anger surged, and I flexed my hand, aware of the cool metal of the bracelet circling my wrist. Most collectors limited their pieces to the old and unusual, but Scallywag seemed like the exact sort of filth to take his interest to the next level.

I had only crossed paths with two male werewolves, and I had given them a wide berth, slipping away from them in thick New York crowds, unwilling to take the risk of meeting them. My wolf's uncertainty on how other males would react kept me at a distance, scoping out everywhere I went with my nose as much as my eyes.

No one knew I was a werewolf, and while I wanted to keep it that way, others of my kind would know the instant they caught a sniff of me unless I was really careful. Digging through my purse, I pulled out the bottle of perfume, which was a mix of cinnamon and lilac, two scents I found confused my nose and masked my nature.

Dousing myself in it would buy me time to find out the truth of what was hidden in Scallywag's castle. I sprayed myself until the scent clogged my nose and made me dizzy before returning the bottle to my purse. If there were women—werewolf or otherwise—locked away as hostages, I'd steal them away and set them free.

After all, I was a thief, and limiting myself wasn't my style. I'd never stolen anything living before, which intrigued me.

If there were women trapped in Scallywag's castle, I would find them. What I would do with them, I had no idea. My wolf had a few ideas, but the last thing I needed was multiple females knowing I was one of them.

As long as my wolf didn't slip into the winter rut, I could ignore the temptation of female werewolves. If I didn't, I'd risk a lot more than the chance of securing a mate.

My wolf wasn't pleased by my thoughts, but he didn't fight me over it, either. That was something we agreed on; our on-going existence came first, and our life wasn't worth the risk of any female, werewolf or otherwise.

Freedom, however, was. The thought of anyone being held captive as a piece of a living collection infuriated me so much I could smell it through the cloying perfume clogging my nose.

The only way for me to go was forward. I took hold of the lever and pulled.

A soft click was the only indication something had happened. I pressed my hand to the stone wall and gave a push. It shifted under my hand, and I shoved it open. Sliding my purse off my shoulder, I removed the perfume, my cell, wallet, keys, extra battery case, and passport, and cruise ticket and stuffed them into one of the pouches I had strapped to my thigh. Hopefully, the leather and remaining odds and ends inside would keep the door from closing behind me.

I slipped inside, hoping I wasn't about to make a critical mistake.

Chapter Four

DECLAN: 0, PACK OF ANGRY WOMEN: 1.

Most men would have found the idea of being plowed over by a group of scantily clad ladies appealing, but all I could concentrate on was the fact I had a new bump on the back of my head, bruised or cracked ribs, and a blinding headache. I wasn't even sure how I'd ended up on the floor pinned beneath a lingerie-clad woman, but she and her friends moved fast, and after my tumble down a staircase, I was no match for them.

A delicate foot pinned my throat to the floor, and my blurred vision denied me the opportunity to take stock of those surrounding me. Since one pinning me down wasn't enough, one of her friends joined in.

I didn't even bother to fight them. They'd win, and I knew it. I couldn't even make out more than a blur of skin broken by splashes of color marking their bras and panties.

The next time I got anywhere near Scallywag, I was going to rip him to shreds and toss his body into the ocean, to hell with the consequences.

"You're not him." The woman had a pretty enough voice, a little smoky, a lot husky, and with just enough of a growl my wolf was ready to roll over and submit to her. "Who are you?"

My cell chose that moment to ring. "Answer that," I rasped. "Thigh holster. Right leg."

My already ruined dress ripped as one of the werewolves dug for my phone, locating it and answering with a swipe. To my surprise, she held it to my ear.

From what little I could see of her, she was a blonde.

"McGrady," I answered.

"Any luck, Declan?" Anthony demanded.

"Declan?" the woman straddling me hissed, and I felt her hand fist over my chest, grabbing the front of my dress.

I flicked my thumb over my ring to take a picture of my captor. "Check the stream in a minute. Hey. How long does it take for a concussion to heal? I think I have a new one."

"Declan, now is *not* the time."

"Sure it is. I just cracked my head on the floor again, but at least this time, instead of six stories of stairs, I got…" I squinted in my effort to count the women staring down at me. "A gaggle of ladies."

"A gaggle of ladies," Anthony echoed.

"What do you call a group of women?

Colony? Herd? Stampede? I'd count them, but things are a bit blurry right now."

"Jesus Christ, Declan. Are you okay?"

The woman straddling me stole my phone and enabled the speaker. "Who the fuck are you?"

"He wasn't joking about the gaggle of ladies, was he?" Anthony sighed. "Hey, client. I think he found your ladies."

"He?"

"Declan is the scout portion of your extraction team," my client replied, and judging from the clarity of his voice, he had claimed the phone from Anthony. "Is Patricia there?"

"Patricia, some dude is asking for you," my captor said, disabling the speaker and offering my phone to one of the other women.

A moment later, someone laughed, soft and content. "No kidding, eh? No wonder I couldn't tell; he's wearing so much perfume it's burning my nose."

It was rare, but I loved it when a plan worked as intended.

"You want us to follow *his* lead? He's half-dead, covered in blood, and wearing a dress that went out of style two hundred years ago. Are you serious?"

The other women giggled. I sighed, closing my eyes while the castle spun in circles around me, and said, "She's probably right on that score. Tell him I'm going to slow you down. I can and will extract myself, thank you very much. I'll figure out a flight plan for you ladies and either serve as a distraction or bait."

Professional Pride: 2, Common Sense: 0.

At least I was being honest with myself. Until I had a chance to change to my wolf and hunt, I'd be useless. While my unnatural heritage kept me alive, I healed a lot slower as a human. Given a couple of days, I'd probably recover enough to get out on my own, assuming I could find somewhere quiet to hole up until I could rest.

I tried not to think too hard about the logistics, including the lack of water in the castle's hidden hallways.

"He wants to talk to you." My phone was passed back to me.

"McGrady," I answered, closing my eyes to ward off my headache long enough to deal with the conversation.

"Do you think you can get them out of the castle?"

My client didn't pull his punches, and I sighed, wondering what the hell I had gotten myself into for only half a million dollars. "Hostage situations are a little above my pay grade and skill set, sir. I can try, but I'm used to working solo. I can give them directions on how to navigate the galleries and get to the ground level. I don't know the lay of the land around the castle, only that the cliff has a one-person lift. The shore below is pretty minimal, and I have no idea how far it extends."

It wasn't really a lie; extractions involving living people had, once upon a time, been my speciality, but I had left that life behind a decade ago, and for good reason.

"You aren't capable of joining them?"

"I'm a liability. I'll cover their six and serve as a distraction to buy them time to get off the castle's grounds."

"You're ex-military."

I grimaced. I had never officially served in the military, but I had picked up things over the years working in operations, and my partner before Anthony had been a retired SEAL. "Not quite, sir. I learned a few tricks from a former SEAL."

That was a safe enough admission. While I had once done some relocation for the US government, I tried my hardest to forget those days.

At least I'd been smart enough to use a false identity back then, one so complex the government believed in its authenticity. Living openly as Declan McGrady was the pinnacle of my accomplishments, although I wondered how much longer that would last.

It wouldn't be much longer until no one believed my real age; I had already gotten to the point my youthful appearance drew unwanted attention.

My client clearing his throat dragged my focus back to my phone. "Make a plan and get the ladies out of the castle. I will text your phone with a link to a GPS tracking app. Install it, use the code I will send you, and make sure it stays running. That will make certain your phone can be tracked by the extraction team."

"I'll give my phone to the ladies once it's set up," I promised.

"What about you?"

"Contract rules still apply." I hung up before my client could argue with me. When he called back half a minute later, I declined the call, silenced my phone, pulled up a map app, and went to work, ignoring the stares of the women surrounding me.

LYING prone on the floor for an hour gave my head some time to recover, though not enough to put an end to my dizzy spells and blurred vision. After I declined ten calls, my client took the hint and sent over the details for the tracking app, which I loaded up and set up to his specifications.

The French version of Castle Transylvania was located north and west of Paris, which made it ideal for planning an escape. The castle wasn't too far away from civilization, and if the satellite maps of the surrounding area were to be believed, terrain wouldn't be an issue for the women.

The nearest town was ten kilometers out, which wasn't much for a healthy, motivated werewolf.

"Okay, ladies, listen up," I ordered, my gaze locked on the screen, which was the only thing my uncooperative eyes could focus on without putting up a fight. "You've got a ten kilometer run east from here to the nearest town, and it's through vineyards and farmland. It should be an easy hike. Satellite imagery isn't showing any notable obstacles, so you should be able to wait for extraction in relative safety. Moving targets are harder to hit, so once you go, keep moving and don't stop until your contact team picks you up."

After adjusting the zoom on the map, I charted a plan for their escape, setting my phone up to relay instructions to reach the waypoints I had set. "This is your flight plan. Stick to it. I'll be sending the coord list over to the team so they can plan an interception."

I turned the display to face them. The blonde insisted on staying right where she was, straddled over my stomach. As far as I could tell, she was quiet unless annoyed and capable of reining in the other women with a single word.

She snatched the phone out of my hand and muttered complaints about me while looking over the map. "Why set a route like this? It circles in on itself three times and zigzags all over the place. This is fucking stupid."

I didn't have the time or will to explain the concept of confusing the trail, so I ignored her complaints and replied, "Logistics.

If you're following a set flight plan, the extraction team can intercept you. With the tracking program running on the phone, they'll be able to pinpoint when you should arrive at the next waypoint. That'll help make sure you connect with them. You should be able to move fast enough on this terrain, especially since you're fresh and ready to make a run for it."

What, exactly, had I gotten myself into? Assessing the art collection of a spoiled rich lordling was far different from making certain a bunch of female werewolves made it from Point A to Point B without running into trouble; I was in no condition to keep up with them.

My wolf understood the irony of having finally found females of our kind, only to send them on their way without having a chance to court any of them. I had no choice but to resign myself to the bitter reality of the situation.

"We're fresh," she replied, her tone taking a hard edge. "Fine. We follow the phone to each waypoint. What then?"

Her guess was probably as good as mine, although I understood how extractions were supposed to work from my military ops experience.

My job was to extract myself, and different rules applied

Steadying myself with a deep breath, I replied, "You meet with the extraction team and they take care of the rest. Go with the flow and don't put up a fight. Your job is to cooperate with them."

"What about you?"

"I'm not a factor in the operation as soon as you seven ladies are clear of the castle grounds." Either I would make my escape or I wouldn't. Dancing around the subject wouldn't change things. "My extraction is my problem, ladies. That's the way this operation works. I'll be on rear guard duty and covering your backs. I'll make my own way out."

With luck, less than a week from now, I'd be on my way back to the United States on a cruise out of Hamburg. If I missed the ship and had no other choice, I'd catch a flight out of Germany back to my home turf and put the entire job behind me once and for all.

"That's bullshit."

My wolf growled his appreciation in my head, and I ignored him. "That's the terms of my contract, sweetheart. You'll just have to live with it. You and your friends will be leaving the castle, you'll be following the assigned route and hitting each planned waypoint, and you'll be extracted and on your way back to the United States, probably by the end of the day."

For the first time since tackling me to the floor, the woman straddling me rose to her feet, my cell still in her hand. I didn't need to see her face to know she glared at me. I got to my feet, shaking my head to clear it of the vertigo still plaguing me.

"We're wasting time. Let's not give him any extra time to make preparations." I turned, clenched my teeth, and marched through the hallways in the direction of the staircase leading to the storage room six stories up, wondering how I'd get them out of the castle without killing someone in the process.

Blood was a finite resource, and the quantity I had left on the staircase stopped me dead in my tracks. It puddled on the landing, and smears of it marked the steps and walls. I winced, gingerly touching the back of my head.

My reintroduction with the floor hadn't helped matters for me, and at least one of the gashes had a tendency to open up and resume bleeding when I moved my head the wrong way.

I'd need the nineteen-day cruise complete with a stop in the Caribbean to recover from my misadventures in Scallywag's castle.

"What the fuck?"

"There's a reason I'm a liability," I muttered, shaking my head. "Look, lady. Maybe instead of questioning my methods, get your head into the game. Your job is to get you and your friends to the extraction point. Let me worry about my problems."

"Julie. My name is Julie, not lady, not sweetheart, and not any other idiotic cutesy nonsense you might try to come up with."

"Fine, Julie. You worry about your job and let me worry about mine. You get one try at this, and if you twiddle your thumbs, you'll hurt yourself and your friends without meeting up with the extraction team. You'll end up stuck in France with Benjamin Scully. Got it?"

The other women kept their mouths shut, staring between me and Julie. From what I could tell through my blurred vision, they worried. The horrific amount of perfume I had bathed myself in did a good job of masking their scents in addition to my own, which was probably a good thing.

I disliked that they knew my real name, but at least they couldn't tell I was a werewolf like them.

"Understood, Mr. McGrady." Julie clacked her teeth together, glared at me, and stomped up the staircase, hesitating at one of the dark splotches several steps up. She shook her head and kept going.

I waited for the other women to begin the long hike up to the sixth floor before joining them, grimacing at having to climb so many stairs. In the effort of preserving my dignity, I took my time, pausing to take in the stains marking where I had splattered my blood in the stairwell.

A normal human should have died after such a tumble.

"How the hell did you survive that fall?" Julie demanded in a whisper when I reached the top of the staircase.

"Your guess is as good as mine. I spent twelve hours out cold at the bottom, for what it's worth. Got lucky." Being inflicted with lycanthropy helped, but I couldn't tell them that. I hesitated, taking in the wall, and sighing in relief when I spotted a lever near the stone wall. "Once I open this, you're on the clock. I know absolutely nothing about the castle's security systems, except for the fact I saw surveillance cameras through the gallery. This opens to a store room. Your best bet is to take advantage of the fact you're fast and know where you're going."

I grilled them all on the way out until every last woman was able to repeat the directions back to me, complete with landmarks, which I showed them on my phone by accessing the catalog of images.

They'd be able to find their way out one way or another.

Julie glared at me, looking like she wanted to give me a shove down the staircase. I scowled back at her, wondering what I had done to irritate her so much. "Ready to move, ladies?"

"Ready," the others chorused. Julie

growled something under her breath, grabbed hold of the lever, and yanked.

As it had with me, the doorway swung silently open, revealing the unlit storage room. Like me, the women showed no signs of needing light, and Julie led the way, squeezing through the crates on her way to the doorway leading to the main galleries.

I stalked after them, waiting for the ax to fall and our escape to be revealed. The door shut after me of its own volition, and the thump of stone on stone chilled my blood.

If luck was on our side, we'd be gone before the security system and those monitoring it registered we were present. If all hell broke loose, I didn't know what I would do.

Once the ladies were free and clear, I'd make my way back to Hamburg to the hotel I had booked, change into real clothes, and pretend I had never taken the job from hell. I'd board my cruise home, take my half million dollars, and disappear for as long as possible. I'd wash my hands of meddling clients and the risky world of high-end theft.

Anthony would understand. Some risks weren't worth taking, and I'd finally bit off way more than I could chew.

All I had to do was get the women out of the castle and on route to the waypoints so they could return to the United States.

How hard could it be?

Chapter Five

A SUCCESSFUL HEIST hinged on the timing, and my twelve-hour nap at the bottom of the staircase coupled with the lost hours exploring abandoned corridors set our escape window at shortly before dawn.

I'd take every bit of good luck to come my way. I needed it.

The galleries were completely dark, which made navigating through the castle a tricky affair. My eyes were good in the dark, but not *that* good, and I relied on the gleams and reflections of the rooms with windows to guide me, and the rest I did by feel.

The soft patter of bare feet in front of me allowed me to track the pack of female werewolves, who kept silent without any coaching from me. As I feared and expected, they did move a lot faster than I could after my tumble down the stairs.

By the time I reached the third floor, the female werewolves were so far ahead of me I could no longer hear their feet on the cold stone. I kept my pace slow.

The last thing I needed was to hit my head again. The pounding in my skull was accompanied by the throb of abused muscles and bruised bones, but there was nothing I could do about it. There would be time enough for resting after I made my escape. Once I left the castle, I'd risk the cliffs, although I'd risk them in a way no one anticipated. Thanks to my trip on the yacht, I knew the waters were deep enough for cliff diving, although the cliff's height still worried me.

I hadn't done any jumps higher than fifty feet, and the cliff was closer to a hundred if my guess was correct. In the dark, I'd have to rely on my wolf's strength and speed to jump far enough over the shore to miss the shallow waters.

Sending seven women out in lingerie was bad enough, but at least they had direction. Without my phone to guide me and looking like an attempted murder victim, if I came too close to civilization, I'd face a lot of unwanted attention.

My best bet was to head for the ocean, shift to my wolf, and make a mad dash for Hamburg following the coast. Once in the city, I could sneak into the lodge serving as my hotel, change into clean clothes, rid my face of makeup, and pull out the extensions lengthening my hair.

I'd even be able to cut the two months of

growth I'd added to help me pull off my infiltration. In one or two hours, I'd be a whole new man.

The castle remained dark and quiet, and by the time I reached the ground floor, the only sign of the women's passage was the front door, which they had left open in their wake. I slipped through and shut it behind me.

The first light of dawn touched the sky, and I eyed the distance from the castle to the cliff. The anchor for the lift waited, and in its shadow, I saw the last person I wanted to see.

Scallywag was alone, and he was armed with a pistol. In the gloom, I couldn't tell the model. He saw me moments later, and he straightened, stepping towards me.

"You whore," he snarled at me, his voice booming. "You have no idea what you have cost me."

I restrained the urge to laugh. "Lose something?" Taunting an armed man was a good way to get myself killed, but unless I could cross the distance to the cliff and make my jump before he shot me, I was already in trouble.

"How did you find them? How did you know they were here?" Scallywag's voice rose in pitch.

I risked taking a few steps forward, my body tensing as I prepared myself for the stupidest plan of my entire life. Jumping from a cliff while trying to outrun a bullet was suicidal, but I lacked another out.

Even if I rushed him, he'd have plenty of time to aim and fire. I wasn't impervious to bullets. In that, I was as mortal as my enemy.

"I didn't know. I was here to see your collection, and I don't mean of unwilling women. You wanted to add me to their numbers, didn't you?" I flexed my hands and kept my chin high and my stride steady.

Scallywag lifted his gun, aiming it at me. "That's right. Come over here nice and quietly. Maybe I lost them, but I can begin again with you."

"I'm not in their class, I'm afraid."

It was true; they were all spitfires, and Julie was their queen. I considered myself fortunate she hadn't decided to squish me like a bug. My masochistic wolf wanted more of Julie's attentions.

I ignored my wolf and focused all of my attention on Scallywag. The man's grip on the weapon was weak but he held his finger safely away from the trigger. With my vision so blurred, I couldn't tell if the safety was engaged.

Either way, I needed to take risks if I wanted to make my getaway.

Scallywag grunted and clacked his teeth. "I'll get rid of you once I have others again, don't worry. Although, given enough time with ladies of that caliber, you may become just like them."

I read between the lines: he meant to coerce the next werewolf female he caught to change me into one, too. Swallowing my laughter, I shook my head. "I'd rather die."

"I can arrange that."

I dipped into a crouch, balanced my weight on my toes, and surged forward, sacrificing speed to zig zag and make it harder for him to hit me. His first shot smacked into the dirt in front of me. Focusing all of my attention on the cliff, I broke into my fastest run.

The second shot grazed my shoulder, and I stumbled before recovering. White capped water stretched to the lightening horizon, and I cursed the black clouds blanketing the sky over the churning sea.

My feet slapped on the wooden deck leading up the lift, and when I reached the edge, I jumped and plummeted to the ocean far below.

CLIFF DIVING WAS all about angles and hitting the water just right. Without knowing the depth of the water, my plunge into the ocean might end with a broken and battered body before the surf pounded me into the stony shore.

I twisted my body, hoping I wouldn't break my toes, ankles, and legs when I smacked into the ocean feet first. The last time I had done something as stupid as jump off a cliff into the sea, I'd done just that. Only the fact I'd done the jump solo had prevented some uncomfortable questions, although changing to my wolf had lessened the damage from a full break to a fracture.

I didn't have long to consider the painful ways I could die before I hit the churning waves. Blowing air out of my nose and mouth as I sank down, I kicked and swam for the surface. The water caught my clothes and jerked me towards the shore. It wasn't until my feet hit bottom I was able to propel myself upward and gasp for breath.

The crack of gunfire heralded a splash beside me. I yelped and recoiled, and the second shot came so close to my shoulder the splash of the bullet hitting the water struck me in the face. I took a deep breath and dove, fighting with the dress coiling around my legs.

Unless I made distance or found a place to hide, I was as good as dead.

The open water offered the best chance of long-term survival, so I propelled myself deeper into the ocean, surfacing long enough to catch a breath of air before submerging again. Even with my wolf lending me his strength, it didn't take long for my energy to flag and the weight of my dress to pull me down.

I broke the surface long enough to catch my breath, twisting to watch the cliff. I had washed out several hundred feet, but my wolf-enhanced vision caught the motion of the lift lowering to the shore beneath the castle.

Scallywag pursued me, and he had a motorboat still tethered to the dock.

"Mongrel," I hissed.

The dress wasn't fit to be worn by anyone ever again, so I ripped through the material in my effort to escape its heavy confines. The skirt went first, and the current ripped the fabric out of my hand. The rest I pulled over my head, although I ended up tearing the sleeves off, which were determined to cling to my arms. The bra took me the longest, and I cursed the clasp behind my back, submerging several times before I managed to free myself.

There wasn't anything I could do about the stockings or tattered ruins of the sleeves, not without drowning myself in the process.

The backfiring of the motorboat's engine warned me I'd run out of time. Cursing my luck, I dove and let the outbound currents catch me and propel me far from shore, where no sane man wanted to go.

Then again, no one in a small motorboat had any business risking the open ocean with a storm brewing on the horizon. One or both of us would drown, and I had no idea which one of us would succumb first.

With my luck, probably me.

WITHOUT THE DRESS weighing me down, I could tread water. The thundering sky, surging winds, and capped waves offered a measure of protection from Scallywag, who trolled the waters in search of me.

When he spotted me, he screamed curses at me and fired his gun, but I ducked beneath the water and evaded his attempts to kill me. The storm swept in, and the rolling seas turned vicious, dragging me towards the cliffs, like it or not.

I definitely didn't like it, especially because the same waves were driving Scallywag back to his dock. With no idea how many rounds he had left in his gun, if I wasn't careful, our game of silent Marco Polo would come to a tragic end—for me. Snarling a curse, I angled towards shore to make distance from the madman and the cliff skirting his castle.

My wolf wanted me to put an end to the man permanently, but I didn't dare.

I remembered too well what had happened to my mother. No matter how much Scallywag deserved it, I couldn't reveal my true nature to the man *or* kill him. If I wanted to do more than survive through the day, I needed to make a clean getaway without anyone learning of my dual nature.

Focusing all of my attention on an outcropping of stone jutting up from the ocean, I swam across the current, allowing the waves to propel me towards shore while distancing myself from Scallywag.

I checked over my shoulder in time to watch the man drive his boat right up onto the stone shore and jump out before running in my direction. I snarled and dove, continuing towards my goal. When I surfaced, the crack of gunfire echoed against the cliffs.

The thump against my upper arm shocked the breath out of me, and the ocean pulled at my legs and dragged me under the waves. Conflicting currents spun me in a circle, tossed me to the surface long enough for me to splutter before sucking me down again.

Water swirled around me, and fire seared through my right arm despite the ocean's chill.

A strong current snatched my feet, yanked me out of my spin, and jerked me out to sea. I clawed my way to the surface, although my right arm refused to obey me, leaving me using my legs to keep afloat. I twisted in a circle and hissed my shock at how far from shore the current had dragged me.

The ocean was full of perils, and rip tides drowned swimmers every year without fail. My only chance of escaping was to swim across the current and find calmer seas. With the full brunt of the storm stirring the water, my options were limited. Shuddering, I inspected my right arm, relieved and alarmed the bullet had gone through.

The hole wouldn't completely close when

I shifted, but with luck, I'd be able to swim as a wolf. Otherwise, I'd drown, and there wasn't anything I could do about it. I drew in a deep breath, called on my wolf, and shifted.

UNDER NORMAL CIRCUMSTANCES, shapeshifting from human to wolf involved a flash of pain that felt like it lasted an hour but took less than a second. Time slowed, stalling around me while my body twisted on itself, bones snapping and reforming while muscles snapped and regrew. My skin dissolved away before sprouting fur.

Shifting in the ocean hurt unlike anything I had ever experienced. While the waves froze around me, the frigid waters pierced through me, and the salt burned when I remained trapped between shapes.

I never quite understood the logistics of how my clothing and possessions shifted with me, but I was grateful for it; my identity and way to resume my life remained with me, one certainty I could rely on.

This time, however, something was different. Warmth surrounded my right foreleg, soothing and spreading through me to numb the pain of my transformation. When it reached my head, time snapped back to its proper order and waves crashed over me, dragging me beneath the water.

A soft, blue-white luminescence surrounded me, and where the light touched, I sensed life teeming in the water. Bubbles burst in the churning surf, and energy flowed as the storm unleashed all its fury on the uncaring sea.

The waters cared nothing for who—or what—lurked in them, lifeless yet full of life, leaving me to the mercies of fate. A fish, drawn in by my flickering glow, darted away, startled. My awareness of it winked out the instant it retreated.

Tearing my focus away from the unwanted insight, I forced myself into motion, paddling for all I was worth to the surface. I panted, tossing my head up high so the spray wouldn't drown me before I had a chance to orient myself.

The currents tugged at my fur, but I fought them, and once I located the storm-battered coast, I angled towards shore while the rip tide clawed at me in its effort to sweep me farther from the safety of the cliffs.

Thunder rumbled overhead, and lightning flashed across the sky. The ocean trembled, and a jolt of electricity surging through the water made my body tingle. A second bolt zapped into the sea between me and the shore, and bursts of blue and white danced across my vision.

Several dead fish, victims of the storm's fury, flowed by me on the currents, winking in and out of my awareness as they passed through my field of vision. My wolf's hunger surged, but I wrestled control from him before he could chase down a free meal instead of swimming for the safety of shore.

By the time I swam free of the rip tide, the coast and its cliffs were distant. Huffing my displeasure, I shifted how I swam, catching one of the plethora of waves pounding the shore. As though bored of me, the sea willingly released me from its embraced, regurgitated me onto the pebbled coast, and left me lying where the land and water met, the surf tugging at my fur but lacking the strength to reclaim me.

It took a long time for me to catch my breath, and as my frantic heartbeat settled to a steadier rhythm, my body sent me a bill for all of the abuse I had put it through. While shifting helped mend broken bones and other injuries, they left their mark on me. The jump from the cliffs hadn't helped any; my hind legs twitched and throbbed from the bruising impact with the water, and sharper pains warned me I had likely fractured something when I had hit the ocean. To make matters worse, a gradual but increasing throb in my head promised even more misery later.

At least the rip tide had helped in one way; I couldn't spot any sign of Scallywag. The cliffs, while still towering overhead, were sheltered by a curve in the coast, buffering me from the full fury of the ocean and the storm churning it. Rain pattered down on me, accompanied by the rumbles of thunder and gusting winds.

Stifling a groan, I rolled over, got my paws under me, and staggered upright, my head hanging low as I braced my legs so I wouldn't flop back to the pebbled beach. A glint of gold drew my eye to my right forepaw.

The bane of my heritage, the bright pink fur of my paws fading to a brilliant tawny gold frosted in white, was offset by the blue scarab cuff secured to my foreleg. During my transformation, it must have shifted, too, for it fit well. The metal and stones gleamed in the flashes of lightning, and it glowed a pale yellow, its color lost in the shimmer cast by my fur.

I bumped it with my nose. Warmth radiated from the metal and gemstones, and faint steam wafted from my fur, which fluffed as though someone brushed and dried it. I shook myself off, spraying water off my coat.

Later, I would ponder the mystery of the bracelet and why it hadn't shifted and become a part of me like everything else I owned. Later, I'd worry about how and why it had attached itself to me.

First, I needed to get to Hamburg and make my escape from Europe before I caught a severe case of death, for which there was no cure.

Chapter Six

TIME WAS NOT on my side. In my current state, even if I ran my fastest without stopping to hunt, it would take two days too long to reach Hamburg, Germany. There was no way I would catch my ship back to the United States, which left me with Plan B.

Plan B involved using an old passport set to expire in a few months and picking up the mantle of an identity I had left behind long ago. In all honesty, I was ex-military, although not in the way most people expected. It was the truth I had learned the finer points of military-level extraction from a former SEAL, but I had been far more involved than I liked to think about.

I'd never gone to boot camp; agents like me endured more unconventional training. I'd never served, not in the way that earned respect. I had a fake title, and it ranked among the officership, but it had been earned through subterfuge and special operations instead of traditional warfare or paper shuffling. Officially, I was a name in the records no one ever saw.

I would've given a great deal to be a traditional paper shuffler. Those with comfortable desk jobs didn't throw themselves out of airplanes on the government's command, slink into places they didn't belong, or involve themselves in operations no sane man wanted a part of.

I had survived far more suicide missions than I wanted to think about.

Perhaps if I had started in the military instead of being shunted from military branch to military branch, I would have had more traditional training, but I was a ghost, someone who appeared unexpectedly in the night and vanishing as soon as my job was completed.

Right before I'd made my great escape from the government's chokehold on my life, some spur-galled incompetent had thought it wise to elevate Daniel McClain, my name within the military, to the rank of Major in the Marine Corps as part of the ongoing coverup meant to help me slide from operation to operation, a fiasco that had ensured I hadn't used the passport I'd been issued a week before a botched op had offered me freedom.

There was probably still a missing person's report out on me somewhere, which would result in some very uncomfortable questions if my passport was flagged. The government didn't like when their officers vanished, and they had taught me many of the tricks I knew. I had new ones up my sleeve, but if I wanted to make it back to the United States undetected, I couldn't do it as Declan McGrady.

The fact my client had sussed out Anthony's location worried me. Fortunately, almost a decade had gone by since Daniel McClain had disappeared. All I needed to do was make it on board a cruise liner without being picked up.

I shuffled into a ground-eating lope heading north along the coast. I needed to traverse a great deal of France, the entirety of Belgium, and the Netherlands before following the German shore to Hamburg, where I'd book the next cruise out.

Fortunately for me, I had planned for some problems, and the lodge I had reserved in Hamburg was in my name for a full month, giving me plenty of time to make the journey before I had to worry about anyone invading the place searching for my whereabouts. The lodge knew I was scheduled to travel across Europe, resulting in me being gone for days or weeks at a time.

While inconvenient, the lodge's location would even allow me to skirt the city and approach as a wolf without running risk of anyone seeing me half-naked in the tattered ruins of a dress.

I had done my job, and considering I had been working with a stacked deck in the dealer's favor, I had done it well. Sighing my resignation, I searched the cliffs for a way up.

If I wanted to reach Hamburg alive and in tolerable health, I needed to hunt. Then I'd run for as long and fast as I could, hoping I could get on board a cruise liner westbound before my strained body failed me.

FRANCE WAS NOT the optimal place for a werewolf. The few forests lining the vineyards and farms were thin and low on prey, and I didn't dare approach the herds owned by humans. While I'd be long gone before the loss of the animals was discovered, I hadn't survived for so long by taking unnecessary risks.

Most importantly, I didn't dare get too close to civilization. The last thing I needed was someone reporting a ghost wolf with pink paws, nose, and tail. The tips of my ears also being pink was the insult to injury. When I was in my prime, I could almost control how much my fur glowed, though I could never quite get rid of the pale blue and white luminescence radiating from my fur. It made hunting difficult, giving my prey plenty of warning I was around.

Humans, especially the superstitious ones, tended to think the worst when they caught a glimpse of me. Some thought I was a demon dog coming to end their lives. Others thought I was more like a will o' the wisp, luring them close so I could eat their souls while leaving their bodies alive.

I'd made the mistake of getting too close to people as a wolf once, and I swore it would never happen again. While I hadn't been caught, I'd been forced to move away from the forest I'd called home, beginning my habit of changing territory every now and then to prevent people from finding me in the winter.

With my pain hampering me, I had no control over the shimmering of my fur, leaving me to hunt prey too slow to evade me even when alerted by my glow. My wolf's disgust and dismay over the situation annoyed me into unnecessarily tearing at prey I'd otherwise crunch once and swallow whole.

The larger and more satisfying prey fled long before I could catch them, the fresh scent of their fear lingering in the air. Mice and rabbits couldn't sustain me long, and I knew it, as did my wolf.

I really needed to stop and sleep for a week, but I didn't dare.

Once I made it to the safety of Hamburg and a cruise liner destined for home, I could sleep, eat my way across the ship, and recover. Until then, my only choice was to run and hope for the best.

HAMBURG, Germany teemed with charm, but I was too exhausted to enjoy it. Hidden by the bright early morning light, I skirted civilization, made my way to the lodge, and shifted so I could retrieve my keys and slip inside.

The pain was even worse than when I had transformed in the ocean.

With the fear of discovery driving me, I battled with the keys, my hands shaking so badly it took several tries to get the door open. I staggered inside, using my back to shut the door behind me. Sinking down to the floor, I struggled to catch my breath, which burst in and out of me in wheezing pants.

I had made it, but I had no idea how much time had passed since my haphazard plunge into the ocean. A few days felt right for my level of exhaustion. While tempted to fall asleep on the floor, I gathered my flagging strength and dragged myself into the bathroom to shower. The cold roused me enough to execute the next stage of my plan.

No matter what, I would be on the next cruise out of Europe, even if I had to take a one-month tour to make it happen. While the shipwreck had destroyed most of my things, I'd purchased a cheap laptop to finish my preparations. I booted it up, digging out my old passport from its hiding place between the bed's mattresses. The passport, along with other important information, had survived thanks to my decision to return to my room before making my escape from the sinking ship.

After carrying the damned thing with me for almost a decade, the fact I needed it now annoyed me almost as needing to give myself a short hair cut to match the old image. Some of my hair had to go anyway; I didn't know how to remove the extensions allowing me to masquerade as a woman. My clippers would let me shear it down to an inch, although I'd be forced to spike my hair in some hip and horrible fashion to hide that I had cut it myself.

If time allowed before my cruise, I'd go to a barber to undo the damage.

Once the laptop finished booting, I browsed a cruise booking site to explore my options. I groaned, staring at the screen in dismay. It had taken me eight days to reach Hamburg.

I had one choice, the last cruise of the season, which left port in six hours. Spitting curses, I checked the available staterooms. If I wanted to leave Germany by ship, I'd spend a fortune to do it.

The only cabin available was the most expensive suite on board—over ten thousand dollars for the voyage. I groaned, bowed my head, and dug out my credit cards, muttering curses. The suite would require me to dress my best, something I hadn't anticipated when

I purchased clothing for myself after arriving in Hamburg following the loss of my luggage.

I had exactly one suit, and if I wanted to pull off staying in a luxury suite, I needed more. Six hours didn't leave me with a lot of time.

At least my cabin had a printer. I hooked it up to my laptop so I could print my boarding ticket, which I reserved under the name of Daniel McClain. I lost thirty minutes hacking the extensions out of my hair, resulting in an acceptable style as long as the beholder was a rat seeking a nest.

Packing didn't take long; everything fit in a single duffle, which I tossed over my shoulder. I dressed in my suit, checked out of the lodge, and prepared for a second blitzkrieg through Hamburg.

THREE CLOTHING STORES, one mobile shop, and a haircut later, I felt like a new man. The barber had worked wonders, restoring my sense of masculinity while leaving me looking far better than I felt. I wished I hadn't waxed my face; the growth of a beard would have gone a long way towards adding a few years, but there wasn't anything I could do about it.

At least the frantic pace of my shopping kept me awake when I was so tired I stifled yawns every other minute.

Armed with six jackets, an equal number of slacks, and twice as many shirts and ties, I had everything I needed to look the part of a wealthy traveling businessman. My new cell phone had a German number and a ridiculously expensive plan offering long distance and the data I'd need to make it to the United States.

I hoped I wouldn't need it, but if I did, I'd have it, and no self-respecting businessman traveled without a good phone. The laptop wasn't quite what I needed, but if anyone asked, I'd claim my regular machine had broken, which was true enough.

No one would be getting anything off my original laptop after its extended stay at the bottom of the ocean.

I was one of the last people in line to board the ship, a white monstrosity someone had dubbed the *Snow Princess*. In far too many ways for my comfort, its shape reminded me of the Titanic, and I had already reenacted that misadventure once. It was so new the stench of paint, varnish, and new-forged metal stung my nose. Careful to select the correct identification, I handed over my boarding pass, which was checked against my passport.

The man maintained his bored expression, muttered something in a mix of German and English, and waved me through to the next gate to pick up my room key and everything I'd need for my stay on board the ship. I smothered my urge to grin at the pitiful excuse for security. Considering the ship's first stop was in the Caribbean, the lack of scrutiny didn't surprise me much.

The real test would happen when we reached port in the United States, where I'd face customs and immigrations as Declan McGrady, a trick I'd use to my full advantage. Satisfied with my plan and my ability to execute it, I trudged across the cruise ship to my stateroom.

THE SUITE WAS LARGER than my NYC apartment. I had no idea how the staff had managed to beat me to the room, but my bags were waiting inside, tucked in a corner in the entry, which opened to a spacious sitting room. I lowered my duffle to the floor, the one bag I hadn't allowed the busboys to claim while I was getting my suite's key.

I flicked on the light, stifled a groan at the full body ache I had been dealing with the entire day. Somewhere in the room was a jacuzzi, and the first thing I intended to do was soak. Once I'd transformed into a living prune, I would flop into bed until my stomach demanded as much food as it could hold.

Maybe the *Snow Princess* was new, but unlike most cruise ships, it hadn't retired the tradition of the buffet, and I meant to take advantage of it. There were proper restaurants on board as well, but I wouldn't indulge in those until I had satisfied my biting hunger.

The rustle of fabric on fabric was the only warning I got before someone jumped out at me from around the corner of the room leading into the hallway. I caught a glimpse of blue before an arm cracked across my shoulders.

My work involved flexibility and strength, and I partnered gymnastics with Aikido, a defensive martial art, and extreme sports to stay fit. I rolled with the blow, twisted around, and dipped into a back flip, sticking the landing and sliding into a defensive stance. My suit somehow survived the stunt without ripping; if it had been fitted to me properly, I probably would've torn it.

I caught a glimpse of tanned skin, blue eyes, and blond hair before my assailant lunged for me again in an unarmed strike at my shoulder. By size alone, I determined he was male, easily several inches taller than me with a substantial amount of extra muscle. Lifting my left arm, I caught hold of his wrist, shifted my weight, and used my hip to toss him.

The move should've bought me time to escape, but no sooner had I released him, he twisted, landed on his feet, spun, and knocked my legs out from under me in a sweeping kick. I hit the floor hard, the air rushing out of my lungs. Bracing my arms, I brought my legs up to build momentum to surge to my feet.

I made it halfway before an elbow to the chest drove me back to the floor. A knee to my side finished knocking the rest of my breath out of me, and a shove rolled me onto my stomach. Blinding pain stabbed through my left wrist and elbow, and in the split second of shock, my assailant had me pinned, one hand on the back of my head, a knee jammed into the small of my back against my spine, and my left arm twisted behind my back.

His booted toe rested on my right hand with just enough pressure to keep me down. I froze, every muscle in my body tense while I debated my options. All it would take for him to do a lot of damage would be jam his knee against my spine harder or twist my wrist. His hand on my head hampered my mobility and further limited my ability to break free.

A passing interest and a brown belt in Aikido was no match for the hold he had on me. The ship doing lazy flip flops and circles around me didn't help matters any, either. While being a werewolf should have given me an edge, I'd worn myself so thin on the journey from France to Germany I couldn't muster the strength to even attempt to free myself.

I sighed my surrender. "You could have knocked."

"Would you have let me in?" From the accent, he was American, although I couldn't pinpoint where he was from. He wasn't a New Yorker; the accent was wrong. I couldn't think of any east coast city with quite the same cadence, nor did he sound southern, which left a west coast state or a northern border state.

"Probably not," I admitted. "Since you went through so much trouble, who are you and what do you want?"

The pressure on my spine eased, although he kept a firm grip on my head. His fingers shifted, and I hissed as he found one of the knots still marking my skull. "Are you all right, sir?"

Sir? There was only one group of people who would sir *me*, and they were all associated with the government or military. I hadn't seen any of them since I had pulled my disappearing trick for a quieter criminal life of high-classed thievery.

I groaned. "You have got to be kidding me."

No matter what I did, I just couldn't catch a break. Six hours shouldn't have been enough time for someone to get the passenger list for a cruise liner, run it through the government databases, flag it, and send someone out to confirm my identity. There were hundreds upon hundreds of men named Daniel McClain.

My passport number, a required field for

booking my ticket, must have been what triggered the flag, although why would anyone be actively monitoring cruise ships for my passport?

"Sir?"

"Marine, SEAL, or Ranger?" It took every bit of my willpower to swallow my sigh.

"SEAL, sir."

"You know they care when they send the best."

"Of course, sir."

"What the bloody hell did you do, steal a rocket to get here in time to set up your ambush? I only booked six hours ago."

"I was stationed in London, sir, and was briefed in the air."

"How about you go station yourself on the couch," I suggested, fighting the urge to spew a string of modern curses worthy of a former military officer. Closing my eyes was a mistake. The darkness I'd spent days fighting sucked me in and refused to let me go.

Chapter Seven

THE PRESENCE of something icy on my brow jerked me awake, dumped me in a body that hurt far too much, and startled me into motion, which was aborted by an elbow to the chest.

"Easy, sir."

It took several long moments for my brain to catch up with my body. A SEAL had kicked my ass across my suite. I had no recollection of how I had gotten off the floor, but I was on the couch with my feet propped up on the far arm. A bag of ice across my forehead proved to be the source of the chill.

The SEAL had stripped me of my jacket and had unbuttoned my shirt, revealing the mottling of bruises I had earned at Scallywag's castle.

"And here I hoped you were a figment of my imagination. Marvelous." I contemplated getting up, thought better of it, and reached to touch the back of my head, which throbbed far more than I thought it should.

"It looks like you got on the end of a bad op, sir. I haven't seen so many bruises since my first week of boot camp."

"Your CO must have gone soft."

The SEAL sat back on his heels and watched me through narrowed eyes. "Hardly. The briefing neglected to mention you were still in operations, sir."

That the government wasn't involved with the women held hostage in Scallywag's castle both bothered and annoyed me. Their American accents worried me; the government had a responsibility to protect its citizens. My wolf agreed, but he took it a step further.

He wanted to protect women and children over all, something I agreed with.

My desire to safeguard others had kept me serving the United States government for longer than I cared to think about. I had no doubts the man who had taken me down was a good operative; he possessed the hardened look of someone who hadn't just seen the fires of war but had danced in the flames and emerged a changed man. "I missed the memo, too. I'm not. Haven't been for a decade. I didn't know I was involved with an extraction until I was neck deep and running it from the inside."

Cocking his head to the side, the SEAL stared at me, probably wondering if I had lost my mind. Unplanned ops with no contingencies often meant a death sentence for the sod stuck with it, and no agent of any sort wanted to run an S mission, not without some hope of survival.

Until I found out what the government wanted, I had to play the SEAL's game—or find out if I remembered half of what I'd learned decades ago in my piecemeal training. I couldn't escape by sea; SEALs spent weeks upon weeks mastering surf and pool skills for aquatic combat, including neutralizing and restraining hostiles.

"What are your orders?" I asked, resigning myself to either an interrogation or an escort. If the SEAL had been ordered to neutralize me, I wouldn't have woken up at all.

"I'll be escorting you back to the United States, sir, where you'll be debriefed."

"Debriefed," I echoed, unable to hide my astonishment. Was debriefed another term for interrogating the life out of me?

I'd been out of the game for far too long.

"Yes, sir."

"Your name?"

"Lane Fredrick, Petty Officer Second Class, sir."

"I don't suppose if I order you to cut the sir poppycock you'll actually listen, will you?"

"No, sir."

"Damned SEALs," I muttered, and against my better judgment, I lurched upright, wincing at the way the healing bullet wound across my shoulder stretched. The hole in my arm wasn't much better, and I extended my hand and gave it a good shake to test the injury. A splotch of red marred my white shirt. "Ah, bloody mangled strumpet."

Fredrick coughed. "Sir?"

"Don't worry about it. Nothing a bandage and some time won't fix. I've been going nonstop for a week. I need a shower, something to eat, and some sleep, and not necessarily in that order. Are we going to have a problem, Fredrick?"

"No, sir. My orders are to extract you to the United States without incident. Your health is my top priority."

I couldn't stop myself from laughing. "Good luck with that. You're going to need it."

I SLEPT through the entire first day and night of the cruise, waking long enough to appease the obnoxious SEAL determined to shove food down my throat whether I liked it or not. I had a vague recollection of soaking in the jacuzzi, and I did it solely to annoy my unwanted bodyguard. My wolf turned coat, more than happy to ignore the military's return to our life and leave the task of protecting our temporary den to Fredrick.

My head still hurt, but I pretended the pain didn't exist; no amount of regular painkillers would work even if I took them. Medication rarely worked, which I considered a shitty price to pay for the advantages of being a werewolf. Some of the hospital-grade drugs packed enough of a punch to help, but I hadn't tried any in almost a decade.

Lane Fredrick was conked out on the couch, and in the time since flooring me, he had relaxed enough to remove his suit jacket. Shaking my head, I headed into the suite's kitchenette to coerce the coffee machine into doing its job.

I should've stuck with my real name and risked my client forcing Anthony to expose my location. My hell client was likely easier and safer to handle than the US government with a SEAL representative to ensure they kept me right where they wanted me.

Debriefing would be followed by—or include—a desertion charge, although they might consider my training and MO as justification for my disappearance. My last job hadn't ended well, not for me or anyone on my team.

Considering the government had been the one to teach me the finer points of dropping off their radar, I needed to get into gear or I'd end up in even more trouble.

I still wondered sometimes what had been so important to be worth five lives, and I wasn't sure I wanted to know. Blanking out the more torrid details of my past served me well, but with a SEAL determined to drag me back, I needed to come to terms with it or make my next great escape.

Unfortunately for me, the SEAL likely knew about my second passport and my real name, which would require me to dig out the antiquated identity I'd used when serving as the government's lap dog and concoct a cover story to explain why I had no valid identification.

It'd be easier to hit a black market somewhere and start fresh, assuming I could give a SEAL with modern training the slip long enough to pull it off. The challenge tempted me; I had built my reputation as Declan McGrady on pulling off impossible heists and risky stunts.

All it took to make a new man was some creativity and enough money. If my client had paid up, half a million dollars could make it happen. My thoughts circled around in my head, and I considered the viability of such an idea.

When the coffee was ready, I added a pinch of salt and sipped it. I headed to the suite's balcony, sweeping aside the curtain to look out over the sea.

"According to my briefing, you had very unconventional training for a Marine, Major. Do you even know how to swim, sir?" The humor in Lane Fredrick's voice partnered with the competitive edge I expected from a SEAL.

"I jumped off a hundred-foot cliff into the ocean about a week ago and only got shot twice in the process. I'd like to see you do that, Petty Officer Fredrick." I took another sip of my coffee. The waves swelled and rolled, large enough to give the cruise ship the slight rocking motion I liked about traveling at sea.

Had things been different, I probably would've enjoyed a life in the military, especially within the Navy, held at the whims of the fickle ocean.

"You're a cliff diver? I didn't take you for the extreme sports type."

"I'm also a gymnast and figure skater." Both were true, though I hadn't laced up in well over a year. I hadn't done traditional gymnastics in ages, although I found practical uses for the skill.

"That explains that rather untraditional usage of Aikido during our scuffle."

"It comes in useful from time to time."

"What made you resurface now?"

"If I had known I'd be ambushed by a SEAL, I would've taken the risk of being tracked by my client. Being railroaded into performing an unexpected extraction is safer, and I think I would've preferred it." Voicing a dissatisfied huff, I turned to face my new detail, looking him over from head to toe. I pegged him at twenty-five, in the height of his prime, with a single scar across his cheek, which I figured came from a too close call with a high-caliber weapon. "Before you start with your sir poppycock again, I'll set the record straight. My name is Declan McGrady. I'll answer to Declan or McGrady, and I'll even pay attention if you use both if you want to be uptight about it. You toss a sir at me, and I'll pretend I didn't hear a word you said. Understood?"

"That's the name on your other passport."

"Sure is, Fredrick. Good to know basic reading comprehension is still a requirement for a SEAL."

Laughter answered my taunt. "If you call me Lane, I'll call you Declan."

"Deal. I've been out for almost a decade, Lane. The last thing on my agenda is to make any form of return to military service. I don't know what sort of swill you've been fed, but I'm not your caliber, never was, and never will be. That so-called promotion to Major was part of some cover up on route to my last op, and that's where the story begins and ends. I'm out, and fully intend to stay that way. I was never technically an actual Marine despite the bullshit promotion they tried to foist on me. I wasn't *officially* anything."

"You are now officially a major, Major. I was told you'd likely feel that way during my briefing. However, from my understanding, you rank among the elite extraction specialists despite your unconventional training. Compliments don't come down the line readily, and but there were a lot of pretty words being tossed around by the uppers. They certainly don't send a SEAL on a manhunt for a nobody."

I snorted. "I've worked with enough Marines, SEALs, and Rangers to know exactly how your ilk feels about pretty words. Did you wipe your ass with them before or after they dropped you in Hamburg? Did they loosen the restrictions on drug use? It sounds to me like a lot of commanding officers were dropping acid over the weekend."

I drained my coffee and limped my way to the kitchenette to refill my mug.

"The limp from your op?"

"How many ops have you gone on where you walked away clean, Lane?"

"Plenty," he replied, his tone full of pride.

"How many S missions?"

Pouring my coffee and adding my pinch of salt filled the silence, and when the SEAL remained silent, I strolled back to the window, staring out over the sea. "Every time you get your assignment, you probably offer thanks your mission isn't one you know you're being sent on with the expectation you're not coming back."

"I won't deny it."

The past always found a way of biting me in the ass, but I was running out of ways to avoid it. I'd lied to my client more than I liked; maybe I wasn't traditional, but I was ex-military. I defined what it meant to be expendable, and everyone knew it. "When they briefed you, did they tell you some of my nicknames they liked to call me?"

"They called you the Bard, I assume due to your enjoyment of dated language. It was the only nickname they mentioned."

I laughed long and hard. "That part's a little true, but that's not the reason they gave it to me. It's a lot more nefarious than that. The full title was 'the Man the Bard Couldn't Kill.' My commanding officer was the original Bard." Sighing, I fiddled with my mug, staring down at my coffee. Knowing the man, he probably was still around, haunting some government facility. "I spent the last three years of service sliding from S mission to S mission. The government aborted my last mission after we were on the ground and we had already extracted what they were after. Some say the S means suicide, others claim it means sacrifice, but either way, my team was laid out on the altar with knives at our throats, cut off with no back up and no hope of extraction. Five of the team died on the way out. I was split from the others and decided to go underground."

Underground was exactly where I wanted to go again, and I once again evaluated my chances of dodging a SEAL in his prime. I canted my head so I could watch Lane in the window's reflection.

If my words bothered him, he showed no sign of it. "Part of my orders are to determine if you're the real deal or an enemy with a stolen passport."

"What do you think?"

"You haven't aged much."

"Good genes."

"You might be interested to know you're the last asset that hasn't been recovered from that mission."

I grimaced. Ten men had gone in, five had died during the mission, I had escaped, and the last thing I saw of my other four teammates were their backs while I drew fire away from them.

A decade hadn't been long enough to erase their names and faces from my memories.

"Is that what they're going with this time? Asset?"

My client had called me an asset, too.

"A very valuable one. When I signaled mission success, they flew in someone else to make certain there were no difficulties on board until this ship reaches a set coordinate, after which we'll be joining a submarine."

I choked on my coffee. "Is there a second SEAL on board?"

"You'll meet him later. He's scouting the ship and doing recon."

"Is he a SEAL or someone playing pretend?" I knew all about playing pretend, and the last thing I wanted was to have to dodge around someone after the secrets I wasn't ready to reveal on my own.

"I'm pretty sure that's above your pay grade and clearance, Major."

"I'd have to get paid to have a pay grade, Lane. Do I still have clearance? If so, someone's botched things up."

"Point," he conceded.

"You people really aren't going to let me enjoy my cruise, are you?"

"Afraid not. For mission security, the exact time and location of the transfer is confidential."

"You're going to make me jump into the ocean again, aren't you?"

"Don't worry. We won't let you drown, Marine."

"Fucking SEALs!"

Lane laughed.

WITH MY UNWANTED AUDIENCE, taking full advantage of the buffet wasn't an option. I sighed and stared at the selection of meats. I needed protein and a lot of calories to sustain my wolf. My flight across Europe and my inability to hunt thanks to my glowing fur coat had reduced my healing to human average.

Grumbling over the effort involved in filling my plate to a normal man's standards, I trudged back to the table Lane had chosen, tucked to the side with two easy routes of escape while a wall guarded our backs.

The SEAL's eyes narrowed as he considered my choices. "Your file stated you had a high metabolism and required protein additives. That can't be nearly enough food."

The temptation to dump the plate over Lane's head before beating him with it almost got the better of me. Instead of venting my frustration, I sat, picked up my fork, and took a dainty bite, meeting him glare for glare.

"He's worse than a bitch with a bone, McClain. Or, should I say McGrady? Give it up and do what he wants, or he'll annoy you to death."

I inhaled my food and choked on it, wheezing as I got a lungful of roast beef. By the time I dislodged it, the shock of someone sneaking up behind me wore off enough to realize I recognized the voice. The roughened, gravelly voice hadn't changed much over the past decade, and the years hadn't erased the instinctual need to rise and salute, though I capped it before I got to my feet.

The real Bard of the US Navy, Rear Admiral Jack Haney, sat between me and Lane, setting a plate piled high with fried chicken in front of him. When I had last seen him, his hair had been solid black. Streaks of gray ran through it now, but there were few other signs of his age. The hours before deployment on my final S mission remained a bitter memory, and his presence served as living proof I hadn't been an official anything and passed around the branches of the US military.

I'd only seen him in uniform, and his black suit bothered me almost as much as his presence on the cruise ship. My wolf cowered, his presence retreating to the back of my head, leaving me to face off against the man who had successfully brought my entire life to ruin.

He didn't smile, but there was amusement in his dark blue eyes. "He's right, you know. I've seen you eat, boy, and that ain't nothin' more than a bloody appetizer."

Several pieces of chicken made their way onto my plate, and Haney's subtle squinting warned me against arguing.

I turned my glare to Lane, pointing my fork at my former commanding officer. "This rump-fed, pickled liver nuisance is the Bard. If I throw him overboard, do you think anyone would notice? He's gotta be at least ten years over his expiration date."

"You two have become friendly. Fill me in on the details, Lane."

"Probable concussion, two gunshot wounds, potential fractures, substantial bruising, and probable malnutrition," Lane reported.

Haney grunted, and I felt his gaze focus on me, sending shivers running through me all the way down to my toes. Even after a decade, the man put me on edge, and I tensed, waiting for him to play his hand.

Instead of launching into a lecture or dishing out orders, Haney remained silent.

If he wanted to play, I'd play, and I meant to test his mood with my opening volley. The man had more layers than a Picasso and was equally difficult to categorize.

"Of all of the louses the military could send, they sent you?" I muttered, stabbing at a piece of meat so I wouldn't be tempted to assault an officer of the US Navy. I ignored the chicken, although by the time I finished my roast beef, my wolf's appetite would likely demand I accept the man's offering.

"I sent myself, son. It happens from time to time. I like the new name; it suits you better than McClain. I like it so much I've decided you get to keep it. Been sitting on it long?"

"What, didn't bother with running my passport through the system? You're losing your touch, Haney."

"Vice Admiral Haney to you, son."

"Don't you mean Petty Officer, with the emphasis on petty?" At the rate I was stabbing my roast, I'd break the plate in half and shred the meat long before I finished eating it. "Did you run the passport or not?"

"You've put some steel in your spine over the years. Good. You'll need it."

When I said nothing, Haney shrugged and took a bite of his chicken. I waited for him to chew a few times, timing my words for right when he was about to swallow. "McClain's the one with the fake passport, *sir*."

Payback was a bitch, and I got a certain

amount of satisfaction watching my former commanding officer cough, splutter, and choke on his meal. Unfortunately for me, he recovered, leveling a glare at me. "You were investigated and vetted, son. Don't think you can pull that bullshit on me."

I held my hands up in surrender, allowing myself a smirk. "You didn't vet and investigate hard enough."

"You smug little son of a bitch." Haney's admiring tone surprised me, and keeping a wary eye on the man, I turned most of my attention back on my dinner. When I kept quiet, both of the other men followed my lead, eating without a word.

I finished first, setting my plate aside and wondering if it was worth the effort to get up and get more. Life as a werewolf was a constant Catch 22; if I didn't eat enough, my body pillaged the little reserves I did build, making it that much harder to scrounge the energy to be bothered with eating.

I was at the point I wanted to crawl back to my suite, collapse on the bed, and sleep for a month. Throwing myself overboard was also looking like a viable alternative to dealing with the circumstances life threw my way. Instead of holding onto the past, I should've burned my old passport so I never would've been tempted to use it.

"You can either go get yourself a proper plate of food, or I will get one for you," Haney threatened, pointing a drumstick in my direction. "March, son."

I wasn't his son, nor would I ever be, but I was too tired to argue with him. Sometimes obedience paid off, and maybe if I did what he wanted, he'd leave me alone. I had my doubts.

The real bitch with a bone was Haney, and I knew it. He'd keep gnawing away at me until he got exactly what he wanted, and as always, I'd be powerless to do a single thing about it.

Chapter Eight

COMMON SENSE DICTATED I stop eating when I matched the normal amount of food a man consumed, but Haney and Lane joined forces, coercing me into just one more plate of food.

Five mountainous plates later, the sharp bite of my hunger eased.

Declan: 0, SEALs: 1.

I wasn't sure Haney had ever been a SEAL; there was a lot I didn't know about the man, including his fixation on fried chicken, half of which ended up on my plate. My wolf was both wary and intrigued by the man's determination to turn me into a glutton.

At least the waiters took away the empty plates as we emptied them, and all I could smell from them over the myriad of scents in the air was their amusement.

Almost two hours later, I signaled my defeat with a shake of my head and a wave of my hand when Haney tried to pawn off yet another piece of chicken onto my plate.

There was a fine line between full, functional, and comatose, and I toed it. It was tempting to flop onto the table and sleep it off, although I doubted anyone would appreciate it. "Eat your own ruddy chicken."

"I suppose you've eaten a satisfactory amount," he replied, and at the doubt in the man's voice, I jerked my head up to stare at him.

"I'm impressed at how much you can pack away." Lane chuckled, shaking his head. "Healing takes a lot out of a man, and you have a long way to go until you're fit. Did you acquire a cabin of your own, sir?"

"Plenty of room for the three of us in McGrady's suite if my understanding of the situation is correct. We can talk there, and I'll brief you both on the situation."

"Debrief," I corrected.

"That, too."

With my stomach full, my wolf passed out in a content, satiated daze, once again leaving me to deal with the human element of our lives. I swallowed my sigh, staggered to my feet, and hissed at the ache in both my ankles.

Haney stood and caught my elbow before I had a chance to regain my balance. "You're moving like you've been flogged, son."

"Partially my fault, sir. We had a scuffle when he first arrived," Lane replied.

"Of course you did. McGrady's jumpy on a good day, and he's as much of the fight type as he is the flight type." Once I straightened, Haney released me. "Where's the suite?"

The problem with my suite was its location; for the convenience of the majority of passengers, the buffet was located in the heart of the ship, requiring us to traverse the *Snow Princess,* which meant we had a long walk ahead of us. Lane adopted a brisk stride, which was matched by Haney. Pride dictated I keep up to prove I hadn't gone soft.

In some ways, I had. I felt thin, and I was glad my suite didn't have a scale, because I suspected I was at least thirty below par. One forced feeding at a buffet wouldn't restore what I'd lost, and if my guess was correct, I'd need an entire winter of hunting as wolf and man to build myself back up to what I had been prior to accepting my client's job.

Two months of slimming down hadn't done me any favors.

Lane entered the suite first, his body tense as he scouted for trouble. I waited in the entry with Haney while he did a sweep of the entire place. Only after Lane signaled the all clear did the Vice Admiral close the suite's door and head for the couch.

I was tempted to flop on the floor and sleep, but instead, I made my way to the kitchenette and brewed a new pot of coffee. Several cups and staying on my feet would keep me conscious long enough to find out what my former CO was up to.

"The answer is no," I informed Haney,

drumming my fingers on the counter while waiting for the coffee to brew. "I don't need briefed. I need debriefed."

"You might change your mind once you hear the situation, McGrady."

I had heard those words before, and we both knew they were the truth. All it took was a good sob story to rile my wolf up, and once he demanded justice, I was powerless to say no. "You sound confident."

"Seven Americans have disappeared, are suspected to be in Europe, and we want you to be a part of the rescue and extraction team, McGrady. You've a knack for finding things people don't want found, and we haven't been able to locate these civilians. We have limited information, but we're of the opinion they have been kidnapped in order to manipulate some rather influential American businessmen."

I groaned and slumped, bowing my head. "This is not my type of op, Bard."

"We've run out of leads, and we need you. You're the only operative I know who can find things people don't want found. Your ability to infiltrate sticky situations and get out alive makes you invaluable. You'll have a full support team, the best intel the government can provide, and no leash. We need these people back alive, and you're the ideal man for the job."

"Until I was stupid enough to use my passport to book this cruise, Haney, I wasn't even a factor. I'm not your live-body extraction guy. You have far better, more qualified men for that."

"And you'll be working with our best. We need your intel, we need your plan building, and we need your ability to execute unexpected extractions."

The coffee maker gurgled, and I grabbed a mug to pour myself a cup. I glared at the Vice Admiral. "I wasn't even a factor until recently."

"That alone should make you aware of the severity of the situation. I need you for this op, son."

Instead of my usual salt, I went for the cream and sugar, which raised brows from both men, who watched me butcher my coffee until it turned pale gray and my spoon all but stood up in the syrupy mess. I drank it all back without stopping, shuddered at its sickly sweetness, and made another.

"Fine. Brief me, and you better make it good, or I'm tossing myself overboard and swimming for shore."

"There are seven notable businessmen in the United States and Canada who have had people close to them kidnapped and taken as hostages. We believe they will be used as bargaining chips to prevent certain business transactions with the US government from happening. These transactions are rather sensitive. All of the individuals missing are women. They are close enough to these men that they're important bargaining chips. They were all kidnapped within a three-month window."

"No hostage terms or ransom demands?" I asked before treating my second coffee as I had my first.

I needed the sugar to function, and the extra calories wouldn't hurt me any. I gave my third cup a single pinch of salt before making my way into the sitting room.

"The only contact we've had include some anonymous warnings against working with firms with known government connections, which were sent to the businessmen along with lewd photographs of the hostages."

"Lewd." Rape was a likelihood, depending on who was behind the kidnappings. "Okay. They're potential rape victims. Do we have any solid information?"

"That's the problem. We can't get a trace-back to where the messages are originating; they're being sent expedited mail, clean of fingerprints, from all over Europe and Asia. The correspondences are weekly, and the culprit is using a new set of contacts each time to send the packages. The few times we've gotten a hit, the chain has been broken, usually by a murder, effectively preventing us from figuring out who is behind it."

Setting my mug down on the coffee table, I paced across the sitting room, clacking my teeth as I considered the situation. "Why do you think I can do any better than trained CIA field agents?"

"You have the devil's luck."

"I hate you," I muttered.

Haney didn't seem concerned by my complaint, chuckling and relaxing enough to prop his feet up on the coffee table near my mug. "We don't have jack shit on this case. We have their names, we know who they're connected to, and we have some half-baked theories on the kidnapper's goals. There have been no ransom requests, and our concern is that the kidnapper has no intention of releasing the women, preferring a holding pattern. If he wanted a ransom..."

The man sighed, and I echoed him. "If he was after a ransom, he'd be a lot easier to find, but the ladies would likely already be dead."

"I thought you'd understand. The real problem is the fact these disappearances are high-profile enough to worry other investors and companies, adding more delays to a very important contract we need."

"The culprit is likely targeting the military or government, using intimidation tactics." I paced to the window, staring out into the darkness. The waxing moon was on the rise, and I was aware of it as a tingling throughout my entire body. As always, I ignored it, and my wolf stirred enough to sigh his disappointment we couldn't answer its call. In a few days, his disappointment would crest when the moon reached its peak, and we'd suffer together in silence as always.

When we finally found our way deep into a snowy wood, we'd howl for forgiveness at ignoring the moon's silvery glow. Until then, we would wait.

"We have a two-part mission. First, we extract the women and return them to their families. Second, we locate and neutralize the party behind their disappearances," Haney announced. "Pull out the file, Fredrick. You may as well see exactly what you're getting into, McGrady."

"I'm not a neutralizer, Haney."

"You're going to serve as our scout and nothing more. You won't be on the kill team unless you want to be. Your role will be intel, scouting, planning, and analysis."

"It's the scouting part that tries to get me killed," I grumbled, rubbing my forehead in the futile attempt to drive away my growing headache. "Self-extraction after the scout?"

"You'll have an extraction team for you and the hostages should you locate them. We're planning the op as a one and done. If you find them, you'll bag them and bring them home."

"You know, I could have been sitting behind a desk for the past ten years pushing papers around for all you know, Haney. You have no idea if I'm still qualified for this work."

"I know you, son. You don't sit on your

laurels. You've been up to something over the years, though hell if I know what."

I glanced at Lane, who studiously examined one of the paintings on the wall. Following his stare, I took in the replication of Monet's *Waterlilies,* unable to smother my smile. "That's a shoddy print. The colors are dull, and the strokes aren't visible."

Lane snorted. "You're unique, I'll give you that. First, your bracelet is calling from ancient Egypt and wants to go home. Second, did you take an art major or something? What sort of Marine are you?"

I pulled up my sleeve to glance down at the scarab bracelet. For its size, the thing didn't weigh nearly as much as I thought it should, and I had a tendency to forget about it. It was thin enough it fit under my dress shirt, loose enough I could shunt it up my arm so I could button the sleeve, and light enough I didn't care too much I hadn't figured out how to remove it. "The hinges are busted," I improvised. "I'll get it fixed later."

"McGrady has a certain reputation for helping others misplace their things," Haney muttered, shaking his head. "Check your pockets before you leave."

"Too much effort today. You're safe." I sighed, headed for the arm chair beside the couch, and slumped onto it. "Who are the businessmen being targeted?"

"This is classified information and does

not leave this room," Haney ordered. "Understood?"

I straightened, reaching for my coffee to have a sip while I considered if I really wanted to become irrevocably involved in a hostage crisis. "Understood, Vice Admiral. What classification?"

"Higher than your normal pay grade, Major."

The slight emphasis on Major worried me, and unnerved, I used my coffee as a distraction and a chance to steady my nerves. "I already went over this with Lane. I have to be paid to have a pay grade."

I really didn't like the way Haney smirked at me. "You'll find all back pay for the past ten years is ready to be deposited into an active account, on or off-shore. They've been in holding for your recovery, as you have not been debriefed. You've been technically on active duty roster, serving on a top secret undercover mission involving complete radio silence. Of course, I may have used your circumstances as part of some high-level training exercises to test the mettle of potential recruits, although none of them were able to determine your whereabouts."

"I'm pretty sure that isn't legal, Haney."

"We all have our faults."

"Who are the targeted civilians?"

"While I said seven, there are ten businessmen in particular affected by the kidnappings. I have a suspicion one of the hostages was specifically chosen to corner three specific men associated with one woman. Richard Murphy is the closest to one of the hostages, although she also has close ties to Dante Anderson, who is an active supplier for the military. In addition to this, Richard Murphy's father-in-law, Charles Desmond, is a respected lawyer and also a rather successful businessman. Of the three, Mr. Anderson is the most important, as he serves as a negotiator between the United States and several other nations."

"Why hasn't the culprit targeted them for kidnapping, then?"

"All three gentlemen have been, ah, troubled over the past few months, especially Mr. Anderson. He has been assigned a six-man squad to ensure his safety. Unfortunately, Mr. Murphy and Mr. Desmond are both headstrong men who have certain opinions on how they should spend their time. Despite our continued suggestions they leave the extraction to trained professionals, they insist on trying to involve themselves in the case." Haney sighed. "They're rather like you in that regard. In order to muddle their efforts, we may have leveled some accusations of their disappearances at Mr. Desmond. Unfortunately, our ploy motivated all three rather than discouraged their efforts."

I hid my wince by taking another sip of coffee. "In addition to having to extract seven women, we also…"

Something clicked in my head, and I spluttered, trailing off to consider the unlikeliest of possibilities. Benjamin Scully had held seven women in his castle. My client had mentioned being accused of the kidnappings of seven women, one of whom he knew by name.

The evidence I had already extracted the women in question mounted. The more I learned about the situation, the less I wanted to be involved in it. Groaning, I set my mug down, bowed my head, and ran my fingers through my hair.

"Problem, Major?"

"I was just thinking about the idea of having to extract a bunch of loose cannons during an already convoluted operation, sir." It wasn't quite a lie, but it wasn't the truth, either. I regretted not having delved for more information on the two-man team set to complete the extraction I had organized. "How are these men involving themselves?"

"Private investigators, mostly," Haney complained. "Fortunately, they haven't done anything excessive or illegal yet. The only good they've done is establish an exact timeline of each and every kidnapping, including the method used to grab each of the women."

"That's substantial information."

"We could put it to good use if we could anticipate the targets. Unfortunately, we have limited information on why the culprit chose the victims he has." Haney sighed. "We've been chasing dry lead after dry lead for almost six months. We have reason to believe they are still alive, but we do not know how long that will be the case."

"How influential are these three men?"

"Extremely. They're quiet, so far as multi-millionaires and billionaires go. They prefer to stay off the radar. They're all married, and Mr. Anderson and Mr. Desmond both have children. Mr. Murphy's wife is almost as successful as he is, which is another thorn in our side. If she becomes involved, I foresee a lot of problems for the ground team."

"She's not involved?"

"Not yet, no. She only involves herself if she believes Mr. Murphy is in danger. We're worried the hostage situation will escalate to involve them. It's in our best interest to make certain none of these individuals fall into the wrong hands." Haney refused to meet my gaze, which set me on edge.

"You have no clue in hell where Mr. Murphy is right now, do you?"

Silence answered my question in more ways than one. I groaned, leaning back into my chair and wishing I had never been so stupid to accept half a million dollars to take photographs of a snobby collector's middling art collection.

"The woman's about to involve herself, isn't she?"

"She assured me if I put my best men on the mission, she would give me two weeks to locate her husband. She originally wanted forty-eight hours."

"When was that?"

"A little over a week ago."

The timing matched when I had extracted the seven women from Scallywag's castle. I glanced in the direction of the moon, narrowing my eyes in speculation. The women would likely need to become wolves to answer the moon's calling in a few days. If they were wise, they would have gone somewhere secluded and far from civilization.

I'd never had a pack, but I understood my wolf's desire for one; if Mr. Murphy was associated with one of the werewolf women, he, too, was likely one. It was always safer to operate under the worst-case assumption, and if I assumed Mr. Murphy was a werewolf and Patricia was a part of his pack, I had no doubt he would've crossed the ocean to retrieve her himself.

I would've done far more than cross the sea to come to the aid of a teammate, which came as close to having pack as I got. The men had come and gone from my life in a steady stream, but I remembered the names and faces of every man lost. The survivors soothed some of the ache of my failures, though not by much.

"What are you thinking, McGrady?" Haney asked, his tone sharp with impatience.

How the hell was I supposed to find a bunch of werewolves darting around Europe before Scallyway got his act together and hunted them down? If he had managed to catch seven and hold them, two men wouldn't be enough to stop him.

"I need a new job. This one is a load of fucking bullshit. I'm going to need the details on the kidnappings, the timelines, and any information on how they were transported from the United States to Europe. I'm also going to need every scrap of information you have on Mr. Murphy and what I can expect if I have to extract his meddling ass out of this mess. If Mr. Murphy has any potential accomplices working with him, I'll need to know who they are and what they're capable of. So help me god, if you are bullshitting me about a team and a full extraction, I'm going to feed you to a fucking shark."

"Welcome aboard, son."

Declan: 0, SEALs: 2.

Chapter Nine

CONFIRMATION of my suspicions came in the form of seven photographs. While my vision had been blurred when I met the women, I recognized Julie, as did my wolf.

He was far more enthused about the idea of meeting her again than I was. According to her information sheet, she was twenty-seven, had worked as an executive secretary for one of the targeted businessmen, and had won several local karate competitions. My wolf was eager to learn the werewolf female was listed as single. Her father had been former military and had died in combat several years ago.

Her mother lived in New Hampshire while Julie lived in New York City.

The other women were either married or engaged; Patricia was listed as a close friend of Mr. Murphy's, and she was engaged to the son of another friend of his. On paper, the relationships of the women to their respective businessmen made no sense, but when I factored in the possibility all of them were also werewolves, the situation disturbed me.

I had never experienced it for myself, but I understood my wolf's longing for a pack and a mate. The thought of having a pack and losing a precious member of it sickened me.

Setting aside the sheets on the women, I snatched up the second file, grabbed my new cell out of my pocket, and tossed it up and down as I considered my options. Contacting Anthony and my client would probably give me the best leads, but if I did, I'd have to reveal I knew exactly what had happened to the women, and I wasn't sure if I wanted to play that card yet.

There was no way of knowing if Scallywag had a mole inside the military.

"McGrady—"

"Declan," I corrected, flipping through the sheets on the businessmen involved with the kidnapped women. I froze when I reached Mr. Anderson's file. The familiar face staring up at me startled me into straightening. "Hello, hello. Who do we have here?"

I knew him by a different name, which didn't surprise me; those who worked under the government's radar always hid behind a mask. When we had started working together, neither one of us had been willing to give a name at all, resulting in an ongoing joke. He was Bob, I was Bob, and neither one of us had dug any deeper than that. I hadn't seen him in a few years, instead working with one of his close associates for what I needed, but I liked the man.

In a world of cutthroat dealings, there were few who had such clear eyes.

"That's Mr. Anderson, the liaison I was telling you about." Haney sighed. "Perhaps we should deal with this later. If you're that tir—"

"Stop your whining," I muttered, dialing my contacts number and holding my phone to my ear.

Four rings later, a sleepy voice answered, "Hello?"

"Hey, Brandon. I need you to patch me through to Bob." Struggling against my urge to laugh, I focused on the sheet in front of me in my effort to avoid betraying myself. "Sorry to wake you."

"Oh, hey. You haven't gotten yourself killed yet? What the hell are you doing calling me this time of day?"

"Work, what else? You know me; if it wasn't important, I wouldn't be calling you."

"From Germany? What the hell are you doing in Germany?"

"Doing Bob a big favor, apparently."

"I'll one up you; got a pen handy?"

I reached across the coffee table and stole Haney's pen out of his hand. "Ready."

Brandon gave me a phone number, which I dutifully wrote down. "That's his private cell, so you should be able to get a hold of him. When are you coming back to Miami? We need to get together for a beer."

"Beer sounds good." Picking up the sheet of paper with Bob's number, I got to my feet and headed to the window. "Might be a while, though. I'll give you a call when I'm in the area. Thanks for Bob's number."

"Sure thing. I'm going back to bed now. Take care of yourself and keep out of trouble. You're as bad as Bob for that shit, and it gives me a headache." Brandon hung up on me before I had a chance to reply. Laughing, I dialed Bob.

He answered on the second ring. "Who is this?"

"Bob, it's been a while."

"Oh, great. I'm going to have to change my number again."

I arched a brow at the quip. "When did you develop a sense of humor?"

"Eh, a while back."

"You also seem to have developed an unfortunate case of Canadian." I chuckled, shaking my head. "Grapevine says there's some interesting things going on with you."

"That's an understatement. Are you still up for hire?"

"For you, always. What do you have for me? I'm on an unsecured line, and I have some friends in the room with me."

My 'friends' glared daggers into my back, but I ignored the sense of being watched and scrutinized.

"I know this is outside of your normal work, but how do you feel about a trip to Europe to hunt someone down for me? My hands are tied."

"I can get to Europe. Where?"

"That I can't tell you. I don't know. I lost contact with a friend of mine three days ago. At the time, he was in Switzerland. I need you to find him."

I grunted to acknowledge him and considered the timing. Three days was promising; if the extraction had worked to plan, Switzerland was a good place to make a run for it. There was a healthy tourism trade in the Swiss Alps, and with the full moon rising in a few days, there were a lot of places for a half dozen or so werewolves to hunt and hide. "Email me the basics. No names, just an overview of the circumstances."

"It'll be to you in ten minutes. Can I call you on this number?"

"It's a disposable, so be aware of that."

"Understood. How much do you want for the work?"

"We'll deal with that afterwards. For now, at cost."

"You're not going to bleed my wallet dry? I'm shocked. I'm absolutely shocked."

Laughing, I shook my head. "Not this time, old friend. I still owe you a favor, so let's call it at cost and consider us even."

"Deal. I'll get off the line and send you the info. I'll send the encryption key as a text."

"Sounds good. Take care." I hung up, pocketed my cell, and fetched my mug so I could refill it.

Haney and Lane stared at me, and both of them shifted, their unease reflecting in their expressions. Unable to resist the urge, I smirked at them. Railroading wasn't my style, usually, but there was something satisfying about toying with them as they had toyed with me.

"That was the vaguest bit of business I've heard in a long time," the Vice Admiral admitted, crossing his arms over his chest. "What are you up to?"

"That's above your pay grade, sir," I countered, taking a sip of my coffee.

"I'm starting to dislike that steel in your spine, son."

"How likely is it that there's a mole?"

Both men winced, which was the only answer I needed.

Nodding my acknowledgement of the admission, I returned to my chair, looking over Richard Murphy's file. "I have a few ideas, but if there's a mole, I'm going to need the smallest team I can gather, access to gear, and as much radio silence as you can get me."

"How small of a team do you need?" Haney demanded, sitting straighter.

"One or two men I can trust not to botch the job. They need to be able to handle unwanted surprises and keep their mouths shut."

Haney's smile chilled me. "It's been far too long since I've done any field work. Feel like taking a stroll, Fredrick?"

"You're the boss," the SEAL replied.

Declan, 0, SEALs: 3.

NEXT TIME, there was no way I was allowing Haney to arrange transport. While operating on less than three hours of sleep, the last place I wanted to be was on the top level of the cruise ship watching a helicopter come in for a landing.

Haney and Lane were already in flight suits, and I wore one of my expensive black suits, complete with gold cufflinks and tie. All of my gadgets, including my new cell phone, were in the single duffle Lane carried over his shoulder. The time of day, fortunately, meant most passengers were either asleep or below decks having breakfast.

The last thing I wanted was someone snapping photographs of me boarding a war bird with a military escort. I was rusty enough I couldn't identify the type of helicopter, but I doubted it was meant for long-range flights, which filled me with foreboding at the thought of an air-to-ship transfer and another pickup to reach shore.

The *Snow Princess* had a respectable flight deck, which was the only reason the fiasco wasn't aborted; with enough space for three helicopters, there was room for error, though not enough to soothe my agitated nerves.

The pilot didn't need the room, although he took his sweet time hitting his mark. Once he landed, Lane ducked and ran for the opening door, leaving me and Haney to follow in his wake.

Haney tailed me, probably to make sure I went where he wanted me to go. It was probably wise of him; I was tempted to throw myself overboard to avoid the flight. Helicopter crashes and hard landings *hurt,* and I'd been in several, all of which had involved the ocean in some fashion or another.

When I reached the parked bird, Lane offered me a helmet, which I stuffed over my head. The bird could seat six, and I enjoyed having an empty seat beside me.

I buckled in, grateful I hadn't forgotten everything over the years, and signaled I was ready once I double checked my helmet and belt. With the efficiency I expected—and on some level, missed—the helicopter was skybound and on the way.

Twenty minutes into the flight, I regretted agreeing to anything. The already choppy air churned, and the helicopter bucked like a demented bronco. I kept my mouth shut, although I cast glares in Haney's direction.

The man shrugged. A moment later, he said, "Wait until you see the drop-off point."

"Five minutes, sir," the pilot said. "Nice morning for a swim."

I leaned over and glanced out the side window. White-capped waves crashed below. It reminded me a lot about the conditions in the hours before the cruise liner had sunk on route to Europe.

Yep, the pilot was a SEAL, no doubt about it. Only a SEAL would be insane enough to view the rough waters as a potential place to go for a swim. Then again, I knew a few operatives who would be up for the challenge.

I wasn't one of them.

Four minutes later, the helicopter approached a surfaced submarine, and the waves crashing into it sent spray high into the air. Several men in dive equipment waited on deck. Closing my eyes, I counted to twenty. When that didn't help settle my fraying nerves, I focused on drawing deep breaths.

The submarine was large enough the water wasn't rolling it as bad as I feared, considering the ocean's conditions, but the only way we were getting off the bird and on deck was by jumping. If I made a single misstep, I'd end up in the water, requiring the dive team to haul me out before I drowned.

I sighed. If the pilot was good, he'd hover the helicopter like it was some sort of mechanical hummingbird, allowing me to drop down on a harness and line to the waiting crew below. If he was stellar, he'd bring the damned thing within a few feet of landing, allowing for a free fall jump.

Neither option appealed to me at all.

"If you're ready, I'll hover the bird over the deck," the pilot stated.

I truly did have the devil's luck. I muttered curses and shook my head. Lane and Haney stared at me. While tempted to flip them both off, I went to work unbuckling, keeping an eye on the submarine below as the pilot eased into position.

"Fredrick, you're first. Follow him, McGrady."

I nodded. Lane muscled open the door and secured it, taking his position to jump down to the water-slicked deck below. After taking off his helmet and tossing it to Haney, who stashed it in its proper place, Lane tensed, waited for his moment, and dropped out of the bird to the submarine.

Both his feet slid out from under him on landing, and he hit the metal hard enough I winced in sympathy. Before he was pitched overboard, one of the sailors hauled him to his feet, clearing the way for me to make my jump.

I took off my helmet and hung it up, taking the few extra seconds to brace myself for the transfer, berating myself for becoming entangled in a military mission. The only thing worse than the deck of a submarine was the smothering confines of its insides. My wolf whined in my head, but I ignored his complaints and prepared for the short leap down, ruing my choice of attire, the stormy seas, and the circumstances.

Oxfords were not the ideal shoes for attempting a helicopter-to-submarine transfer. I clenched my teeth and hopped out, ready to drop into a crouch so I wouldn't tumble and roll overboard. Watching Lane slip and slide prepared me for the slick metal.

The pilot hovered the helicopter close enough to the deck that the landing didn't jar my aching bones too much, although I still went down to one knee. A diver took hold of my elbow, pulling me upright to make space for Haney.

The Vice Admiral followed moments behind me, and the instant his feet touched the deck, the pilot left. The spray and rain drenched me, plastering my suit to my body. It didn't take long for the chill to stab at my skin, and I shivered.

I made it inside the submarine without incident, and only one rogue wave washed over the submarine, ensuring I was utterly soaked before descending into the cramped confines of the ship.

As the only one without the benefit of a protective flight suit or wet suit, by the time I got out of the ocean spray and deep into the maze of the submarine, my teeth chattered. It wouldn't have surprised me if someone told me my lips were turning blue.

On the way across the submarine, I peeled

out of my soaked jacket, which Lane took. One of the sailors offered me a dry towel. Until I had a dry change of clothes to go with it, it was pretty pointless, but instead of complaining about it, I went to work on my hair.

While I got curious looks from the working men and women, they ignored me the moment they caught sight of Haney. Salutes were shot off in rapid fire, which the Vice Admiral waved off.

"Hanging in there, McGrady?" Haney gave my shoulder a slap over my healing gunshot wound, hard enough to propel me forward a step.

I hissed. "You're really trying to kill me, aren't you?"

"Would I do that?"

"Yes, you would, Bard, and you know it." I turned, twisted my towel, and whipped the Vice Admiral with it, cracking him in the arm. "Watch the shoulder. It hurts enough without your help."

Several of the sailors close enough to watch my breach of etiquette paled, their stares flicking to Haney before they found work to do. I snorted, shaking my head.

A decade ago, I probably never would have had the balls to towel-whip a commanding officer, but times had changed, and until I had a uniform and they forced me into it, I considered myself a civilian with the misfortune of being roped into a mission.

It wouldn't fly for long, but as long as Haney let me get away with it, I'd toe the line.

"Shit, son. Forgot."

It was as close to as an apology as I'd get from him, which was startling enough I turned my full attention to the man, who gave a one-shoulder shrug at my silent, questioning stare. I narrowed my eyes before returning to the task of drying my hair so I wouldn't freeze to death in the time it took me to hunt down some dry clothes, most of which I was certain was still on board the cruise ship destined for the Caribbean.

In a sane world, I wouldn't have had a reason to be jealous of my luggage.

Haney took the lead, guiding us to the captain's quarters. "Try to remember your manners, son."

"I might even remember how to salute, sir." I draped the towel over my shoulder. It'd been so long since I had been on any military ship I couldn't remember the protocol for boarding, although I was pretty certain dripping all over the captain's quarters wasn't a standard part of operations.

With my luck, Haney meant to make nice with the captain of the submarine he had diverted from its regular mission before hauling me back up top for another flight to shore.

The only thing worse than a stormy-sea drop off was a pick up, and with my luck, instead of holding my own against the waves,

I'd end up in the drink. Being fished out of the ocean by a SEAL ranked pretty close to the top of things I wanted to avoid on the trip.

Haney stared at me for a long moment, sighed, and knocked on the captain's door.

Chapter Ten

I WAS REALLY GETTING tired of people jumping out at me. Submarines didn't offer a whole lot of room to move, and with Haney and Lane blocking my routes of escape, the khaki-clad man had a straight run at me. I recognized the service uniform of an officer, but not in time to stop myself from dropping my shoulder, grabbing him by the front of his uniform, and twisting so I could flip him over me and into Lane.

Both men hit the ground in a tangle of arms and legs. The duffle containing the little we had brought onto the helicopter flew up in the air, and with a dry chuckle, Haney caught it.

"Toad-spotted ratsbane!" I spun, the blood draining from my face as it sank in I had thrown a Navy captain over my shoulder into a SEAL.

"That's not minding your manners, son," Haney chided, lowering the bag to the floor before reaching down to offer his hand to the fallen captain. "My apologies, Captain Williams. Are you all right?"

"I have always wanted to get thrown by a Marine. It was one of my aspirations in life," the captain replied, hopping to his feet without accepting the Vice Admiral's help. He dusted himself off, straightened, and snapped a salute. "Welcome aboard, Vice Admiral, sir."

My salute wasn't as crisp as Lane's nor did it last as long. I should've made a better than half-hearted attempt to mind my manners as Haney had warned, but I was tired—too damned tired to deal with the military, its rigidness, and everything it represented in my life.

"My apologies, Captain, sir."

Captain Williams turned to me and looked me over head to toe. With no sign of gray in his brown hair and bright blue eyes, the man didn't seem very old, likely in his late thirties, which made me wonder how he had elevated his rank so early in his career.

His eyebrow arched as he took in my drenched shirt and rumpled suit. I had no doubts he could see the dark bruises showing through the thin material. Breaking the silence with a laugh, he thrust his hand out to me. "Nonsense, Major. When word down the line said I'd have an interesting Marine coming on board, I thought I'd have a look for myself. Looks like Vice Admiral Haney still hasn't managed to kill you yet."

The name Williams didn't ring any bells in my memory, which made me wonder just what the captain had been told about me or what—and who—I had forgotten over the years. His age would have put him in active duty when I had bounced around the various branches of the military. I shook hands with him, and I appreciated the fact he didn't engage in a strength challenge. "Not yet, sir."

"Please forgive the cramped quarters. One day they'll figure out how to make these tin cans more spacious. No incidents?"

"It's a bit choppy out there," Haney replied, herding me into the captain's quarters. "Thanks for the lift."

"Glad to be of service, sir. Minor detour on route to our next exercise. We'll rendezvous for your next transfer in four hours. Make yourselves comfortable in the meantime. I'm technically off duty until your departure." Captain Williams went to his desk and gestured to the two chairs crammed into the room before looking me in the eyes. "Do you want to keep dripping all over my submarine, or would you like a dry uniform?"

"We could all use a dry change, if you've got the spares in stock," Haney admitted.

"I'm sure we can round something up." After a brief conversation on the submarine's com, Williams gestured to the chairs again. "Take a load off."

"Sit, son."

"I'll pass, sir. If I sit, you're going to need a

crowbar to get me up again." Standing would help keep my aching muscles and joints limber enough to cope with another flight off the submarine, especially if the seas remained stormy.

Haney sat, twisting around to stare at Lane, who shook his head. The SEAL stood with his hands clasped behind his back, at full attention. Old habits die hard, and I assumed the same straight-backed posture before I realized I had moved.

"Close the door, Petty Officer," Captain Williams ordered, and the seriousness of the man's tone put me on edge. Lane obeyed before returning to his position beside me. "You're a very difficult man to track down, Major. Unless I'm way off my mark, they'll be studying your case to help train our spooks for years to come."

I kept still, watching the captain. "Thank you, sir."

"It wasn't a compliment, Major."

Haney chuckled, leaning back in his chair and stretching his arms. "Williams is competitive in nature, Major, and you've dodged every spook interested in making a name for himself over the past decade. He wrote an interesting paper focusing on Marine and SEAL missions with a focus on rogue, burned, and missing operatives. I'm afraid he'll have to write a revision considering your reappearance—and pay up on a certain friendly bet we made a while back."

"I'll write you a check," the captain grumbled. "I'd love to know how you've managed to stay off the radar for a decade. You're going to have one hell of a debriefing."

"My orders were clear, sir. If the mission was compromised, we were to disappear. The plug was yanked, so I followed orders." I paused, glancing at Haney, who gave me a subtle nod. "It's not difficult to stay hidden if you keep on the move and use a different name, sir."

"You've been the subject of numerous manhunts, all of which you've avoided. That is no easy feat."

"I was careful." Not careful enough, but my presence on board the submarine was evidence enough of that.

Captain Williams turned his attention to Haney. "How'd you catch him?"

"His circumstances forced him to use his real passport, which was flagged. We got lucky; we were in range to take advantage of the opportunity. The details are classified."

I found it interesting Haney trusted the man enough to drop some information but not any of the major details.

"I take it the exact details of your transfer are likewise classified?"

Haney clasped his hands behind his head and smiled his smug smile, his eyes twinkling. "We have a code name and everything."

"I saw. Why do you get all the nice mission names? Did you bribe someone to assign you WOLF HUNT? You don't want to know the code name for the exercise we're about to do."

I held my breath and was glad I could blame my shiver on my wet clothes. A knock at the door put an end to the conversation.

"Enter," Captain Williams ordered.

A young woman in officer's khakis held uniforms in one arm and snapped a salute with the other. "I've brought the uniforms, sir."

Lane relaxed and took them from the woman. Instead of service khakis, they were dress blues, and I masked my grimace by clenching my teeth. Once the door was closed, the SEAL went through the uniforms, thrusting a set to me. "You should get yourself dried and changed before you catch your death, Major."

Before I had a chance to say a word, Captain Williams directed me to the door beside his desk, which led to his bunk. When I closed the door, the sound reminded me of a jail cell locking me in and sealing my fate.

I HAD no idea why they had a Marine major's dress blues on board, but with staying in my wet clothes as my only alternative, I changed. Williams's officer had included everything I needed, including a cap. The short exposure to the elements hadn't done me any favors, and my entire body throbbed by the time I emerged from the captain's sleeping quarters.

All three men inspected me from head to toe. Haney nodded his approval. "You clean up nice, son."

"Dress blues make anyone look good, sir," I countered, squeezing by the desk to stand beside Lane. Both men had changed, and considering both of them were dressed in uniforms appropriate for their rank, someone had made preparations before our arrival.

I thought it was a waste, but I kept my opinion to myself.

"The next transfer should be easier." Captain Williams pulled out a map and spread it over his desk. "If I've been given a good weather report, we'll be clear of the storm in time for the rendezvous. Gear will be waiting for you on shore. You're going to have a pretty tight schedule until you make landfall. Unfortunately, I have no details on what that schedule will be. Why don't you three head down to the mess? I have a feeling you're not going to get a chance for even a cup of coffee once you're on the move."

"Appreciate it, Captain," Haney replied, adjusting his uniform to his satisfaction. "We'll take you up on that."

The two men exchanged pleasantries for a few more minutes, and when they finished, Lane and I snapped salutes to the submarine's captain before making a strategic retreat from his quarters. Haney led the way, at home in the tight passages and general confines of the sub.

My wolf hated the lack of natural light and pressure of the ocean around us. When we squeezed against the walls to allow working sailors to pass us, I fidgeted, drawing a disapproving scowl from the Vice Admiral.

"Relax, Major. There's no need to be so jumpy."

"Hell is a tour of duty on a submarine," I muttered under my breath.

Lane snorted and jabbed me with his elbow. "You're supposed to like working at sea, sir. You're a Marine."

"I thought I told you to cut the sirs," I hissed back.

"You're in uniform, sir."

"Point," I conceded before glaring at Haney's back. "How did they get a Marine uniform in dress blues in my size on such short notice?"

The Vice Admiral chuckled. "Magic, son."

"Is there a reason we're dressed up, sir?"

"Yes."

I waited. When Haney didn't elaborate, I was sorely tempted to bang my head into something hard. Instead, I kept my mouth shut.

Sometimes I could mind my manners, especially when there was nothing I could do to change my situation. Unless Haney had changed over the years, all questioning him would do was encourage him to find a way to make the situation even more unpleasant for me.

The mess, like the rest of the submarine, was a work of engineering art, maximizing every bit of space possible. I used up what little good fortune I had; the mess wasn't as busy as it could have been, allowing us to find a place to sit. One perk of submarine duty was the food, which was superior to everything else I had sampled while flitting through the various military branches.

Any other day, I probably would have enjoyed the corned beef and cabbage, but I picked at it, earning frowns from Lane and Haney. I spent more time pushing food around my plate than eating, a habit I had thought I had broken years ago.

"You're going to scrape a hole through the plate if you keep that up," Haney chided.

I wondered if the werewolves in Europe would mind an addition to their numbers, assuming I could escape the military one more time. The sigh from my wolf didn't fill me with hope.

Once a lone wolf, always a lone wolf.

THE OCEAN WAS calm enough the helicopter pilot hovered his craft within a foot of the deck, allowing us to board without having to harness up for a lift. I was grateful for the flight suit over my uniform, which helped keep the chill off.

The haze of a distant shore offered me the hope we wouldn't be in the air for long.

I buckled in and adjusted my helmet, listening to the chatter. I kept quiet, my gaze locked on the land. Once I had my feet back on solid ground, I'd be better equipped to come up with a plan on dealing with the nightmare my life had become.

As always, my sense of duty would sink me, and while I loathed the idea of being sucked back into military operations, I also understood the importance of what I'd been asked to do.

That the op involved civilians made me itch to dive into the action. When I had been recruited, I'd been in love with the idea of making a difference. The government, however, hadn't wanted me involved with helping *people,* instead using me for other acquisitions.

More often than not, I had been expected to lay down my life for intel. Sometimes the intel led me to rescue ops, but sometimes the intel led others on my team to neutralize threats to the United States.

The work had, no matter how much I loathed to admit it, given me all the skills I needed for my less-than-legal relocation of art and other goods.

If Haney ever found out how I'd spent the last decade, he'd probably shoot me himself.

In the twisted world of warfare, ethics and integrity mattered.

I'd thrown mine away when my team and I had been left for dead and forced to scatter to the four winds. Regretting the mistake of having used my original passport, I stared out over the ocean.

Lane tapped my shoulder and pointed somewhere below us. Leaning towards the window, I glanced down. A massive battle ship flying the Union Jack cut through the waters below.

"You're bloody kidding me," I blurted, closing my eyes, swallowing my groan, and wishing throwing myself into the sea was an option. The dress blues made a lot more sense; if the US was calling on the Brits for a favor, we needed to look our best.

I was surprised they hadn't sent over a box of medals to go with the uniform. I had no idea if I was entitled for any legitimate decorations beyond my starred Purple Heart, which I had never actually picked up; I'd always found an excuse to worm my way out of attending any award ceremonies.

"They're headed to Devonport and kindly offered to give us a ride. They'll be making port tonight." Haney shrugged. "I thought you liked the Brits, Major McGrady. You've worked with them before."

It took every bit of my willpower to rein in my temper and keep my voice calm and even. "I prefer subtlety, and there's absolutely nothing subtle about this, sir."

If Haney wanted to announce to everyone everywhere the US was moving on something, he was doing a textbook job of it. Spies were probably having a field day speculating why the US Navy's Vice Admiral Haney was globe-trotting with a Marine and a SEAL in tow.

In my opinion, the mission was already compromised; if Scallywag and his accomplices had any contacts in Europe, he was probably aware of some major movement. If his goal was to undermine government acquisitions through American businessmen, he likely did.

"You don't have to like it, Major. You just have to follow orders."

I should've taken my chances with my client, and as soon as I had half a chance, I would. At the rate Haney was going, he'd botch the operation before it got off the ground.

Recovering botched operations was as much of a specialty as lifting priceless pieces of art for the highest bidder. In that, Haney had been right to want me on his team.

Unlike him, I still had my head screwed onto my shoulders. Perhaps the price of command was a lack of vision of what was on the ground, and the longer I stared at the Royal Navy ship below, the more I was certain Haney had lost his touch.

My wolf growled, and tinging his displeasure was his agreement of my assessment.

Before I could act, I needed a plan. To make a plan, I needed information. To get the information, I needed my laptop or cell phone, a chance to check my emails, and the time to make a discreet call to Anthony.

The real work would begin in Devonport.

Chapter Eleven

Compared to Vice Admiral Haney, I was invisible, just another sailor among many. Grateful to avoid the attention, I stuck close to Lane, who likewise seemed happy to avoid bumping shoulders and talking with the Brits.

"Dog shit in the spring," Lane muttered, shaking his head.

While I had a different metaphor for the situation, his was apt, and I nodded my agreement. "Fish rotting in the sun."

"Cat farts."

"Blooming corpse flower."

There was a trick to directing someone's attention to something while standing at attention, and Lane was a master of the subtle nod. Two British sailors in dress uniforms saluted Vice Admiral Haney and the captain of the Royal Navy ship, talking in soft enough whispers even my sensitive ears couldn't pick up what they were saying.

Like us, they were undecorated. While Lane and I were technically sailors, I had my doubts the pair had actually done real time on a ship or as a part of amphibious warfare.

At least I had some experience jumping out of boats and sea-deployed planes in order to reach land.

I shifted my weight, straightened my back, and ignored the ache across my shoulders, watching Haney continue his conversation with the Brits. "Methane."

A sniff of methane would turn someone into a ghost pretty quick, and if those two Brits weren't spooks, I'd chew boot leather.

Lane made a soft sound, a mix of a chuckle and a snort. "Thallium."

I huffed, appreciating the SEAL's knowledge; thallium was a good way of killing someone and turning them into a ghost, although far slower than inhaling methane. It was also a good comparison to what could happen to spooks caught over enemy lines. "Poison dart frog."

"Polonium."

I gave a slight nod in Haney's direction. "Tuna."

Lane's sigh was so soft I barely heard it. "Rotting in the sun."

"Australia's supposed to be nice this time of year."

"Sure, if you don't mind everything there trying to kill you."

"How about New Zealand?"

"Maybe."

With the ship cruising closer than I liked to top speed, the wind whipped and chilled me through my uniform despite the fact I was no longer wet. Standing in the same position cramped my muscles, but I kept still.

Maybe I didn't want to be on board a Royal Navy ship as a representative of the United States, but I respected the uniform—and the real men and women who wore it—too much to put on a poor showing. If Haney meant for us to stand as sentinels for the inspection of our British counterparts, I could play the role easily enough.

In addition to the two undecorated officers mingling with the ship's captain and Vice Admiral Haney, one of the women standing at attention kept staring in our direction, her gaze shifting away whenever I was too obvious about scoping her out. Two other men had a more-than-healthy interest in us as well.

"You'd think they'd be more interested in Vice Admiral Haney than a Marine and a SEAL," Lane observed, clucking his tongue. "That sailor over there's been giving you the eye ever since we boarded."

"Probably a spook hoping a spotting will nab her a promotion over in spookville," I grumbled. "It's a game. I call it Whack-a-Decky. Person who gets the highest number of positive hits wins."

"I heard him call you Major McGrady

during the introductions. He's cut off your easy way out."

Clenching my teeth together, I parted my lips so I could talk without betraying what I was saying in case there was a lipreader in the curious crowd of sailors. "This is a botch."

It came out mumbled but a lot clearer than I thought it would.

Lane grunted, and mimicking my method, he replied, "He botched it on purpose. Why, though?"

I didn't have an answer, so I switched gears back to places I'd really like to run away to if a chance provided itself. "If New Zealand doesn't grab you, how about Antarctica?"

"Bit cold for me. Bermuda's nice."

"I know some guys."

"I figured." He drew in a deep breath, and without moving his lips, he mumbled, "I didn't sign up to fuck over one of our own."

"We'll figure something out." I had no idea how, but I'd come up with something. Something fishy was going on, but unfortunately, I didn't know what or why, and I had a feeling it had everything to do with my client's involvement in the case of seven missing women and the two men sent to extract them from France.

THE MINUTES DRAGGED INTO HOURS, and Vice Admiral Haney seemed determined to stay on deck, leaving Lane and me to rot standing at attention. The ship's captain sent his sailors back to work while we stood a respectable distance away, too far to overhear what was being discussed.

"It's a game of 'our sailors are more disciplined than yours.'" Lane shifted his weight, straightened his shoulders and back, and sighed. "We won at least twenty minutes ago. Why did the uppers even let him leave his post for this? He's not field ops."

"He said he sent himself, remember?"

Lane narrowed his eyes. "I had forgotten that. Think they'll court martial us for following orders?"

"Yep."

"Fucked if we do, fucked if we don't."

"Sounds about right." I eyed the coastline, which the ship skirted. "There's no reason that helicopter couldn't have dropped us on shore."

"I noticed."

"If we jumped overboard, how long do you think it would take for them to notice?" I eyed the water; the ship was moving at a fast-enough clip hitting the water would hurt. Then again, it would take such a large vessel time to come to a halt and turn around.

"They'd notice." Lane tilted his head up a fraction, his gaze darting to one of the ship's towers. "I think they were warned you're the field ops version of Houdini."

"Bermuda is sounding nice right now. We

could go diving for shipwrecks. Make a career out of it."

"The Bermuda Triangle is a myth." The corners of Lane's mouth twitched upward. "If they ever let you out, what are you planning on doing?"

I snorted. "I hold little hope of them letting me out. I fully expect to be spending the foreseeable future in detainment, no matter what happy songs the Bard likes croaking."

"Dead fish rotting in the sun."

"This entire thing is a fiasco, and for the life of me, I can't tell who is having the wool pulled over their eyes." I shifted my gaze to Haney, who was gesturing at the shore with his back facing us. "He has a history of assigning people I'll like to my teams to keep me in line. Then he sends us on suicide missions to see how many of us he can kill off. Of course, the one time he sends me on a mission I can buy into, he botches it before we can get it off the ground."

"I've heard rumors of that nature, but I thought they were exaggerations. You think this is really a full botch?"

"He has us standing on display so we're seen. He wants it known we're around and about. He's putting himself out there, and when such a high-ranking officer starts strutting across the pond, people notice. The wrong people notice. The instant we head in the direction of the hot zone, they'll figure things out." I sighed, curling my toes in my shoes in an attempt to ease the ache in my feet. "Who does he want seeing us? Why? That's what I want to know."

"Maybe we're doing a joint mission with the Brits? We do that from time to time."

"Hell of a lot of spook types on board for a joint op, don't you think? I feel like we're on display in a zoo."

"If we were in a zoo, we'd at least get set feeding times."

I cast a longing glance at the shore. "Aren't SEALs supposed to be masters of the sea? Surely you could swim to shore without breaking a sweat."

"I don't feel like dragging your half-drowned ass to the beach, Major."

"I'm an expert in fine arts, painting identification and authentication, and I've dabbled in restoration. I like history, too. I'm also pretty good at getting into and out of places I don't belong." Wiggling my toes wasn't helping my feet, so I shifted my weight and stance to find a little relief from standing still for so long. "If I ever get free and clear, I'd like to curate a gallery."

"That explains the bracelet. Takes a man with real backbone to wear something like that. You're interested in Egypt? Is that why you got a replica made?"

"It's the real deal. Couldn't resist trying it on." I shrugged. It was mostly the truth; I hadn't been able to resist the cuff attaching itself to me. "Oops."

"It's the real deal," Lane echoed.

"Yep."

"The real deal as in you couldn't help trying on a museum piece and it got stuck. You're joking, right?"

"I didn't steal it from a museum."

"Who *did* you steal it from?"

I widened my eyes. "Me? Steal something? Why would you think that?"

"I paid attention during briefing, that's why."

"Rubbish and poppycock, Petty Officer Fredrick."

"If you say so, Major McGrady."

"Fucking SEALs."

"Lunatic Marines."

We both snickered under our breaths and waited for Vice Admiral Haney to have mercy on us.

HANEY HAD a mean streak a mile wide, and he kept us on deck right up until we reached port, where we were forced to get out of the way of the sailors bringing the ship into dock. Every muscle in my body protested, and Lane winced when we stepped off to the side to observe.

As he had since we had boarded the Royal Navy ship, he kept the British officers company, ignoring our existence except when we made a nuisance of ourselves by standing in the wrong place at the wrong time. I stayed at attention, and Lane followed my lead.

If I leaned on anything, I'd probably ooze to the deck in a limp and unconscious heap, which wouldn't leave a very good impression. Maybe I wasn't a real Marine, but if Lane could keep standing straight and tall, so could I.

Professional Pride: 3, Common Sense: 0.

"I need a beer," Lane muttered. "At least you can trust the Brits to have decent pubs."

"Do you really think he'll let us go to a pub? You're joking, right?"

If looks could kill, I'd be long dead, riddled with holes from Lane's glare. "The man has to sleep sometime."

"So do we. The deck's starting to look pretty comfortable, actually."

"Don't even think it, McGrady."

"Too late. Bloody hell, Fredrick, I'm dead on my feet."

"You look it."

The Devonport Naval Base bustled with activity, but as soon as the ship was secured, Haney waved for us to join him. An escort of several Royal Navy officers met us on the docks. The introductions went by in a blur of salutes, polite greetings, and stiff formality. I should've paid more attention to who was who, but it took most of my effort to stay on my feet.

Salvation came in the form of a two-starred officer who pulled Haney aside, leaving Lane and me in the hands of two Royal Navy representatives. Neither man seemed interested in making small talk, which worked for me.

Instead of guiding us to the visitor's on-base lodging, something I'd experienced a few times in the United Kingdom while on mission, we were led to a black, unmarked car. One of the men opened the back door for us, saluted, and left, while the other, a dark-haired man with a stern expression, slid into the driver's seat.

I doubted I'd ever get used to the way the British drove on the wrong side of the road. Without fail, the reversed seat positions threw me off, making me grateful I wasn't the one behind the wheel. With how tired I was, I'd probably get in an accident before making it off base.

Lane frowned, adjusted his grip on our shared duffle bag, and flexed his hand near where he'd normally have a handgun holstered.

My fingers itched to have a weapon on hand, too, but I hid my unease by getting into the vehicle and buckling up. Lane followed my lead, although I could see the tension in his posture and in the lines etched across his brow.

"Relax, Lane," I murmured, staring out through the tinted window as the car drove us through the base towards the city of Devonport. "The Brits don't bite."

"Often," the driver corrected with a soft chuckle. "Welcome to our side of the pond, Major McGrady, Petty Officer Fredrick. I have orders to take you to your lodgings for tonight and permission to take you anywhere you may need to go, within reason, of course. The name's Ethan. Ethan Jones. What can I do you for?"

"Pub," Lane and I chorused before staring at each other and chuckling.

"Jolly good, sirs. I know just the place. You been here before?"

"I was stationed in London until recently," Lane said, glancing at me with an arched brow.

"I've been here before, but it's been a while," I admitted.

The last time I'd been in the United Kingdom, I'd visited a museum or two, leaving with a few things I didn't own. I fought the urge to grin at the memory of the heist. It'd been one of my better jobs. By raiding several barbers and salons for hair, I ruined the investigator's chances of using DNA evidence by scattering the strands through the entire place.

Leaving evidence like hair behind was a good way to get sunk, and my ruse had worked as well as I could've hoped. Even if investigators tested the thousands of individual strands, which I had cut in variances to mask the length of my hair in case I left any at the crime scene, it'd be near to impossible to discover who'd committed my crime.

All they had on me was video evidence, and I had gone to great lengths to disguise my appearance and trick the cameras.

Ten minutes later, Ethan parked in front of a two-storied stone building. The Anchor's Rest was the type of pub I expected to exist hundreds of years ago. Its wooden doors were banded with iron, and I clenched my teeth, shivering at the metal's close proximity.

Iron didn't hurt me, but even without touching it, numbness spread through my head and settled into my bones. I clenched my teeth and followed after Lane, my legs shaking. Ethan held the door open, and I eased my way through, careful not to touch the black metal.

I'd never live down collapsing in a British pub. Fortunately, the door seemed to be the only source of pure iron, and once inside, the clinging lethargy eased. Ethan waved at the barkeep, who pointed at a table tucked in a corner.

I took the seat closest to the wall, which put me as far from the iron-bound door as possible and gave me a clear view of the entire pub. Lane sat, positioning himself between me and the majority of the patrons, who stared at us.

Americans in dress blues probably didn't come around often. My wolf growled his dislike of their scrutiny. The iron helped me in a way, so soon after its influence, I was too tired and fuzzy-headed to bristle at the unwanted attention.

Ethan penned me in, grinning as he scooted his chair closer to the table. "The food here is pretty good. Get what you want; it's on us. Figured you'd like something like this after being at sea. Got a favorite beer?"

"Guinness," I replied, though I was tempted to go straight for a glass of scotch. "How's the fish and chips here?"

"You won't regret it, but the bangers and mash can't be beat."

"Bangers and mash it is, then."

Lane narrowed his eyes. "Do you even know what that is?"

"I have been to enough pubs in these parts to know. The cockles tempt me, but no sane man can turn down good bangers and mash."

Ethan chuckled and shook his head. "Americans. You're all randy bastards."

"I'm in on the bangers and mash, too," Lane said, leaning back in his chair and balancing it on two legs. "It's a rule of international travel. If the local says something can't be beat, order that. I'll take whatever cream ale you think is the best."

When a waitress came by, Ethan ordered for us, which worked for me. She brought our beers right away, and Lane and I shared twin sighs of satisfaction.

Chuckling, Ethan shook his head. "When was the last time you two had a bloody beer?"

"Too long," I admitted. "And my limit is one."

Taking a sip, I closed my eyes, and enjoyed my Guinness, right down to the thick froth and its strong flavor.

Lane snickered. "That is the expression of a happy man."

"He looks like a cat who got into the cream. Fancy seeing you here, Declan. You're dressed up."

At the sound of Anthony's voice, I choked on my beer. Someone rescued my glass before a few hard slaps to my back knocked my breath and my beer out of my lungs. I wheezed, coughed, and cracked open an eye. "Anthony, you impertinent motley-minded horn-beast! What are you doing here?"

"Finding you. Mind if we have a seat?"

I waved, giving my chest a thump to finish getting the beer out of my lungs before turning my attention to Anthony's company. A dark-haired man in a crisp blue suit watched me, his expression guarded. He didn't look very old, but there was something about his dark eyes that put me on edge.

Drawing a deep breath was a mistake; the sweet and spicy scent of cinnamon filled my nose, and when my eyes widened, Anthony's companion smirked. "I've been looking forward to meeting you, Mr. McGrady."

"Major McGrady," Lane corrected, and the SEAL sat straighter, his cheek twitching.

My client lifted his hands in surrender. "I

meant no offense. My apologies, Major McGrady. Navy?"

When I didn't say a word, Lane answered, "Marines."

"Sit," I invited, reaching for my beer, wondering how my client had found me, why he'd dragged Anthony along with him, and how I'd survive my first meeting with another male werewolf.

Chapter Twelve

THERE WAS no way Anthony could have found me without help, and when Ethan cleared his throat to put an end to the silent standoff, we all turned in his direction. "Major McGrady, this is Charles Desmond, a friend."

"We've spoken," I acknowledged, setting my beer down, rising to my feet, and thrusting my hand across the table. "I didn't think I'd be meeting you here, Mr. Desmond."

Desmond grinned, took my hand, and gave a firm shake, hard enough I recognized his strength but not so tight I felt challenged by his grip. "I called in a few favors for the privilege, Major McGrady. Anthony is a pleasant traveling companion."

"It seems we have something in common, Tony. We both have done some unexpected and unwanted traveling recently. Did you have a nice flight?"

Anthony snorted. "He's even more restless than you are when you don't get your way."

"I see you already know Mr. Hammond." Ethan shifted his seat to make room for Desmond, and Lane made space for Anthony. "Sorry for the subterfuge, Major. I was under orders."

"I'm pretty sure we both requested to be taken to a pub." I shrugged. "Are the folks in London behind this?"

"That would be telling, Major."

Desmond looked me over, his gaze fixing on my undecorated chest. "Is the uniform for appearances?"

Lane stiffened, and before the SEAL lost his temper, I nudged him with my elbow to catch his attention. "Medals aren't my style, Mr. Desmond."

"You're decorated, then. I thought you said you weren't ex-military."

"It's complicated."

"I see."

Lane grabbed his beer and drank it down, tapping the empty glass to the table. "I think I need another one. Maybe two."

"Are you two hungry? We already ordered dinner, but no reason you two can't join us," Ethan said.

Desmond nodded. "Whatever you recommend."

"Ditto."

Raising his hand to catch the attention of the waitress, Ethan ordered bangers and mash for them and another beer for Lane.

Desmond ordered the best scotch the pub

had, and Anthony declined a drink, which didn't surprise me. The man was more of a lightweight than I was, and he often opted to serve as the designated driver and babysitter of drunks.

While tempted to order another beer, I kept my mouth shut. One would be enough to get me into trouble. After two I wouldn't remember half the night.

Lane glared at Desmond. "It'd be difficult to get Major McGrady's full decorations on short notice, Mr. Desmond. He has a five-star Purple Heart, a Medal of Honor—"

"I have a what?" I jerked in Lane's direction. The Purple Heart with stars I already knew about; I'd taken far more than six injuries while on missions on behalf of some government agency or branch of the military.

"It was awarded after your last mission, sir."

"Now *that's* a load of poppycock if I've ever heard it," I grumbled, shaking my head. "I'm not sure I want to know what else they've foisted on me without my knowledge."

"A few ribbons and a couple of other medals, sir. You're very well decorated."

"Is there a back door of this joint so I can sneak out? I think I'm developing a severe case of wanderlust." I sighed, rubbing my temples. "This is turning out to be the week from hell."

"Vice Admiral Haney had us on deck at

attention from the moment we boarded until we made shore," Lane explained. "I'm exhausted, and I don't have two bullet holes in me."

"One was only a graze. No big deal."

"Don't make me recite the entire list, Major."

"Fucking SEALs," I muttered under my breath.

"You were shot?" Desmond demanded.

"Count Dracula wasn't very happy that I let his brides out of Castle Transylvania. He took some pot shots after I went into the drink. No big deal."

"Count Dracula? Brides?" Lane blinked at me, his expression puzzled.

I was saved from having to answer by the waitress returning, bringing dinner with her. Taking a deep breath, I savored the scent of sausage partnered with garlic and potatoes. I focused on my food, taking my time cutting everything up.

There was a benefit to being exhausted; I lacked the energy to focus on more than one thing at a time, allowing me to filter out the conversation around me and worry about nothing other than my food.

The serving size was large enough it took the edge off, allowing me to keep a firm leash on my wolf, who whined restlessly at the presence of another werewolf in such close proximity.

If Charles Desmond didn't expose me, I'd

pretend he wasn't anything other than a normal man, too.

"Declan?" Anthony's voice dragged me back to the conversation. I looked up from my food, staring at him.

He wasn't the only one who sighed.

"What?"

"When was the last time you got a full night's sleep?"

It was a good question, and I turned to Lane. "When did we last get some sleep, anyway?"

"On the cruise. I think we had three hours before our rendezvous with the first helicopter."

"How long ago was that?"

"Hell if I know. It's become a blur," the SEAL admitted. "What day is it?"

"You're Navy. What division?" Desmond asked.

Lane straightened. "I'm a SEAL, Mr. Desmond. Petty Officer Second Class."

"Fredrick was assigned as Major Declan's detail. As such, I thought it'd be best to bring him along. My orders only said to ditch Vice Admiral Haney. Knowing how ruddy annoying SEALs can get, I thought I'd keep him happy by bringing him along for the ride," Ethan said, grinning at Lane and lifting his beer up in salute.

The SEAL snorted and lifted his glass. "You're smart for a spook."

"Me? A spook? Why would you think that?"

"Your boat was crawling with them, so I figured something was up." Lane smirked, leaning back in his chair to balance it on two legs. "Major McGrady is a very popular man."

"I noticed. Trust me, I noticed." I poked and prodded at my food. "So, how did you coerce the Brits into working an op? That's a hell of a favor to call in, Mr. Desmond."

"I have friends."

"I know." I straightened, twisting to face Lane. "Guess what? So do I. I need my phone."

Bending down, Lane grabbed the duffle and dug through it, handing me my cell, which was enclosed in a plastic bag. I dug it out, turned it back on, and checked my email. Bob had sent me the information I needed, and I sifted through several other emails, wrinkled my nose, and dialed his number.

He answered on the second ring. "What do you have for me, Bob?"

"If you keep losing people, I'm going to come over and kick your ass, Bob," I answered.

Bob groaned. "Which one did you find?"

"Take a guess. I'm in Devonport. Should I send this loose cannon back to you? How many have you lost track of?"

"Just one. He's with you?"

"Apparently. He kidnapped one of my friends for the ride, too."

Desmond snickered. "I encouraged. I did not kidnap."

"No, I'm pretty sure you kidnapped him. He has a severe allergy to guns."

"I didn't bring it with me on the plane."

"So, Bob. The loose cannon. What do you want me to do with him?"

"His wife and his children are ready to kill him. Please let him know this. The eldest daughter is about ten minutes from a murder."

I chuckled, glancing at Desmond. "I have been informed your wife and children are ready to kill you, and that your eldest is about ten minutes from a murder. It is unclear who will be murdered, though."

Desmond scowled. "Who are you talking to?"

"Bob."

"Who, exactly, is Bob?"

My wolf was as eager as I was to challenge the rival male, and I smiled. "Bob is Bob."

"You're calling me for a reason, Bob," Bob said, his tone turning serious. "What do you need?"

"Did you contact the Brits?"

"Would I do that?" Innocence oozed in the man's tone, and I snorted my disbelief. When I remained silent, he sighed and said, "I may have greased the gears a bit. In my defense, I didn't know if the loose cannon would actually contact them. I take it he did?"

"Oh, yeah. He did, all right. I'm having

dinner with him, my kidnapped friend, a SEAL, and a Brit who looks far too smug for his own good."

Ethan laughed. "You're an irreverent chap."

"Good. I'm going to owe you a lot more than a favor if you can keep an eye on him."

"That's promising. When I'm done with you, your wallet is going to be crying tears of blood and begging for mercy. I'm also going to need a new ID. I'll be expecting a bullet-proof one. The best you've got, except better."

For a long moment, I thought Bob was going to hang up on me, but then he sighed. "Got it. Career field?"

"Something interesting with good long-term options. And I want a good financial package. Also, I want a nice cabin somewhere nice and quiet, deep in the woods, where I don't have to come out and deal with your people again for at *least* a few years."

Snickers dissolved into hysterical laughter on the other end of the line. "I think I can do something about that. Hey. Do me a favor, would you?"

"No, Bob. You already called in your favor. Pay me."

"Can you talk to my friend's wife before she kills someone? Please? Maybe if you talk to her, she'll relax a little."

"There'd better be a good tip in this package. Okay."

"Hold on a second."

While I waited, I pointed the phone at Desmond. "This is your fault. Also, I should have charged you three times what I did."

The man grinned at me. "Who are you talking to?"

"We've already been over this."

"You're playing coy with me."

"You'll survive."

I returned the phone to my ear and waited, taking advantage of the wait to have a few more bites of my dinner.

"Hello?" The woman's voice was sharp yet silky, and my wolf liked what he heard. I ignored his interest and wondered how I'd handle a woman who managed to intimidate men capable of negotiating with foreign nations and military officials.

"Good evening, ma'am. Bob told me you wanted to talk to someone about a certain situation?"

Laughter burst out of her. "Bob? You make this poor man call you Bob? That's terrible."

"That's okay, he calls me Bob, too. He might know my real name, maybe. Probably not. Don't ask, don't tell. It's worked well for us, ma'am. So, what do you want to know?"

"I want to know if you can find my father and beat the fucking shit out of him."

It was my turn to chuckle. "Done, and as for the second, ask me again tomorrow, ma'am. It'd be rude to interrupt a man who is enjoying his bangers and mash."

"Who is enjoying his *what*?"

I struggled to maintain my composure. "Sausage. He's enjoying his sausage."

If looks could kill, Charles Desmond would have had me in my grave the instant his glare fixed on me. I smiled at him.

Declan: 1, Charles Desmond: 0.

"He's in the UK, isn't he? That fucking no good piece of shit! Tell him to get his ass back to Seattle where he belongs. Does he have any idea what sort of trouble he's causing by disappearing without telling anyone? Mom's on a war path, and she's gone and gotten Sara riled up."

I had no idea who Sara was, but I had a feeling if she was anything like the woman Bob had put on the phone, she'd end up causing *me* a lot of trouble. "I can certainly try, ma'am, but it might be prudent to allow me and a friend to keep a very close eye on him instead. With his resources at the ready, he could be quite useful in my operation."

"Your operation. And who, exactly, are you?"

"My name's Major Declan McGrady, ma'am, and I'm the gentleman who stormed the castle. I'm a Marine, and my partner is a SEAL. I think between the two of us, we might be able to keep your loose cannon under containment."

Lane preened, watching me with a satisfied expression on his face.

"I'm listening."

"Good, ma'am. I'd like to keep him on hand for information. He can provide intel on our targets, which will help us track them easier. We'll take good care of him and try to return him intact to you."

"You actually want him? Fine, keep him. Toss him in the ocean when you're done with him. Let's talk about Richard."

"Let's," I agreed, grinning over the feisty woman's antics on the phone. "How difficult of a mark is he going to be?"

"He's going to be trouble. I'm sorry. He's an idiot and gets carried away, rather like my father."

"My condolences, ma'am. I'll do everything I can to bring him in. Have Bob give you my number. Shoot me a text. If I'm not operating under radio silence, I'll answer as soon as I can. Let us do our job."

"You might need my help with him."

I closed my eyes and sighed. "What do *you* bring to the table, ma'am?"

"You're not saying no?" The wariness in the woman's voice was almost enough to draw a chuckle out of me.

"I'm not saying yes, but I'm not saying no, either. Here's the deal. Convince me you won't be in the way, and I'll be open to being convinced to have you sitting in a hotel nearby to work as backup. What tricks do you have up your sleeve?"

"I'm good with a gun. I can browbeat my

husband into line when he gives you trouble. What else do you want?"

"Obedience. You follow orders from me, or you're out. Understood?"

Her hesitation pleased me; she was thinking, and I gave her all the time she needed. "Understood, sir," she hissed.

"Text me your number, and I will give you directions." I hung up on her and slipped my phone into my pocket. "Sorry about that, gentlemen."

Desmond stared at me with narrowed eyes. "Who, exactly, were you on the phone with?"

"I'm going to give you the exact same deal I gave her, Mr. Desmond. This is my operation. You listen and obey my orders, or you're out. There will be no loose cannons on this operation. That can get people killed. If your people are in trouble, chances are *they'll* be the ones who get hurt as a consequence. Am I understood?"

Like his daughter, Desmond hesitated. "Understood, Major."

"Good. There's just one problem. How are we supposed to deal with Vice Admiral Haney?"

Ethan smiled. "We're taking care of that, sir. He's going to be so busy for the next week he won't even remember you exist. Don't worry, we've assured him that you'll be enjoying the best of British hospitality during your stay. As soon as you've finished dinner,

Mr. Desmond, Mr. Hammond, and I will leave the pub; we have matched cars. You'll go with him. In four hours, you'll arrive in London, where you'll be staying for the night. From there, you'll be headed to France. Mr. Desmond has British passports for your use."

"Why does it feel like my life has become an elaborate game of spy versus spy?" I complained, glancing at Lane.

"Because it has," the SEAL muttered, shaking his head before holding his hands up in surrender. "I'm not even going to ask how you have passports for us, Mr. Jones."

"It's the magic of British hospitality, sir. We're glad to be of service."

I wondered what sort of favors Charles Desmond and Dante Anderson had to call in to have the British government dancing to their tune. Maybe one day, I'd ask.

Then again, maybe I wouldn't. Some things were better left a mystery.

Chapter Thirteen

Most men and women serving in the military shared the uncanny ability to fall asleep anywhere instantaneously. When we left, sliding into the car Anthony was driving with Desmond in the front passenger seat, Lane paused long enough to toss our duffle in the trunk, get in, buckle up, and wait for me to climb in beside him before he passed out.

The cinnamon scent of werewolf filled my nose, put my wolf on edge, and made me hesitate to join Lane in exhausted slumber.

Desmond twisted around in his seat, his gaze sliding over Lane before settling on me. "You going to be all right for a four-hour drive? Mr. Fredrick mentioned you'd been shot?"

"Twice. One was a graze, which has mostly healed. Other isn't too bad. I'll manage."

"If there are any problems, let us know.

Better not screw around with gunshot wounds."

"They've had time to heal. It's fine."

Anthony snorted. "You could be on your death bed and wouldn't even dream of complaining, Declan. Maybe you can fool Mr. Desmond, but you can't fool me. How's your head doing?"

"It could be worse. The headache is tolerable. It's getting better by the day."

"How the hell did you survive that fall? That was insane. I was certain you'd cracked your head open and were dead." Anthony spat curses before sighing. "Are you sure you're okay?"

"It was touch and go for a bit, but I'll be fine. Promise. Nothing some good sleep won't cure."

"And a few good meals, too. You look gaunt, Major," Desmond said, his eyes narrowing as he looked me over. "You barely had more than a snack at the pub. You military types eat more than horses."

I had a feeling Desmond had exchanged werewolf for military type in his statement. There was no way he didn't know what I was. His scent, a pervasive cinnamon with a subtle, sweet undertone I couldn't quite identify, was making my wolf anxious, and he whined in my head. The scent markers went undetected by human noses, something that had spared me from discovery long ago.

While I had no substantial experience

with other werewolves, I operated on the assumption if I could identify him by smell, he could identify me, too.

"Too tired to be hungry," I admitted, glad it was the truth. The buffet on the cruise had helped, too. Buffets always helped.

I tried to hit one at least once a week to help maintain the illusion I ate a normal amount the rest of the time. When I did my buffet runs, I often went to two to hide the vast quantity I could eat.

The trick only worked in cities with buffets, although I did try to plan my travels around where I could eat my fill. If I stayed under the thumb of the military, I'd probably lose even more weight.

"Great. You're like Richard. That's just what I need right now." Desmond sighed, shaking his head and turning to face forward. "If you get hungry, let us know, and we'll stop somewhere to get you something to eat. You'll impair your healing."

"Mr. Desmond is used to getting his way," Anthony warned, his tone wry. "I never want another gun pointed at my head ever again."

"The safety was on the entire time."

"That doesn't comfort me at all."

Desmond snorted. "It wasn't even loaded, son. Stop your bellyaching. You were perfectly safe the entire time."

"This guy might even have more issues than you do, Declan. Why do you always cause me so much trouble? At this rate, I'm going to lose my job because I'm out in fucking Europe instead of back home where I belong."

I kneed the back of Anthony's seat. "You can't lose your job, you clay-brained varlet. You're the boss."

"My job sucks. Insufferable clients. I quit."

I kneed the seat again, harder. "You're not allowed to quit."

"Why the hell not?"

"If I can't quit, you can't quit."

"Boys, behave," Desmond chided. "No crashing the car because you're squabbling. No one is quitting, and no one is losing their job. I already told you I would provide capable men to cover your work as needed, Anthony."

"See? He's way too used to getting his way, which is how I ended up on a plane going to Europe. He thinks I'm just going to give access to his henchmen and let him do what he wants with my company. You owe me for this, Declan. You're supposed to be the one who goes to insane places around the world, not me. I don't travel. I'm the guy who does the computer things. You know, the guy with a safe desk job. Keyword: safe."

For someone who claimed he didn't travel and had left England as a child, Anthony handled driving on the wrong side of the road with more grace than I could have managed on a good day. He treated the traffic circles like obstacles to overcome, and I was glad traffic was light, or he wouldn't need my help crashing the vehicle.

I was pretty sure the Brits wouldn't be happy if we totaled one of their cars in an accident.

"So, what happened out there? How exactly did you get shot?" Desmond asked.

I grimaced, glancing at Lane. The SEAL snored, and while the noise was soft, it reassured me he was asleep. "I made them a flight plan, tailed them out, and ended up running into Count Dracula. I didn't see them, so I assume they gave him the slip."

"They did. Before I lost contact with them, they mentioned they'd heard a lot of gunfire."

"I jumped off the cliff into the ocean and played a game of Marco Polo with him. Thanks to the storm and a rip tide, I won. Got shot in the process, but shit happens. Made my way to Hamburg to hop a cruise back to the United States but got nabbed by the sleeping SEAL back here. Long story short, here I am."

"Damn it, Declan! You told me you wouldn't be cliff diving again. What is wrong with you, man? Breaking your legs the first time wasn't bad enough?"

"Small fractures," I muttered.

"What did you break this time?" my friend snapped.

"Why do you always assume I broke something?"

"Because you always break something, asshole."

"I think I came away mostly unscathed this time, believe it or not. I'm not even limping much anymore. I went in feet first and got the angle mostly right." I shrugged and made myself more comfortable, contemplating whether or not I trusted Desmond enough to catch a few winks of sleep.

With Lane down and out for the count, however, I couldn't quite bring myself to relax enough to rest even though I needed it. I stretched my legs, making a point of jostling Anthony's seat again.

"How tall was this cliff?" Desmond twisted around again to face me, tilting his head down to stare at my legs and feet. "You looked a bit wobbly earlier, but I assumed that was because you weren't eating enough and were tired."

"I stood at attention on deck for several hours. I'm fine."

Desmond frowned, narrowed his eyes but nodded acceptance of my words and turned to face the front again. "Get some sleep, Major. We're going to have a long day tomorrow. You'll want to be fresh."

Despite knowing he was right, I couldn't force myself to sleep. I did close my eyes, though I kept a close watch over Lane through my lashes. If the werewolf in the front of the car did decide to get aggressive, I'd be ready.

AN OBJECT at rest stayed at rest, and my body wanted nothing to do with getting out of the car. I'd stayed awake the entire drive, but while I was conscious, my arms and legs weren't thrilled with the idea of getting up and moving.

I made it to the hotel suite before I collapsed on the nearest soft surface, which proved to be the couch. When someone tried to force me to move, I snarled a few threats of dismemberment.

They left me alone.

The vibration of an incoming call woke me, and I fumbled for my phone, rolled off the couch, and hit the floor hard. I swiped my finger across the screen, hoped I answered instead of hanging up, and mumbled, "Hello?"

"Can you pick me up?"

It took me several long moments to recognize the woman's voice as belonging to Richard's wife. I stifled a groan, lurching upright. The sitting room was dark, and there was no sign of Lane, Anthony, or Desmond. "Where are you?"

"The airport."

"Which one?"

"Heathrow. Did I wake you? Sorry. Stupid time zone changes. Stupid planes." The woman's voice wavered, and I heard her swallow. "I *hate* planes."

"Rough flight?" I cradled the phone with

my shoulder so I could rub my eyes and force them to focus in the dark. The duffle bag with our things was near the front door, and the promising shape of keys was on the coffee table not far away.

"A little."

"I can come get you. I don't know how long it'll be. Find an in-security lounge until I reach the airport."

"Okay. Thanks. Uh, what do you look like?"

"I'll text you a picture," I promised. "Sit tight and stay in secured areas until I tell you to come out."

Without waiting for an answer, I hung up. I pressed the palm of my hand over the keys to keep them from jingling and slid them off the table. Once safe and quiet in my pocket, I hunted for a room key, which I found on the computer desk.

I hesitated for a moment at the thought of leaving Lane and Anthony alone with Desmond but considering all was quiet after I had fallen asleep on the couch, I suspected they'd be safe for however long it took me to go to the airport and return. My wolf growled at me for leaving them behind, but I shook my head and refused his desire to bring at least Lane with us.

The SEAL needed sleep almost as much as I did, and the woman in the airport was my responsibility. After a few more annoyed growls, my wolf relented and stopped harassing me. I dug my wallet out of the duffle bag and pocketed it, then tip-toed my way to the door and slipped out of the room, easing it closed behind me. I winced when the lock clicked.

A quick stop at the front desk to get directions later, I was on my way, heading to the hotel's parking garage in search of the black car on loan from the British government. After fifteen frustrating minutes, it beeped at my pressing of the fob's button, and I found it crammed into a spot barely big enough for it.

I cursed the vehicle, the tight space I had to ease it out of, and the convoluted directions to reach the airport. I made my way to the passenger pickup area, texted the woman a picture of my ID, the model and color of the car, and told her where I was waiting.

She either had wings on her feet or had gotten as close to escape as possible, because within two minutes, a dark-haired woman emerged from the departure doors, spotted my car, and hurried over, yanking the passenger side door open.

"Airports," she snarled, fumbling with her seatbelt.

All I could smell in the car was the spice of werewolf, and the woman's scent reminded me of Desmond. I glanced at her out of the corner of my eye. She didn't look like Desmond; even rumpled with her thick hair making an escape from its ponytail confines, she was the type of woman I expected on the silver screen instead of in a car with me.

Desmond, on the other hand, was the type of man I expected to find in the thick of the action, hardened and refined over the years, although deceitfully youthful in appearance.

Being a werewolf probably had something to do with that.

"Sorry it took me so long to get here."

"Appreciate you picking me up. I was going to go mad if I had to stay in there for another minute." She shuddered and hugged herself. "Fucking planes."

"You'll be pleased to know we'll be driving across Europe, then. Faster by plane, but a lot harder to fly under the radar. If we wanted everyone to know where we were going, we would've flown out of Devonport."

"Right. So, you're the one who got them out of the castle? You don't look like all that much."

"I'm not in my prime right now," I confessed, shaking my head and driving in the direction of the hotel. "Sorry to disappoint you, lady."

"Nicole."

"Declan. Anything I should know about the fact you showed up here? I didn't tell you where we'd be going."

"Dante told me."

"Dante?"

Nicole snickered. "Bob. You call him Bob."

"Hey, he calls me Bob, too. Don't knock it,

lady. Bob's a great name. We've done a lot of good business calling each other Bob. Don't spoil a great working relationship with names."

"Speaking of Bob, I should call him."

I tightened my grip on the wheel with one hand, dug my phone out with the other, unlocked it with my thumb print, and offered it to her. "It's a German number and Bob already knows it. It'll save you a pretty penny in long-distance charges."

"Considerate. Thanks." She took the phone, dialed a number, and held it to her ear. "Hey, Dante. I made it. Bob's driving me somewhere now."

"We're going to a hotel."

"A hotel, apparently," she relayed. "Yes, Bob picked me up. What is wrong with you two? Bob and Bob? His name's Declan. Declan. I can spell it for you if I need to. Don't make me start spelling, Dante. It's fuck-it-all o'clock, and I just spent fifteen fucking hours flying here."

My phone was set to a soft volume because of my sensitive hearing, but I heard faint laughter on the other end of the line.

"Seriously? He said the exact same thing, word for word. Did you two plan this?" Nicole sighed. "No. He's driving right now."

"Put it on speaker."

"No. You'll crash into something."

I laughed. "It's not just planes you have a problem with, is it?"

"Shut up, Declan," she hissed.

I turned my attention to the road and bit my lip so I wouldn't laugh. While I had no idea what sort of man Richard was, I had a feeling I'd like him if he was able to handle such a short-tempered lady as his wife.

THIRTY MINUTES after leaving the airport, I parked the car in the same tight spot I had left well over an hour ago. Stifling a yawn, I rolled my shoulders and debated the pros and cons of sleeping slumped over the steering wheel.

"I'll go get checked in," Nicole said, sliding out of the car.

"Don't bother. I'll just tell the front desk there's an extra in our room. We've got a suite, but no promises you won't end up on the couch."

"Couch is fine. Thanks."

I forced myself into motion with a low groan, double-checked I locked the car, and tailed Nicole, stuffing my hands into my pockets. I stopped long enough to inform the front desk of an additional person in the room before heading to the elevator. Nicole pressed the up button, shifting her weight from foot to foot, pausing to hop as we waited. When the door dinged and opened, she bounced in, watching me with wide, expectant eyes.

Watching her fidget was enough to tire me out. I yawned and dug the room key out of my pocket.

Nicole snatched it out of my hand and bolted for the room, not quite hitting a full run before she made it to the other end of the hallway. She waited until I caught up before opening the door.

A growl from within was answered by Nicole, who dove into the room. I heard Desmond grunt, and when I peeked through the doorway, Nicole had the man on the floor, pummeling him with her fists. I leaned against the frame, crossed my arms over my chest, and arched a brow as the pair tussled.

"What the fuck do you think you're doing?" Nicole shrieked, reaching for Desmond's throat.

I stepped inside and closed the door before one of the other guests reported a murder. My wolf's interest and amusement were marred by growing hints of concern. Holding the woman back with both hands, Desmond ducked his chin to protect his throat, the corners of his mouth twitching.

I couldn't tell if the man was trying not to scowl or grin.

"You're the one who kidnapped my Marine? I found him first, daughter."

"Your Marine?" Furrowing my brow, I leveled my best glare at the other werewolf.

"I stole you fair and square. That makes you mine."

"I do not seem to recall you being involved in any extraction operation. The spooks did the work with the help of the Royal Navy. You're second-rate interference at best."

"Dad, don't talk to the Marine while I'm trying to kill you," Nicole hissed, swiping her hands at Desmond in her effort to reach his throat. *"You ran away from home."*

"So did you. You're not supposed to be flying at all, young lady. I'm pretty sure I told you flying was still absolutely out of the question."

"I got on a plane for you, you ungrateful asshole!"

"Why am I supposed to be grateful? I told you I'd handle everything. I promised I would drag Richard back home where he belongs, specifically so you wouldn't have to fly anywhere."

Nicole snarled curses and struggled to break free of her father's hold. As she kept fighting Desmond, his scent warmed with his amusement.

I couldn't tell if Richard was a lucky man or not. One of the pair seemed like a handful, but both of them?

I decided I didn't envy the man at all.

I tossed the keys to the car onto the coffee table along with the room key and dropped onto the couch, stretched my legs, and peeled out of my oxfords. I bent over, grabbed my shoes, and tossed them in the general direction of the door. "When Bob told me she was a few minutes away from a murder, I didn't think you'd be her victim, Desmond. Can't say I blame her. Want some help, lady?"

"See? Even your Marine is on my side. Thanks for the offer, but I can handle him."

"Your knee's about an inch south of a soft spot. Hit him there hard, and he should be easier to deal with," I advised.

Nicole jammed her knee into Desmond's side right beneath his ribcage, hard enough he yelped and lost his hold on her. The pair rolled, and Nicole flicked her finger against the side of his throat.

Desmond's pained yowl brought Lane staggering into the room, dressed in his uniform slacks and his wrinkled shirt unbuttoned. "What the fuck?"

"Father and daughter dispute," I informed him, propping my feet up on the coffee table. "Good morning. Take a load off."

"Mornin'." Yawning, Lane staggered to the kitchen and fumbled with the coffee machine. "Time to go?"

"I'm not driving. I'm going to sleep until we reach Paris." I echoed Lane's yawn. "I call dibs on the front seat with Desmond behind me. I'm going to lean the chair back and trap him so he stops bothering people."

"I like him, Dad. Can I keep him?"

"No. You already got the Anderson twins. It's my turn. My Marine and my SEAL. You can't have the programmer, either."

"Why are you stealing men from the military, anyway?"

"Felt like it."

"Maybe we should tie him up and throw him in the trunk, Lane," I muttered, dropping my feet from the table and getting to my feet. "I'm taking a shower. Try not to kill each other. No murders. Am I understood?"

"Dear god, Dad. He's channeling Mom." Nicole stared at me with wide eyes. "That's the creepiest thing I've ever heard."

Taking advantage of his daughter's distraction, Desmond flipped her over, pinned her to the floor, and sat on her. "Enjoy your shower, Major. I'll make sure to keep the murdering to a minimum."

I made my escape to the bathroom before anyone could stop me.

Chapter Fourteen

I ENJOYED TRAVELING with a British passport far too much for my own good. In addition to her American and Canadian passports, Nicole had a British one as well, though hers was battered and worn from use.

Desmond's passport was older, too, leaving Anthony, Lane, and I with ones so freshly printed the pages were stiff and had a tendency to stick together. Eight hours after leaving London, we arrived in Paris without drawing any unwanted attention to ourselves.

In a feeding frenzy more appropriate for sharks than people, Desmond and his daughter descended on the first buffet we found while Lane, Anthony, and I gawked at them. With their voracious appetites masking mine, I dared to take more than I normally would, and my wolf groaned his contentment in my head.

"We're going to need a plan," Desmond

announced, sitting down across the table from me with a huge pile of roast beef he had plundered from the buffet. "Declan, what do you think?"

"I think it's too early to make a solid plan," I admitted, shrugging. "Until I have a chance to do some ground work and gather intel, I can give you some ideas but little else. First, we don't know where our mark is. Second, I don't know what he's capable of. Third, the timing is terrible for night reconnaissance; the full moon rises tomorrow evening. Great for if you want to find your way through the woods, miserable if you want to do it without being seen."

Tomorrow evening, I'd be hard-pressed to keep from shifting, and I had no idea what being in such close proximity to other werewolves would do. The last thing I wanted was to find out if there was any substance to werewolf legends, especially regarding hunting in packs and territory disputes.

Lane shrugged. "If we have to do night work we might need the moonlight unless we get goggles."

"Cost is not an issue. If you need goggles, we get goggles." Spearing several pieces of meat with his fork, Desmond transferred them to my plate. "Eat more, son. You're skin and bones, and I don't like it."

My wolf wasn't sure what to make of Desmond's behavior, but it wasn't worth the effort fighting the other werewolf over it. Shrugging, I picked my fork back up and poked at the meat. "I ate."

"About a quarter of what you should be eating."

I frowned and narrowed my eyes, wondering if the man was being serious or not; consuming twice as much as Lane made me uncomfortable, and I was too aware of the other patrons staring at the obscene amount of food at our table. "I'm fine. Nicole, what can we expect from your husband?"

"He can be a bit volatile. He enjoys surprising people, and he's prone to doing the unexpected. It's really troublesome. He's headstrong, and once he decides to do something, he goes and does it." The woman sighed, stabbing a piece of meat with her fork hard enough I was surprised the plate survived unscathed.

Like her father, she reached across the table and dropped it onto my growing pile of offerings. "Dad's right, by the way. Eat. I hate when stubborn men faint because they don't take care of themselves. It's annoying, because I end up having to deal with the consequences."

"She's very experienced with this," Desmond added, his mouth quirking up into a grin. "Richard pushes himself too far all of the time. His brother, Alex, fortunately isn't as bad."

"Be wary about him, you three." Leveling a glare at her father, Nicole pointed her empty fork at him. "They are not up for sale or adoption. You will not take any of them home with you. You will not force them into the prison you call a house, nor will you coerce them into calling you nice names. It's bad enough Richard slips and calls you Dad sometimes now. I will not allow you to abuse these innocent men. Am I understood?"

"I found them first."

"This is not up for negotiation, Father."

"What the fuck have you gotten me into?" Anthony hissed, jabbing me with his elbow. "Those two are insane."

"Stop whining. You're getting paid extra. Two-hundred thousand for a free trip to Europe isn't a bad deal."

"I already paid you, Declan," Desmond grumbled.

"To take pictures, you bloated, mentally crippled marmot."

"That's a new one. Ran out of the good ones?" Shaking his head at me, Anthony rose to his feet. "I need pie. If there is no pie, there better be cake. If there is no cake, I'm hiring you to wage war on this buffet, Declan."

"Do I look like a charity?"

"Yes."

"We'll come to a fair arrangement for payment for your help. I'm prepared to pay a substantial amount for the recovery of my two boys and the ladies with them." Desmond's eyes focused on my plate and remained fixed there until I ate a bite to appease him. "It's a two-part job. First, we need to find them. Second, we need to get all of them back to the United States."

"My specialty is information gathering. Lane is probably better trained for live extractions."

"From my understanding of the situation, your performance in France was superb. The ladies were impressed. They were also quite worried, as they had heard the gunfire."

There was something unnerving about the way Desmond watched me, and I hid my discomfort by focusing my attention on the pile of meat that had been deposited on my plate. While I wasn't very hungry anymore, I ate anyway. If the werewolf women had hearing anywhere near as sensitive as mine, they would have heard the gunfire from miles away.

"Unsurprising. I wasn't far behind them getting out of the castle."

"One of the ladies seemed rather convinced you had gotten killed and was pretty upset about it."

I lifted my gaze to stare at the other werewolf male, wondering where he was going with his commentary. "And?"

"You made quite the impression on her if my understanding of the situation is correct."

"Please feel free to ignore my father, Declan. He thinks he is clever when he is not. He also has an unfortunate tendency to want to play matchmaker. Really, Father, can't you behave yourself for ten minutes?"

"I can when I feel like it."

"Feel like it, then."

The two started bickering, and sighing my relief, I glanced at Lane out of the corner of my eye. "Get the feeling we've jumped right out of the pan and into the fire?"

"It took you how long to figure that out?"

"Fucking SEALs."

Lane laughed. "What have we learned from this, sir?"

"Next time, carry three IDs instead of two and book at boarding."

"Special Ops," the SEAL sighed, shaking his head. "Can't live with them, can't live without them."

It was a small victory, but I'd take what I could. With a smug smile, I got up and headed for the buffet.

Declan: 1, SEALS: 4.

Desmond decided he wanted to stay the night in Paris, but instead of heading to a hotel, he made several phone calls and arranged for us to stay at a friend's vacation home located outside of the city. The mansion stirred my anxiety, and unable to sleep, I went to work.

I needed a plan, one I could build the rest of my work on. The others left me on guard while I worked on my laptop in one of the mansion's three living rooms. The one I had chosen was the smallest of the lot, and it had four couches, compounding my unease.

My entire apartment could fit in the room.

Shaking my head, I forced my attention back to my work. While Bob had provided me with the information he had on Richard Murphy's whereabouts, little was of use. If I wanted to find them, I'd have to go to the Swiss Alps and hunt them down the old-fashioned way.

There was one last thing I could try, but since it had been over a week ago since I had given Julie my phone, I doubted it would work. Pulling up the app to find my phone was basic, and it should have been the first thing I had tried. Shaking my head at my folly, I engaged the app, entered my password for the device, and gave it a shot.

Twenty seconds later, my phone's location popped up on the screen.

It was still in Switzerland, somewhere deep in the Alps—deep enough I was amazed there was cell reception.

I chuckled, dialed my own number, and put my phone to my ear.

"Hello?" a man's deep voice answered in a rumble.

"Richard Murphy?" I asked, gambling it was Bob's friend.

"Who is this?"

"The owner of the phone you're using."

"Yes, I'm Richard," he replied. "I was wondering when you'd call."

"Got sidetracked. What's your situation? I've got a five-man team ready to extract you."

"You get around, Mr. McGrady. Who are you?"

"Someone who wants his phone back. Look, Mr. Murphy. There are a lot of people who want to know where you're at and get you back to where you belong. Some of them are even your friends. We can play this two ways; you can cooperate, give me the details of why you cut communications and dropped off the radar, or I can wander upstairs and tell your wife your coordinates and set her loose. She—"

"Nicolina is there?" Richard boomed, his voice deepening. "That's a German number. What is she doing in Germany?"

"Paris, actually. I bought a replacement phone in Germany. She got here as people typically do, by plane."

"You're serious. She flew to Europe."

"I picked her up from the airport myself. Seemed a bit rattled but otherwise fine."

A string of curses thundered on the other

end of the line, and I waited for the eruption of temper to calm. "Put her on."

"She's sleeping, and I really doubt her father would be very happy with me if I headed into her room in the middle of the night."

There was a long moment of silence. "Desmond's there?"

"He's here, and he's out for blood, Mr. Murphy. He's determined enough to coerce Her Majesty's Navy into providing him with a Marine and a SEAL to fetch your ass out of Switzerland. Help a man out here."

"How the hell did the Royal Navy get a Marine and a SEAL?"

I laughed. "They stole them out from under the nose of a US Navy Vice Admiral at Desmond's request."

"You have got to be kidding me."

"I'm afraid I'm being completely serious."

"What is your part in this, and how did Desmond coerce you?"

"I suppose full introductions are in order. I'm Major Declan McGrady. I'm the Marine. Desmond originally hired me to infiltrate that French castle under the guise of planning an art heist to determine the location of the seven ladies keeping you company. What should have been a scouting job turned into an extraction. You should know the rest of the story."

"From my end, but not yours. Julie's convinced you were killed."

"Just because I jumped off a cliff and was

shot twice doesn't mean I was killed." I shook my head, chuckling at the memory of the headstrong werewolf woman. "My job was to cover their six. I covered their six."

"You're one tough son of a bitch, Major."

"This tough son of a bitch has a job to do. Why are you holed up in Switzerland, and do you need help?"

"We're being tailed by the folks who kidnapped the ladies. We're trying to lie low in the Alps, but they're pretty determined. We've been able to keep ahead of them, but no more than that. It would not be wise for any one of us to kill someone."

I scowled at the memory of my mother and her death, knowing full well what would happen to them if a group of werewolves did kill someone. "You're correct. If you and the man with you have phones, ditch them. They may be tracked. My phone is definitely being tracked, so ditch it, too. It's best if you destroy every piece of electronics you have. Memorize my number and text me updates on a disposable phone. Turn it off between contacts. Understood? If you can get a new disposable in every town, that would be wise."

"Understood. We'll be on the move to keep our tail busy."

"Good. It'll make it harder to track you down but less likely you'll be intercepted by the wrong party. Give me a second." I bent over my laptop and pulled up a map of the Swiss Alps. "There are a bunch of tourist villages in your area from the looks of it. Text me the location of the last one you were in and a reverse direction to the one you're heading to. If someone is intercepting your messages, that should be enough to throw them off at least once."

"I'll one up that; I'll start in reverse order and work counter-clockwise around the compass rose by the number of towns I've texted you to offset it. A little complicated to figure out on the fly, but it should do the trick."

I considered the plan. In order to accurately determine the direction Richard would be headed, I'd have to count the number of towns he had already visited and use that number in combination with his claimed direction. Once I ticked around the compass rose in counter-clockwise order, I'd reverse the resulting direction to find out which way Richard was headed. "I like it. Simple but difficult to crack. We're going to be on our way to Switzerland in the morning."

"Be careful, McGrady. Our tail is armed and dangerous. We're not geared to deal with them even if we decided to use lethal force."

"I don't have to be armed to be dangerous or lethal," I informed him. "Keep yourself and your group alive long enough for us to get there. Keep moving. I'll make sure we're ready for a firefight."

"Thanks."

I hung up and stared at my phone for a

long time. I wanted to believe Scallywag wanted to retrieve the seven women he had lost, but a nagging doubt warned me the real target was Richard Murphy, and that the game was about to become a great deal more dangerous.

Chapter Fifteen

I KEPT my conversation with Richard a secret. The last thing I wanted to do was compromise the man's position. If I did, I wouldn't be the one to pay the price. Protecting Richard and those with him through secrecy was my only option.

Leaving Nicole in the dark bothered me more than hiding the truth from the others did; I caught her staring out the window at nothing, her gaze locked somewhere far to the south east, as though she was somehow homing in on her husband's distant presence.

Despite being the first ready in the morning, I was the one who delayed us, my attention on my choice of routes. With two werewolves for company, I needed to find a place they could answer the moon's call if necessary—a place I could guard over Anthony and Lane if the wolves turned violent.

When the sun set and the moon rose, my troubles would begin. The peak of moonrise would happen a little after two in the morning, and while my wolf and I could resist the urges to change and hunt, I had no idea how strong the moon's call would resonate with the other two werewolves—and if their presence would unbalance me and my wolf.

My wolf's unease grew the longer I hesitated, and I was aware of everyone watching me.

"What's the hold up?" Anthony asked, leaning over my shoulder to peer at my laptop screen. "A map app?"

"I'm driving, and I'm deciding on the route," I informed him, clicking on the map on a promising town tucked at the foot of the Swiss Alps. "I'm also picking a place to stay for the night."

"You are?" Desmond crossed his arms over my chest. "That's my job."

"Loose cannons do not get to pick the routes or safe houses in the hot zone. Lane, if he gives you trouble, shoot him."

"I'd need a gun to shoot him."

"Take the loose cannon and his daughter and find me some guns, then. If they promise to behave and can demonstrate their ability to use a gun, they can even have one each."

"What's your poison, Major?"

"Sig or Glock. If the stars align and you can get me a fully automatic handgun, I'll take it. Biggest punch in the smallest package you can get me."

"You don't use a Beretta?" Desmond asked,

his surprise registering in his scent as well as in his voice.

"I have nothing against them, but they aren't my first choice." I made a shooing gesture at them. "Anthony, stay. The rest of you get out and see about weapons. Lane, you're in charge of a full ops kit."

"That's going to cost a fortune."

"I'm paying," Desmond stated. "And I might just know a few people who can hook us up."

I made a humming noise, dug my cell out of my pocket, and dialed Bob's number.

"Hey, Bob. What can I do for you?" my conspirator and sometimes friend answered.

"Bob, who do you have in Paris who can hook me up with gear?"

"I'll text you a name and number. Give me five. How many will be going for the pickup?"

"Three. Two men, one woman."

"I'll ping you. Costs are on me." Bob hung up.

I set my phone on the coffee table beside my laptop. "Bob's taking care of it."

"I love Bob," Nicole said, smiling at me. "You have him eating right out of your hand, Declan."

"Who the hell is Bob?" Pacing around the sitting room, Desmond came to a halt in front of the coffee table and made a grab for my phone.

I beat him to it, clucked my tongue, and

shook my head. "Loose cannons might compromise my sources."

"I know who Bob is," Nicole sang before sticking her tongue out at her father. "I'm not telling. That's what you get for running away from home and worrying Mom."

"What about *you* running away from home and worrying your mother?"

"I told her where I was going, asshole. She even drove me to the airport."

"She drove you to the airport."

"I flew to Seattle to check in when she called to say you'd flown the coop."

"You flew to Seattle."

Nicole sighed. "You're broken. How else would Mom drive me to the airport? She's at home keeping Sara contained. Declan, where are we going?"

My phone buzzed, and I checked the message. A town and a direction waited for me. I put the phone back down, headed to the map app, and scrolled until I found out where Richard was headed.

I'd be really surprised if he'd have cell reception. I texted him back with one of my obscure email addresses. He texted back a confirmation.

The next text was from Bob, and it listed the name of a store and an address, which I gave to Nicole. "Lane, you're in charge. Prep us as though we're going into a fire fight."

"That doesn't sound promising."

"Good. It wasn't supposed to. See what

Bob can get us, and don't be afraid to get some heavy weaponry." I hesitated, debating whether or not I really wanted to take a nose-dive into armed violence. Sighing, I submitted to the inevitable. "If there's one available, nab me a sniper rifle. We might need it."

"You're a sniper?" Desmond blurted.

"I know my way around a sniper rifle." That my targets were inanimate objects didn't matter; my aim was good, my eyesight was superior, and I didn't miss. Killing someone wasn't my style.

I didn't have to kill someone to disable them.

"I'm trained, too," Lane said. "It's not uncommon for Marines and SEALs to be trained in many different weapons, Mr. Desmond. I'll make sure we have everything we need. Don't you even think of going anywhere without us."

Laughing, I shook my head. "Wouldn't dream of it."

It was the truth. The last thing I wanted to do was go into the woods after eight or nine werewolves with two more at my back hunting me down for giving them the slip. Some called me crazy, but I wasn't completely insane.

IT TOOK LANE, Nicole, and Desmond three hours to get the gear, and when they returned, it was in a silver SUV instead of the black car. I herded Anthony out of the house, locked the door behind me, and turned to face the two werewolves and the SEAL. "Someone bought me a new car. Keys, please."

"Mine. I bought it, I drive it," Desmond growled.

"I'm not sure how you bought a car in three hours, but you know what? I don't care. Give me the keys. I'm the only one who knows where we're going, and I have zero intention of telling any of you the location or the way to get there."

Nicole's face paled, and her gaze skipped to her father. The woman held her breath, and her scent soured from her unease. Hopping down the three steps to the stone walkway, I marched to the other werewolf male, met his gaze, and held out my hand. "No keys, no son-in-law."

Anger had a scent, and Desmond's burned my nose with its strength. I waited, sliding one foot back to assume a subtle defensive stance, waiting and watching. Sighing, Desmond dropped the keys into my palm. "Fine."

I closed my fingers over the keys, nodded, and circled the vehicle, pausing long enough to take a picture of the vehicle and its plates, which I texted to Bob with instructions to attempt to get clearance at the Swiss border. "Get in. We have a long drive. I've already booked us somewhere for the night, and I want to be there by sundown."

I slid behind the wheel and waited for the others to climb in and buckle up before starting the engine. "Lane, how'd the acquisitions go?"

I heard the click of a box opening in the back, and a moment later, Lane thrust a handgun between the front seats. "Your Bob is obsessed with Beretta M9s, sorry. Best of the bunch. I've got clips and magazines for them, enough ammo for all of us, vests, night goggles, and some other toys. I like Bob a lot right now. He even landed you a sniper rifle you'll like."

"Holster."

"Shoulder or hip?"

"Shoulder." I shrugged out of my jacket, grabbed the holster, and eased into it, grimacing at the stiffness in my shoulder and arm. Giving the gun a thorough once over, I nodded my satisfaction and stowed it before putting my jacket back on. "Carry permits and forms for the gear?"

Lane handed over an envelope. "Here."

I reached across Desmond, opened the glove box, and stashed them inside. "Good. Disposable cells?"

"Bob had ten put aside for you. Do you really need that many?"

"Yes. Give me one of their numbers."

Lane did, telling me the passcode as he did so. I texted the number to Richard's cell. In the back seat, a phone pinged with a text message, and I held my hand out for it. The response, from an unknown number, was a name and a direction. I messaged Bob with the new number and tossed my phone to Desmond. "Destroy that, would you? Leave nothing intact."

Scowling at me, the werewolf grabbed the phone, got out of the car, and slammed the device on the ground before crushing the remaining pieces under his heel. "You're a very frustrating man, Major McGrady."

I snorted and cracked my knuckles before revving the engine. "Daylight's wasting, Mr. Desmond."

"You have my permission to call me Dad."

"Can I leave him here, Nicole?"

"I wish," Richard's wife growled. "Father, get back in the car and be quiet for once in your life. Please."

"I'm starting to regret I didn't leave without them," I muttered, waiting long enough for Desmond to get back in the car before putting the vehicle into gear. "Why didn't you talk me into leaving, Anthony? You're supposed to be my spot man."

"Don't you go blaming me for this, Declan. You're the one who got caught by the SEAL. I'm just here for the ride. Can I go home now? I have a severe gun allergy. I think I'm getting hives."

I sighed, shook my head, and wondered what I had gotten myself into yet again.

After being jerked around by far too many people, driving restored my sense of control with the benefit of soothing my wolf's fraying nerves. I pushed my luck and the speed limit, determined to reach our lodgings in Switzerland before nightfall.

I stopped to fill up for gas and grab quick bites to eat on the way, and not even Desmond was willing to question my frantic pace. The close proximity to the full moon made my skin itch, and my wolf whined his restlessness in my head.

As soon as I recovered Nicole's husband, I'd dive right back under the radar with Bob's help, picking up a new life and leaving behind Daniel McClain and Declan McGrady once and for all. I'd retreat to the forests for the winter and begin again in the spring.

Whether by luck or Bob's intervention, we breezed across the border into Switzerland, and I hummed a happy tune while everyone else breathed sighs of relief. I checked the clock, calculating the time to reach where I had made reservations for the night. "Let's find a market."

"A market?" Desmond glanced at me, deep furrows marking his brow. "Why?"

"We're in Switzerland. One simply does not go to Switzerland without acquiring chocolate."

"I'm taking you home with me, Declan,"

Nicole announced. "I'm taking you home with me and putting you in charge of my chocolate stash. I'll pay you a competitive salary for the work."

I was really going to need a good plan to escape the hold of Desmond and his daughter—and a distraction when it was time to fly from the coop after I helped them recover Richard, his partner, and the women they were escorting.

Until then, I'd play along and get a better feel for the werewolves so I'd have a better idea of what I'd need to do in order to escape.

"It is such a shame we don't have the time to make side trip to Belgium." I faked a sigh, shaking my head. "We're getting chocolate and the makings for dinner. I feel like cooking."

In truth, with the full moon on the rise, cooking would help me focus, and gorging would keep my wolf content while I waited out the most difficult hours of the month. I'd make enough to feed all three of us werewolves and the pair of unsuspecting humans.

My wolf liked having his way, and he really liked good food, which meant he wasn't satisfied until I cooked things *he* liked.

If it took me cooking a feast capable of feeding an army of werewolves to keep my wolf contained during the full moon, I would do it without complaint.

Nicole sighed, and it was a happy sound.

"I really need to take you home, then. You cook?"

Anthony groaned. "You're not going to go all gourmet on me again, are you?"

"We're in Switzerland and our place has a world-class kitchen. I'm going so gourmet you'll be ruined on restaurants for a year. Desmond and his daughter have the suite next door with the inferior kitchen."

That the suite next to ours was at least a hundred feet away had been part of the reason I had selected it. If the two werewolves shifted with the rise of the full moon, I had a little distance and a separate building to protect Lane and Anthony.

Anthony sighed. "Damn it, Declan. What the hell is wrong with you? You're a freak of nature. Do you know what happened that one time you did this? Remember that damned full moon on Halloween when everyone went nuts because that's what people do when there's a full moon on Halloween? Do you remember what happened?" Anthony pounded the back of my seat. "Well?"

To keep from shifting when the moon's call was at its absolute worst, I had sequestered myself with Anthony in his apartment, taking over his kitchen and cooking from sunset until sunrise, filling every bit of his freezer and fridge with food. I had made so much I had filled my freezer with enough left over to feed Anthony's parents, his sister, and his brother.

"It's not my fault you gained ten pounds. That's what you get for lazing about instead of exercising."

"You know what happens now? I get calls from my mother asking if you'll be cooking again. That was *years* ago, and she's still asking. You're sick, Declan. Completely sick."

I laughed. "You enjoyed every bite of it and you know it."

"He can't beat Navy cooks," Lane declared.

I shifted my eyes from the road to the rearview mirror and said nothing. I did, however, smile.

Maybe Anthony wasn't a werewolf, but he turned on the SEAL and hissed, "He's better."

"How would you know?"

"My great uncle was one when he was in the service. Ate his cooking all the time. He begs for Declan's food, too. *Begs* for it. He's corrupted my entire family." My friend and conspirator kneed the back of my seat. "He was asking when you'd come and cook for him in his veritable old age again, by the way."

"I told him the only way I'd feed him again was if he gave me his sugar cookie recipe. No recipe, no cooking. That's the deal, Tony."

"You bake, too? I'm really taking you home with me now, Declan." Nicole made a sound suspiciously like a purr. "No one bakes better than Richard, but two bakers is better than one."

"Don't challenge him, please. Please don't. He'll take you up on it. We'll all get fat, and it'll be your fault." Anthony sighed. "I'll beg."

"Baked goods last a while, and with seven stressed women joining us soon, I intend to be prepared." The ladies made a convenient excuse. By the time my wolf was through with the full moon, there wouldn't be a lot of cookies left over for them to enjoy, but that wasn't my problem.

All I cared about was making it through the full moon without sprouting a pink, glowing fur coat in front of anyone.

Chapter Sixteen

In my determination to cook my way through the night, I bought so many ingredients Lane had to reorganize the SUV to make everything fit. Even then, everyone except me ended up holding something on their lap.

As both punishment and a challenge, I made Desmond hold the three dozen eggs I had purchased along with every other fragile object I could find, including a delicate bottle of olive oil. I needed the oil for my cooking, but I had chosen the most fragile bottle I could find just to make the other werewolf carry it, threatening life and limb if the horrifically expensive bottle broke.

"Artisan olive oil," the werewolf snarled at me, his cheek twitching. "Isn't regular olive oil good enough for you?"

"No."

"Now look here, son."

I ignored Desmond snapping and growling, driving with far more care than I had prior to my stop at the market. The place was only twenty minutes out from my destination, but I estimated it'd take me thirty or forty depending on the roads.

If any of my eggs broke, it wouldn't be because I took the twisting, turning roads leading into the Swiss Alps at a reckless speed. It'd been years since I had been to the town, but I remembered the barely there pathways leading to the lodge all too well.

They hadn't changed. The owners of the cabins hadn't, either, although Bodwin had sounded older and far more tired than I liked. He'd been happy to hook me up with both of his cabins, and he hadn't even charged me a fortune for them.

My wolf liked Bodwin and his irreverent ways. He played life by his own rules, and my wolf and I respected that. Add in the fact he enjoyed art almost as much as I did, and we were quite comfortable with each other.

Before I left, I'd have to surprise him with a visit to his reclusive home farther up the mountain. If I brought cookies, he probably wouldn't shoot me again.

Maybe.

"You're far too pleased with yourself, boy." Desmond didn't sound happy, which made it difficult for me to keep from grinning.

"Dad, leave the poor man alone. If he wants to cook, let him cook." Nicole thumped her knees into the back of her father's seat. "You're supposed to be an adult."

"He's really not," Anthony muttered.

"I know. It's terrible. What exactly did he do to you? I will ask Richard and Sanders to straighten him out."

"Kidnapping and armed 'encouragement.' Desmond wanted his help locating me," I supplied. "*International* kidnapping, if that makes a difference."

"Oh, it does, Declan. It does." Nicole cracked her knuckles. "I think I'll help them. Father, did you really kidnap the poor man?"

"I needed his help to meet with Declan. I paid him for it. I'm paying for the entire trip. It's not a kidnapping if I hired him."

"He pointed a gun at my head until I accepted his check and agreed to help. He even walked me to the bank to cash it to make certain there were no problems." At Anthony's faked sniffles, I bit my lip so I wouldn't grin or laugh.

Desmond shifted and fidgeted, and I felt his glare on me.

"Break a single one of my eggs, Desmond, and I really will be pissed." I glanced at the man before turning my full attention to the road. "And since we're on the subject of international kidnappings, you'll triple Tony's pay for pointing a gun at him in addition to hazard pay. You do not want to know what will happen if he gets hurt because you dragged him into this, Desmond."

"If my idiot father doesn't agree, I'll pay

the difference," Nicole offered. "It's my husband you're helping, after all."

Desmond sighed. "I'll pay. I'll also make certain your Anthony's protected while you're working."

"You do that. Now, there are some rules for staying at this safe house," I announced, changing the subject before someone else took control of the conversation. "The owners really, really do not like anyone up on their mountain. If you want to be shot at with a high-powered rifle, go up the trails towards the peak. They might make you dance for them instead of killing you, but I wouldn't make any bets about it."

"What kind of safe house is this?" Lane muttered.

"The best kind. You should see what they do to people who haven't asked permission to be on their property."

"What are the other rules?"

"No one, and I mean no one, goes on the north face of the mountain. It's an avalanche risk. They've already had a few snowfalls at the peak, and one wrong move could trigger one. So, don't go to the north face of the mountain."

"This place sounds safe," Desmond muttered.

"The owners have two dogs. They're big, they're mean, and they like to play on the east face of the mountain. They don't leave that side unless provoked, so I really recommend you avoid the east, too. Our cabin is on the west slope."

Desmond sighed. "What's the problem with the south slope?"

"Ski resort and village. Small place, quiet, nice people. Combined, I think they speak maybe ten words of English. Avoid it, unless you happen to speak Romansh."

"Romansh? Never heard of it."

"Most haven't. It's fairly obscure. I know the basics, but that's about it."

Nicole leaned forward, propping her elbows on the center console between the front seats. "How did you learn Romansh?"

I laughed, and deciding to yank the tails of both werewolves, I replied, "Well, last time I was here, the owners shot me. I stuck around for a while after that."

"The owners shot you?"

"I neglected to bring him cookies the last time I went up to his place."

"He shot you because you didn't bring him cookies."

"My cookies are *that* good, Miss Nicole."

"They really are. I've considered breaking his knee caps to keep him around my place so he'd be forced to cook for me." Anthony chuckled, jostling Nicole aside so he could prod me with his elbow. "Three dozen eggs makes a lot of cookies."

"I'll even let you have some, Tony. Pity cookies for the poor programmer."

"Pity cookies are the best cookies. Can I have a whole batch?"

"If you swear to stay out of trouble and keep out of the line of fire, you can have two batches."

"Richard's not going to be happy if you steal my daughter with your superior baking skills."

Anthony snorted. "You're joking, right? Your daughter's safe. Declan doesn't even like women. He doesn't like men, either. He actually doesn't like anyone. He only tolerates me because I do nice things with computers and keep giving him interesting toys to play with. Declan has a strict no-woman policy."

"And thank you for talking about my sex life," I muttered, reconsidering my stance on baking anyone any cookies at all. I could make omelets with the eggs. I liked omelets.

My wolf, however, growled his disapproval in my head.

"Your lack of one," Anthony shot back.

"That's payback for letting Desmond hire me, isn't it?"

Anthony clapped, slow and deliberate. "It sure is. I did not see almond flour anywhere in your acquisitions."

"You're worse than a dog with a bone." Shaking my head, I turned on my headlights so I wouldn't get caught at dusk on tiny, treacherous, car-eating Swiss roads leading up into the mountains. "Yellow-bellied marmot."

"No almond flour," Anthony hissed.

"What are you, a cat? Sit back where you belong. The peanut gallery doesn't get to be up in the front while I'm driving."

I caught a glimpse of Lane's hand descending on the top of Anthony's head, and moments later, my friend made a startled, indignant squawk before disappearing out of my field of vision.

"I'll keep them contained back here, sir."

"Now, be quiet. We're in wolf country, and I'd rather not hit one or roll the vehicle all the way down the mountain before we get to where we're going."

"I'd rather you not roll it down at all," Desmond muttered.

"If you keep being a bothersome hedge-born lewdster, I'll light it on fire before shoving it off the cliff."

"Please be quiet, Dad. For just this once, please be quiet."

Silence was a precious gift, and for the ten minutes of quiet I got finishing the drive up the mountain on too narrow roads, I'd make sure Nicole got a batch of my best brownies.

THE PAIR of cabins halfway up the mountain required me to drive on a ledge carved into the side of the mountain. The SUV handled like a dream, but the fact I had less than six inches of leeway stirred my wolf.

He liked a challenge, and he loved the forced precision and careful way I maneuvered the vehicle. Adrenaline and his excitement washed through me, and it took every bit of my will to swallow my eager whines.

When I pulled in front of the cabins, which were surrounded by sparse evergreens and thick blankets of snow, everyone in the car breathed out a sigh of relief.

"What the actual *fuck* was that?" Nicole whispered.

"A road?" I put the SUV into park and twisted around in my seat. "I'm pretty sure it's a road."

"That may have been the sexiest handling of a car I have ever seen." Nicole's eyes widened, and her cheeks flushed.

I pulled out my phone and snapped a picture of her, which I promptly texted to her husband. To add insult to injury, I relayed her message word for word. "Thank you, ma'am."

I got out of the car, trudged to the smaller of the two cabins, and lifted the welcome mat, dug up the loose stone, and retrieved the keys in their magnetic box. Once I replaced everything as I found it, I returned to the SUV, holding them out to Desmond. "The keys to your castle, Mr. Desmond. You and your lovely daughter will be sharing that one. I'll have others with me."

My phone pinged, and I checked the message. I laughed at the string of question marks, stepped away from the car, and took a picture of the cliffside road I had traversed to get to the lodge before sending it to him.

"There's actually reception here?" Anthony joined me, burdened with paper bags. "These aren't cabins. They are mini mansions. What sort of safe house is this?"

"The best kind. Difficult to find if you don't know where they are, easily defensible, and multiple ways out if you're cornered." I hurried to the front door where we'd be staying and dug out the key, unlocking it. I had my gun out of its holster and sweeping the dark room. I prowled through the place, checking every corner.

All was quiet, and I relaxed, stowing the Beretta. Returning to the front door, I flicked on the light switch.

Anthony chuckled. "Hey, electricity! Score."

"Did you really think I'd cook so much food without it?" I shook my head. "Of course there's electricity."

"How about internet?"

"Keep dreaming, Tony."

"I'm allergic to places without internet, Declan. You should know this by now. What am I going to do without the internet?"

"Read a book."

"Where am I going to get a book?"

"The library."

"In case you haven't noticed, we are not at a library."

I pointed down the hall leading deeper into the cabin. "Third door on the right."

"There's a library?"

"Help unload the car," I ordered, unpacking the ingredients so I could get to work cooking the night away. "You can read while I cook."

"You're not going to make me serve as your minion tonight?"

"Not this time." With two werewolves in close proximity, the last thing I wanted to do was have anyone hovering nearby. The Halloween I had sequestered myself with Anthony, worrying about turning on my friend had been enough to keep my wolf carefully leashed. It'd be bad enough fighting my wolf's more aggressive tendencies with a SEAL under foot.

If Desmond and his daughter came too close, I wasn't sure if I'd be able to restrain the restless, wild side of my life.

My phone rang, and I checked the display. When I saw Richard's number, I answered, "McGrady."

"I'll be dropping off the radar for a day or two. Need to get rid of this phone."

"Okay. What's your status?"

"Annoyed. This tail is persistent."

"I have a few numbers for you to memorize."

"Okay. I'm ready."

"Sec." I headed to the SUV, dug out the stash of phones, and started relaying them to

Richard while everyone else stared at me. Returning to the cabin, I headed into one of the back bedrooms and closed the door so no one would overhear me. "I want you and your ladies to make as much of a run for it as you can tonight. Work your way into the Alps, preferably in the direction of France, and make it difficult for your tail to follow. Stay away from civilization. Tomorrow night, discreetly find a place you can drop an email or text message to me. Borrow someone's phone if necessary. It's preferred, actually. A hotel can probably send a message on your behalf."

"I can do that."

"Good, I'm destroying this phone as soon as I hang up."

"Understood. And McGrady?"

"Yeah?"

"Keep an eye on Nicole, would you?"

"Was already planning on it. I'm even keeping an eye on that loose cannon of a father-in-law you have, too."

Richard sighed. "Thanks."

"Quick question."

"What?"

"Should I be worried if he wants me to call him Dad?"

"You poor son of a bitch. What did you do?"

"I don't put up with his poppycock."

"That'd do it. Just give them some space tonight."

"Will do. Take care of yourself out there."

Richard hung up. For a long moment, I stared at my phone. Sitting on the bed, I dialed Bob's number.

On the third ring, he answered, "Hello, Bob."

There was a faint murmur of conversation in the background, as well as other ambient noises I recognized as coming from an airport terminal. "Are you at an airport?"

"Damn, Bob. Your hearing is sharp."

"Why are you at an airport?"

"I was bored."

"You were bored."

"Very."

"You were bored so you went to an airport?"

"This is a pretty nice airport. I really should come to Paris more often."

I choked on my own spit. "You're *where*?"

"So, how do I get to you, Bob? Please help. There's a very angry woman with my credit card and more guns than the military, and she doesn't need any one of her weapons to rearrange my spine. I made a severe error of judgement."

Drawing deep breaths, I pinched the bridge of my nose in an effort to keep calm. "Please put the angry woman on the phone."

"That might not be wise."

"Bob."

"Yes, Bob?"

"The woman. Put her on the phone."

"I don't want to."

"Now."

A yelp heralded the clatter of the phone striking a surface. Moments later, a woman asked, "Who the fuck are you?"

"Bob's friend. You can call me Bob."

"Bob."

"That's right, ma'am. Why is Bob in France? Were you aware he's a potential target?"

"I'm aware."

"You evaded six SEALs to get him to France, didn't you?"

"It was entertaining."

Maybe Nicole liked car driving skills, but nothing wound me and my wolf up quite as much as a woman who could handle some of the best-trained men in the world.

"Marry me," I blurted.

She laughed long and hard. "That escalated quickly. You sure do talk sweet, but I'll have to pass. I'm only into men who can shoot better than I can."

"I'm a sniper. I'm even a decent one, though I'm a bit rusty right now."

"You have my attention."

"Major Declan McGrady of the Marines. Pleasure to meet you. Bob hired me."

"Amber. Major, huh? You must be good if, uh, Bob went to you."

"I have my moments."

"So, what can I do for you?"

"Why is Bob in France? It's a possibility he's a main target. Don't feed me a load of poppycock. Can you guard him against a SEAL team if necessary?"

"I can, and I will if necessary."

My wolf was intrigued by the confidence in Amber's voice.

"Have him load you up with as many weapons as you can. I'm going to give you a phone number. Have him call it. When they answer, have him tell them he will bring cookies if they promise not to shoot him. Ask for directions. Bring a vehicle with good tires and handling. I'm expecting you both here by morning. Have Bob destroy his phone, kill every electronic in it, and get disposables."

"Destroying the phone would not be wise."

"Why not?"

"Trust me."

"Get rid of it. Put it in a charging case so it stays on and ship it overseas for all I care, but get rid of the phone. I can't afford *any* tracking devices coming up here. Every piece of electronics and known bugs will be gone or I'm kicking both of your asses off this mountain. Am I understood? Ship them to Timbuktu for all I care, but they will not be on your person."

"Understood."

"Good. Memorize these numbers. I am expecting text check ins on the hour every hour." I gave her all of my cell numbers and had her repeat them back to me. "Tell Bob I want another sniper rifle. It can be a gift for putting up with his shit."

"We have a third person with us."

"Okay. You have a third person with you. Fine. Fine. Same applies to him. Dump all the electronics. Any other surprises I don't want to know about?" I snarled.

"No, sir."

"If you aren't here in eight hours flat, I'm coming to find you. If I have to come find you, all three of you will regret it. Put Bob back on."

"Please don't kill me, Bob," my friend pleaded.

"Death is an easy way out. Don't worry, Bob. You'll live for a nice long time. After all, I need you alive to drain your wallet absolutely dry. We will have words when you arrive, Bob."

"I'll be ready for them. If it helps my case any, Amber kidnapped us both. She really did. Right out from under the team's noses."

"Bob."

"Yes?"

"Tick, tock. You have eight hours to get here. Do *not* make me come for you."

"You won't have to," Bob replied before hanging up.

Heading outside, I took time destroying the phone, snarling curses at the device, at Bob, and at the twisted mess my life had become.

Chapter Seventeen

FURY, the kind born of worry, anxiety, and uncontrollable circumstances, kept the moon's call at bay, and the plethora of ingredients scattered over the kitchen counters gave me an outlet for my restlessness.

The carrots took the brunt of my negativity, leaving me with a huge bowl of minced orange vegetables I needed to use.

They became the foundation for cake. I had purchased extras of everything, anticipating the first few dishes would be the product of anxiety and stress. Carrot cake was on my short list of foods I didn't like, but I wasn't in the habit of wasting ingredients, and until I worked out the worst of my tension, working on something requiring more delicacy wasn't an option.

Force feeding Desmond and his daughter would provide me with some sport and entertainment while ensuring the cake was consumed. I'd take the third one up the mountain to Bodwin as a part of my bribe. Satisfied with how I'd put the food to use, I went back to work, crushing walnuts and pecans.

I somehow managed not to turn them into powder before they made it into the batter. Out of the corner of my eye, I caught Lane and Anthony staring at me, and the SEAL's mouth hung open while his eyes widened.

Standing straight, I glared at the two men. "What is it?"

"I am making a mental note never to get into a knife fight with you, sir."

"If you're going to watch, you will do so sitting down. There will be no nervous fidgeting anywhere near my kitchen." I redirected my attention to the kitchen, stepping over to one of the four ovens to check its temperature. Satisfied it was heated to the appropriate temperature, I went back to work preparing the three cake pans I'd be stuffing inside.

"Your kitchen?" I heard the laughter in Lane's voice and chose to ignore it.

"Mine."

Anthony chuckled and dragged his stool into the kitchen, positioning himself on the fringe of my warpath. "I don't think it's your kitchen, Declan. Please give me something to do."

I glared at the programmer, scanned my available ingredients, and stared at the massive bag of potatoes. "Wash those. Peel half of them, and then cut and separate them into two bowls; with skins in one, without in the other."

"In water?"

"Yes." I drew in a deep breath, held it, and exhaled slowly to purge my agitation from my body. "Even cubes, geek. Don't get sloppy on me and ruin my food."

It wasn't their fault Bob had thrown a stick in the spokes. It wasn't their fault the full moon was on the rise. It wasn't their fault there were two werewolves I didn't trust prowling around.

None of what had happened was their fault.

Anthony snickered. "I would never dream of it. Just don't throw a spoon at me tonight. I'll behave, I promise."

When I turned to Lane, the SEAL held his hands up, slinking over to a stool and sitting down out of my way. "I'll just sit over here and stay out of the way."

"You can run down the inventory while I work. I want to know what I'm working with. I need to start building our strategy."

"Won't that interfere with your kitchen mission?"

"Lane, the inventory."

"Okay, okay. Keep your britches on, Major."

"Declan."

"I've got the inventory in my bag."

"Go get it." While Lane retreated to the

bedroom he had claimed as his, I folded in the crushed nuts and began the process of pouring the batter into the greased baking dishes so I could get them in the oven. I was sliding the last into place when the SEAL returned. While he made himself comfortable, I set the timer for the cake.

"I'll start off with your rifle. According to the briefing, you were stellar at the long ranges, so I conned your Bob out of a L115A3 AWM. I was considering the CheyTac Intervention, but I thought you'd have more fun with the AWM."

"I'm surprised you didn't get an M82."

"I had a feeling if you were wanting a sniper rifle, you were going for distance."

I shook my head, considered my ingredients, and announced, "Beef Wellington."

Anthony paused in his chopping, his eyes going round. "You love me. You truly love me."

"I proposed to some lady on the phone earlier. Sorry, Tony. I don't love you."

With his eyes narrowed in suspicion, my friend replied, "I'm not sure if you're lying to me or not."

"Apparently, she likes men who are a better shot than she is. I told her I was a sniper, but I was rusty. I was rejected."

Lane snickered. "Do you even have any kills in the field, Declan?"

"I'm the 'go in and steal things' guy, not the 'go in and make the kill shot' guy." Killing people wasn't how I operated, though I had been forced to pull the trigger in combat to get my team out alive. "I learned sniper techniques because it made the uppers happy."

"According to my briefing, you made friends with every last weapon they put in your hand. All skill, zero desire to put those skills to good use."

"I prefer to non-fatally disable people."

"You're the oddest Marine I've ever met."

"Don't feel bad, Lane. I didn't even know I was officially a Marine Major until I got dragged back in. I didn't *have* an official military branch. They were all disguises for operations. I've done ops with just about everyone. At least the Marines are straightforward enough."

"What rank were you before they bumped you up?"

I snorted, shaking my head. "Don't know. Don't care. I was the odd jobs guy. I was given a job and told to do it. The Bard was my handler until I took advantage of the blown op to get out. What else do I have to work with?"

"Twelve Beretta M9s, enough ammo for a good run, enough plastics to take out a tank or three, flak vests, standard bullet proof vests, a box of grenades, short-range com kits, a little bit of this, a little bit of that."

"Define a little bit of this and a little bit of that."

"I didn't know what I'd need so I took a bit of everything."

Closing my eyes, I counted to ten, debating the pros and cons of storming out of the cabin and spending the night as a pink, glow in the dark wolf or putting up with Lane. I cracked open an eye and regarded the spread of ingredients with a resigned sigh.

It was going to be a long night.

I COOKED my way around the world, and seven hours after I started, I'd made an obscene amount of food. The quantity I ate would've horrified Anthony and Lane if they hadn't succumbed to a food-induced coma two hours into my spree.

Of the foods I made, most of the Chinese dishes never made it to the refrigerator, ending up down my throat minutes after making it. Sometimes sacrifices had to be made, and my wolf really liked black bean chicken. He also liked anything dealing with ginger, which resulted in the disappearance of an entire three-tray batch of cookies.

I sighed my contentment and looked over my domain. Brownies, cookies, and cakes littered the counters. Most of the main dishes had already made it to the refrigerator or freezer, but the excess took over most of the kitchen, neatly packed away in plastic tubs ready for transport to the smaller cabin for storage.

There was likely enough to feed Richard,

his friend, and the seven ladies once I found them with some left over. Shaking my head at the quantity I had made, I ferried the first load to the other cabin.

Neither Desmond nor his daughter were within, but I wasn't surprised. Wolf prints marred the snow behind their cabin, which suited me well enough. The only trouble they'd find on our side of the mountain were the cliffs, and I doubted a fall would do more than hurt them.

By the time the sun rose, the moon would be setting. If the pair was wise, they'd return under the cover of darkness. The moon had already peaked, and without its call hounding me every other second, I was able to relax.

It took me four trips to transfer everything to the second refrigerator and freezer. When I stepped out of the smaller cabin, I came face to face with Desmond, who was wrapped in a snow-dusted bathrobe.

"What are you doing?" the man growled, and there was more wolf in his voice than man.

"Ran out of room in the refrigerator and freezer, so I'm borrowing yours. If you're hungry, there's plenty to eat. The brownies are for Nicole." I stepped out of the man's way. "Have a pleasant evening?"

Desmond's nose flared as he breathed in my scent. "Where are your friends?"

"Sound asleep. They're victims of food coma." I stepped out of the werewolf's way so he could come into the cabin designated as his territory. "That was my last trip of food, so I'll be out of your hair."

"You didn't go on a run?"

"I didn't. I don't." I shrugged. "Where's Nicole?"

"I'm here," the woman replied. A moment later, she plowed into her father's back, shoving him into the cabin. Like Desmond, she was dressed in a bathrobe. "Did I hear the word brownies?"

I pointed at the counter. "Enjoy."

"First, he gets me a gun. Then he bakes me brownies. Dad, I'm taking him home with me."

"I claimed him first, daughter."

"I'm not for sale." Shaking my head, I headed out the door only to have Desmond snag me by the collar of my shirt.

"Go for a run, son. I can hold down the fort."

I halted at the tug on my collar, pulled out the latest disposable phone from my pocket, and checked the time. "No can do. I've got work to do. Your son-in-law isn't going to rescue himself."

"Rescue?" Nicole demanded.

"Rescue. Someone's tailing him, his friend, and his ladies."

"And how do you know that?" the woman snarled.

My wolf tensed at the anger in the werewolf's voice. I swallowed back my urge to turn, growl, and snap my teeth at her. "I know because it's my job to know. It's a need to know situation, and you do not need to know. When you need to know, I will tell you. Until then, you will sit, keep quiet, and do as you promised, or I'm kicking your ass off this mountain and sending you right back to the United States. There are nine people depending on me not to botch this extraction. I will not tolerate anyone compromising this operation."

"Nicolina Angelica Desmond Murphy, back off and sit down. Eat your brownies, and don't you even *think* about doing what I know you're thinking about doing. No murders."

While I sympathized with the woman, who gave a wordless scream of frustration, I couldn't afford to back down. I remained tense until I heard the scrape of a stool sliding on ceramic tile. "You don't have to like me, you don't have to agree with what I'm doing, but you have to follow orders. If you're going to be a part of this team, you play by my rules like you promised."

"She'll obey," Desmond promised. The man's hold on my collar remained firm.

Instead of snarling like I wanted, I stood still and waited.

"You really should go on a run, son. I'll keep your territory safe."

"I don't run on nights like tonight."

"We all do. Don't be shy. When was the last time you had a good run?"

I found it interesting Desmond referred to shifting shapes as going out for a run. Uncertain of what the male's goal was, I hesitated. He knew what I was; his nose was telling him the truth as much as mine was telling me about him.

"I'm fine, Desmond." I checked the time again. "First, I don't have time for, as you put it, a run. Second, I don't need a run. I need to do a gear check and finish making my game plan."

"I can handle the gear check."

"I haven't seen the stuff yet. I need to do it myself. Back off, Desmond, and let me do my job."

"My job is to make sure snappish Fenerec don't maul their friends during the full moon."

I blinked. *Fenerec*? Pulling free of Desmond's hold, I turned to face him, and some of my puzzlement must have shown in my expression; he sucked in a breath and his eyes widened.

"The only person at risk of being mauled here is you. Back off and let me do my job."

"You're a rogue, aren't you?"

"Well, considering I steal things for a living..."

"That's not what I meant, and you know it."

"I don't, actually. Let's not beat around the

bush. Both of you know from smell alone I'm a werewolf. That's why I rented both cabins instead of the one. You do things your way, I do things mine. I don't run during the full moon, and that's that. Go chase your tail if that makes you feel better about it, but leave me alone."

"Fenerec."

"Werewolf."

"No, the name for our kind is Fenerec."

"I'm pretty sure I'm a werewolf."

Desmond arched his brow. "When was the last time you were in a pack, son?"

Canting my head, I considered the man, shifting my gaze to his daughter, who watched me with wide eyes while devouring a brownie. My wolf whined in my head. Pack was something he desired but couldn't have. "I'll be blunt, so you get the point and leave me alone about it. Until you coerced me into this extraction, I'd never met another werewolf face-to-face."

Nicole choked on her brownie and slapped her chest several times before gasping, "I call dibs."

Closing his eyes, Desmond sighed. "Please forgive my daughter. She has no sense of priority, and as an Alpha female, she lives to expand her pack. She also has no dignity."

"Don't make me shoot you, Dad."

I checked the time. "Can we continue this talk later? I have something I need—" The rumble of an engine cut me off, and I spun around. "Excuse me, I have a murder to attend to."

Before Desmond could stop me, I stalked out into the night, my gaze snapping to the headlight beams illuminating the cliff. The approaching SUV was smaller than Desmond's, and its driver hugged the wall, slow and steady until reaching the broader slope and parking next to our vehicle.

I stalked forward, shoving my phone in my pocket. The front passenger side door opened, and Bob stepped out.

My friend hadn't changed much since the last time I had seen him. He still wore the same clean-cut suit I expected him in, although his brown hair stood up every which way.

When he caught sight of me, he waved. "Bob."

I closed the distance between us, tempted to grab him by the front of his suit and toss him into the snow. "Bob."

The sound of car doors slamming drew my attention away from Bob to his friends. I disregarded the dark-haired woman, who I presumed was Amber, and focused my attention on the man who stepped forward to stand beside Bob.

The only difference between them were a few inches in height and the cut of their suits. Deciding the woman was my best bet, I focused my full attention on her. "There are two of them. One is bad enough. Why are there two of them?"

"Sorry. Had to kidnap both. Bad things happen when I let them stray too far apart. I'm Amber."

"Declan. You're early. Good. You can help me go over the gear and make plans." I turned to come nose to nose with Desmond.

The werewolf's fury stung my nose.

"What are you three doing here?" The way Desmond growled stirred my wolf's ire.

I hadn't lost control to my wolf in years, but he was on the other male before I could stop him. While he was always in my head, I forgot just how much he learned from me. Grabbing hold of Desmond by his bathrobe, my wolf twisted and tossed him into the snow, tensing to lunge for the fallen male.

Bob was mine to protect, and I wasn't about to let a rival male too close.

"Dad!" Nicole squealed from the safety of the cabin's front door.

Bob's hand closed around the back of my neck and squeezed. When I snarled, he firmed his grip, tight enough stabbing pain zapped up and down my spine and froze me in place. "Good morning, Nicole. How are you?"

"Hey. I'm good. Declan made me brownies, and they're really good. Please don't kill my father. He's stupid sometimes, but I like him. Oh, it's Amber. Hi, Amber."

Amber sighed. "Nicole, what do you think you're doing?"

"Eating brownies. Watching Bob keep Declan from killing my father. We're fighting over who gets to keep the stray. You really should have one of these brownies. They're amazing."

"Dante, why is Declan calling you Bob?" Desmond asked, picking himself out of the snow. Shaking his head and sighing, the werewolf brushed the snow off his bathrobe.

I growled. With far more strength than I expected from his tall and slender body, Bob gave me a teeth-rattling shake. "I figured you might need my help with Richard, so I asked Amber to kidnap me. Since she wasn't comfortable leaving Elliot behind, she kidnapped him, too. Amber was happy to help; she figured you might need her help with Nicolina."

"Aren't you supposed to have a protective detail?" Desmond growled again, and I answered him with a snarl and snap of my teeth. "Where are they?"

"Damn it! Relax," Bob ordered, giving me another shake.

My wolf whimpered and abandoned me. Without his influence and energy driving me forward, exhaustion flooded through me, and I slumped to the snow-covered ground, forced to obey a human's command.

Chapter Eighteen

"Damn it, Desmond! Stop snarling at me already. I already accepted the blame. What else do you expect me to do?"

Several facts asserted themselves all at the same time. First, I wasn't cold, and the last thing I remembered was being outside and falling into a snowbank. Second, Bob—no, Dante Anderson, negotiator and black-market specialist—was pissed, and when he was pissed, bad things happened to someone. He'd shaken me like a rag doll, demanded obedience, and had gotten it.

Third, someone was petting my hair, and I was torn between enjoying it and succumbing to the urge to bite. My wolf loved every bit of attention, and when I was ready to launch myself upright, he took over and forced me to endure with someone pawing at my head.

Traitor wolf.

"Fix him," Desmond snarled.

“Mr. Desmond, the poor puppy will be fine. He’s exhausted. It’s not Dante’s fault he’s used to working with Richard, who is really difficult to bring back in line.” It took me a minute to realize the woman speaking was Amber. While I understood each word individually, they didn’t make much sense when strung together.

What did she mean by working with Richard?

My wolf wanted me to play dead, listen, and learn, and I obeyed. Intel was supposed to be my specialty.

Unfortunately, when it came to my own kind, I was about as ignorant as they came.

Did Amber really have to call me a puppy, though? I couldn’t argue with her on the exhausted part; bad habits were hard to break, and I had a tendency to run myself into the ground during a job.

“These brownies are amazing,” Nicole announced. “Dad, you should have one. Eat the fucking brownie and stop snarling at Dante before you tick Elliot off. Remember what happens when you tick Elliot off? Elliot tells Amber to deal with you. Do you remember what happens when Amber is told to deal with you? You get shot at. When you get shot, because Amber doesn’t miss her targets, Mom gets mad. When Mom gets mad, I get mad. Do you remember what happens when I get mad? That’s right. You get shot at again, although I remember I’m not supposed to hit you. Then Lisa gets upset, and she starts shooting, too. Once someone starts shooting, people expect *me* to fix the walls. Do you know what happens when people expect me to fix the walls?"

Desmond sighed. "You get angry and start shooting again."

"That's right. I start shooting. *Again*. So, what are you going to do? You're going to eat that fucking brownie and shut up, Dad."

Somewhere nearby, my phone pinged with an incoming message. A moment later, I heard Nicole blurt, "What the hell is this? Hey, Dad. Read this."

"I'm pretty sure that's gibberish. Why is Declan receiving gibberish on his phone?"

"Let me see," Amber demanded. "Hellschwandbach? What's the E mean?"

"Direction," Dante said, and I realized he was speaking somewhere over my head.

"Swiss name and direction," someone corrected, his voice a curt version of Dante's. "Mountain, road, or town; not sure which. Definitely sounds Swiss, though."

Dante had a twin brother, and I didn't like it. Twins smelled the same. They sounded the same. Twins confused me, my nose, and my eyes.

Things had been so much simpler when I had called Dante Bob. It was probably Dante's fault Desmond had found me. Once my wolf relented, I needed to introduce Dante's face to a snowbank.

Someone stroked their hand over my hair, and my wolf basked in the attention, not caring who was doing it, so long as it didn't stop.

Desmond muttered something under his breath before saying, "You probably want to wake him up and fix whatever you did to him before the SEAL in the other cabin figures out his charge has been floored. The SEAL does not like when anyone touches his charge."

"What SEAL?" Amber demanded.

"Declan's. Declan's programmer and general conspirator is also sleeping in the cabin next door."

"Declan's a stray," Nicole announced, and the sharpening of her tone intrigued me. There was a challenge in her statement, and my wolf's curiosity piqued.

"A stray?" I couldn't tell if the question came from Dante or his brother.

"He made the cutest expression when Dad slipped and said Fenerec. Absolutely confused. I don't think he's seen one of us up close and personal before. Poor pup has been about ready to crawl out of his skin trying to keep Dad out of his territory. He's pretty sensitive when it comes to Lane and Anthony. Watching Declan snarl and commandeer Dad's new SUV was a treat, though."

"Can we not talk about that?" Desmond asked. "He still has my keys."

Amber made a thoughtful noise. "Risk factor?"

"Do you think I would let Dante anywhere near him if I thought he was a risk? It's my fault his temper was fraying. I was pushing him into slipping off and taking a run. He was anxious and stressed. I thought an early morning hunt would do him some good. I didn't know you three were on the way. He didn't shift tonight at all. He hid in the other cabin and cooked the night away. Don't know if it's because he didn't trust us or what."

The hand on my head stilled, and Dante sighed. "Him being a Fenerec explains a lot. I've known him for almost a decade on and off, and I never saw a single sign of him being anything other than a really clever Normal. He broke into one of my smuggling rings and tracked me down. Rascal offered to help me tighten up *my* operations if I supplied for him and hooked him up with work."

"Declan tracked you down from one of your rings?" The shock in Desmond's voice pleased my wolf. "I test your rings for the fun of it at least once a year, and I've never busted one of them."

"He's that good. When I heard he had gotten picked up by the Navy, I started laying the groundwork for you to get him out. Once we're done with this, I'm going to set him up so he disappears into *my* network. He's mine. Hear that, Elliot? *Mine.*"

Why did everyone want me? Before I

could sigh, my wolf snapped control away from me, determined to hear the conversation without tipping off the other werewolves we were awake and listening to them.

"I'll make the arrangements, Dante." I disliked how I struggled to tell Elliot's voice apart from Dante's. Dante's twin sighed. "I'll browbeat the military for you. Just undo whatever you did to him before Desmond jumps out of his skin and you have to tame him, too. No fighting, no murders, and no international incidents. It's bad enough Amber stole my phone, my laptop, and everything else—including my fucking watch—and shipped them back home. My watch. She stole my *watch*."

"Dad, don't you say a word."

Desmond grunted and otherwise kept quiet.

"Declan's orders. He said no tech or we go home, and I wasn't going to argue with the nice Marine who found Patricia for us. Now all we need to do is find Richard."

My phone rang, and my wolf relented control enough for me to reach for it, wiggling my fingers. "Give."

"Good morning, Declan," Amber said, and the cool glass and metal of my phone was set into my hand.

I cracked open an eye enough to figure out how to swipe my finger across the screen to answer and held the device in the general vicinity of my ear. I made sure its volume was on its lowest setting so no one could overhear the other end of the line. "McGrady."

"We've dropped our tail, at least for the moment," Richard informed me.

"Good. What've you got for me?"

"I'm on a cell. Belongs to a nice pair of tourists headed the other direction. If someone tracks it, should lead the other way."

"Give me one of the other phones," I ordered, holding out my other hand. A moment later, one was handed to me. "Sec."

"Sure. Don't be long. Don't want to upset the nice folks who own the phone."

"Coords?"

Richard spelled out the name of his location, and I plugged it into my phone and let the app chart the most direct route.

If my phone was correct, we were less than an hour away. "One hour."

"Got it. We'll stay put unless our tail shows up."

"Perfect." I hung up, sighed, and groaned at the stiffness in my neck and back. I sat up, aware of everyone staring at me. I shook my head to clear it. "Gotta run a quick errand. I need two people to come with me. Whoever the hell drove that little SUV coming in and one other. I need the space for the goods and the hands to get things loaded quick."

Amber dug her hand into her pockets, pulled out a set of keys, and jangled them. "I'm your driver, Declan."

"Take Lane. He's fresh," Desmond suggested. "You sure you're okay to drive? You won't be long, will you?"

"I'll be fine. Won't be long. Just need to pick up a few supplies for the main operation."

It wasn't a lie; for the main operation, I needed Richard, his partner, and the seven ladies. I also needed to make sure his tail was dealt with once and for all.

What Desmond and the others didn't know wouldn't hurt them.

"I don't know how you have so many contacts in Switzerland, but I owe you for this, Declan," Desmond said. "Get the rest of your gear and get your ass back here so we can find my sons."

I eyed the werewolf warily. "Just how many sons do you have, anyway?"

"Four now."

Neither my wolf nor I appreciated the predatory gleam in Desmond's eyes. I glared and retreated, refusing to turn my back on the man until I was out the door.

"He's so shy," Desmond said, his tone amused.

"You're terrible, Dad."

MILITARY TRAINING HAD Lane already awake and fumbling for coffee in the kitchen when I went to retrieve him. It took him less than five minutes to get ready while I made us all coffee for the road.

I delayed long enough to grab my sniper rifle, take it out of its case, and make sure it was assembled and ready to go. I grabbed the ammunition and headed to the SUV, where Amber was waiting.

"You're the lucky bastard who gets the AMW? Nice. You know how to handle that bad boy?"

"You're armed?"

"Knives, two guns, a couple of grenades, and some plastics. Do I need more?"

"That'll work. Follow close. When we arrive, we load fast and hit the road back to here." I handed her one of my cells. "We'll keep in contact with this. I'll call you once you're to your car; put me on speaker and toss the phone on the seat while we're driving. Lane, you're in charge of the other phone in case my contact calls."

The SEAL grunted and got into Desmond's SUV. I set our coffees in the holders before I handed over my sniper rifle and hopped in, buckling up. Before I used one of the spares to call Amber, I waited for her to get into the other car. "We're doing the extraction now. They dropped the tail, and they're an hour away."

"Sounds good. Let's not waste the window. Are we making a run for it once we have them?"

"We're going to regroup, go over the gear, and eliminate the tail."

Lane coughed. "We're going to *what*?"

"Aren't you supposed to be a SEAL?" I glared at Lane, and he glared back. "We can't afford to leave them loose, so we're going to make the opportunity. We're going for the kill shot. Whoever's behind this needs to disappear—permanently."

"Isn't this a little outside of your normal specialty? I hope you know what you're doing."

I glanced in the direction of the cabin. "Desmond's not the type to let something like this go, and Richard's important to him. Those two are important to the United States. The tangos go down. I have a feeling they'll end up tailing all of us if we try to give them the slip. I'd rather lure them onto my territory and take them out. The last thing we want is those men falling into enemy hands."

If Desmond didn't go on a murderous rampage, I had a feeling his daughter would. Something about both of them set the hairs on the back of my neck up on end. While I didn't think they were a threat to me, Anthony, or Lane, I wouldn't want to be the target of their ire.

"Your call, sir."

I dialed the phone Amber was carrying, and she answered on the first ring. "I'm ready."

"Good. This should be a very quick pick

up. Sorry to drag you out at dawn after such a long drive to get here."

"I can handle two hours. Then I'm out for eight minimum."

"Sounds good. Not going to lie; I have similar plans."

I eased the SUV along the cliff road, careful to keep away from the edge without scraping the rock face. Once beyond the most treacherous stretch, I picked up speed, determined to shave off minutes, aware of the seconds ticking by.

An hour was too long in the grand scheme of things; the tail could reappear at any minute, and I wanted to have my marks safe in my custody. If I had to engage, I would.

Anyone capable of tailing werewolves with such finesse worried me. The worry of what would happen if I killed anyone came second to my job—and protecting those who were being hunted.

I was stuck between a rock and a hard place, and I knew it. My wolf did, too, but he was more inclined to hold out hope than I was.

Desmond, Dante, and the others had supplied us to kill if necessary, and they trusted me to make the right decision. It'd been a choice I'd made before, although I usually didn't have to execute the kill order myself.

But, sometimes I did, and I had a feeling I'd be drawing my lines with the werewolves.

Something warned me my decision would make or break me with them.

Did I want to make it with them? My knee-jerk reaction was to make my break the instant I had secured the safety of my marks, disappearing off the radar before Haney could get his hands on me again.

"So, what're we picking up?" Amber asked.

It was tempting to leave the woman hanging. "Who."

"What?"

"Who, not what."

"We're picking up someone? An associate?"

"Nine someones. Discreetly. Not enough room in the SUVs for everyone and the gear if we brought Desmond, his daughter, and Anthony. Richard dropped his tail, and I'm taking advantage of the opportunity."

"You found Richard?" Amber's voice went up an octave.

"I knew where he was the entire time, Amber."

"And you didn't tell us?"

"I didn't tell anyone. The last thing I need is that loose cannon back there barreling off to perform an extraction he has no business being involved in *because he's one of the targets.* I got three prime targets named Dante, Elliot, and Desmond, four if you count Nicole, in that cabin, at least one more on the way, and a bunch of ladies who have been hostage for God only knows how long. It's called security, Amber. It's been compromised enough."

I took several breaths to calm my frayed nerves.

"You're right. Desmond would have gone through the roof and you wouldn't have been able to leave him behind. He is very unreasonable when it comes to Richard and Sanders. He's overprotective to begin with, which is why he came across the pond."

I focused my attention on the twisting Swiss roads descending out of the Alps and into the foothills. If the satellite imagery of the area was correct, Richard had holed up near a valley between mountains, an ideal place for wolves during the full moon. "Sanders. That's Richard's partner, correct? Tell me about him."

"Sanders is a good guy. Steady as they come, decent shot. Good to have in a fight but will avoid them unless necessary. He'd rather be in his greenhouse taking care of his plants. But, Richard's like a brother to him, and when Richard asks for help, Sanders is usually the first in line." Amber paused, making a soft noise in her throat. "You'll like them, I think. Just be wary of Richard when he's around Dante."

"Why?"

Amber chuckled. "Richard had a scare a while back, and he's still touchy about it. If he wants to tell you about it, he will. All you need to know is this: Richard's an overprotective idiot. Desmond's an overprotective idiot. Sanders is an overprotective idiot. Birds of a feather. Just ignore their posturing."

One thing I appreciated about Switzerland was the long stretches of empty road. I drove as fast as I dared on the snow-dusted roads descending the mountain. "You'll be our first contact, Amber. They know you. They'll cooperate with you. I need you to get them in, and I'd like to be burning rubber within a minute of spotting them. They've been dodging a tail long enough I don't want to take any chances on friendly fire. We'll be covering your six when you're doing the pickup."

"Understood."

Chapter Nineteen

We reached Hellschwandbach in a little over half an hour. If Amber objected to my reckless driving, she showed no sign of it as she skidded to a halt on the fringe of the hamlet tucked deep in the heart of a valley. She was out of the SUV and on the move, her gun out and at the ready.

I didn't blame her in the slightest for her wariness; the quiet serenity of the place set me on edge. The calm before the storm was something I'd experienced far too many times. Instead of the sense of security most enjoyed in such a sleepy little place, I expected the shadows to solidify into enemies.

Lane tensed, and his hand hovered over the grip of his gun.

She held my phone to her ear. "Wait here."

Selective hearing was a trait that had gotten me into—and out of—more trouble than I cared to think about. Unbuckling my belt, I slid out of Desmond's SUV, unholstering my gun and doing a sweep of the forest, although I did stay near the vehicles. Lane stayed behind, but his weapon was out and ready.

Covering Amber's six was my first priority, and I slinked after her. The woman strolled towards the trees, her hands in her pockets and her posture relaxed.

"*Amber*?" Richard's voice rumbled, and I sniffed the air. The cinnamon of werewolves filled my nose, so many mingling scents my wolf and I were challenged to identify individual signatures.

"As if I'd stay in Canada when the fun is here. Hustle it; we're on a tight schedule."

I watched the woods, and the shadows did converge into the figures of seven women and two men. I straightened, careful to keep my weapon ready but pointed at the ground rather than at anyone.

"Commandeered yourself a soldier, Amber?" For someone with such a deep voice, Richard was a small man. I wasn't a big man myself, but I still had several inches on him.

The man beside him, who I assumed was Sanders, was lean but muscular and tall enough I'd probably have to lift my chin to look him in the eye. He stared at me. I stared back.

My wolf wanted me to bare my teeth and snarl, but I restrained him.

Richard smiled, gestured with his hand, and the women from Scallywag's castle emerged from the trees. The wear and tear of long-distance travel marked their clothes, clothes they hadn't had when they had fled Scully's castle. Enough dirt layered them I wondered if they had found some mud to roll in during their journey.

Amber snorted. "Get your ass in the car, Richard. Go with him. Patricia, stay with Richard. Sanders, with me." Amber pointed at several of the women. "You're with me. Rest of you go with Richard."

I backed towards Desmond's SUV, ignoring my marks to watch the forest. The stillness of the forest unnerved me almost as much as the silent prowl of the werewolves following me to the vehicles.

Hopping behind the wheel, I turned to Lane. "Take the back. I want you watching our tail."

The SEAL handed over my phone, jumped out, circled the vehicle, and crouched behind the seats.

Richard took Lane's place. "You got here fast."

I grunted, buckling in. Instead of holstering my gun, I offered it and my cell to the werewolf, who took it, checking over the weapon before he nodded.

Three women slid into the SUV. When I had met them, my vision had been too blurred to help me distinguish who was who except for Julie.

It was hard to forget the woman who had

floored me and straddled my chest like she owned me. My wolf hadn't forgotten her, either.

"You really didn't die?" she blurted, taking the seat behind me.

Instead of answering, I checked my rearview mirror, confirmed everyone was in the vehicle and the doors were closed, and put the SUV into drive. I spun the vehicle, taking advantage of the snow to execute a full spin. Amber tailed me.

"Amber, take the lead. Lane's covering our six."

"Yes, sir," she replied.

"Drive like you mean it. I want to be back to the cabin in under thirty."

"Are you insane?" Amber shrieked.

"Marine," I reminded her.

Snarled curses answered me, but the woman floored the gas right up until we reached the steep roads leading up to the cabin.

No one followed us, and I worried.

AMBER MADE me go first over the cliff trail to the cabin, and my wolf egged me into showing off. Desmond's SUV handled like a dream, and I enjoyed the thrill of coaxing the vehicle up and over the final stretch, guiding the vehicle so close to the cliff face I was amazed I didn't scrape the paint.

Richard whistled the moment we were clear, and I parked in front of Desmond's cabin. "Nicole was right. That *is* some of the damned sexiest driving I've seen in a long time."

"You have the strangest family."

Everyone in the vehicle burst into laughter, even Lane.

I slid out of the SUV, stifling a yawn. Amber pulled up beside me, stomped over, and shoved her gun in my face. "Are you *insane*?"

Blinking at her, I pressed my finger to the side of the barrel and redirected her weapon.

Patricia laughed. "Amber, are you really asking him that? He jumped off a cliff while wearing a dress."

"I hadn't heard that part." Amber scowled. "You could have gotten yourself killed driving like that. That's a *cliff*."

"Amber, don't question the man's sexy driving. You just can't *do* that," Richard huffed, circling around the SUV and pointing at her. "Put the gun away. No murders. *No murders.* Why do I have to remind people not to murder anyone? I sound like Mom."

"Richard?" Nicole slammed her way out of the doorway, and I was amazed the thing stayed on its hinges. The woman plowed through the snow and slammed into the man, tackling him to the ground. Howling curses, she pummeled him with her fists.

He laughed, wrapped his arms around her,

and buried his face against her neck. "Good morning, beautiful."

"Don't kill him, Nicole. Please," Sanders said, standing over the pair with a pained expression. "I know he's a pain in the ass, but I like him. No murders. Damnit, now I sound like Wendy, too."

"I'm going to pretend I'm not seeing this," Desmond snarled from the cabin's front porch. "I'm going to pretend you brought back supplies like you said you were. I'm going to keep pretending you three did not sneak out of here without telling me you were doing the extraction!"

"Oh, hey. It's Richard." Dante leaned against the doorway. "I want a turn with him, Nicole."

"No, Dante. We want Richard alive. If you take a turn, Richard might not survive," Dante's brother said, sliding through the pair of men to approach me. "Nice work, Major McGrady. We haven't had a chance to be properly introduced. I'm Elliot Anderson."

I shook with him. Before I could pull free, he tightened his grip. There was something unnerving about the way he stared at me. My wolf's wariness swept through me, and I tensed.

Lane made a strangled noise. I twisted around in time to see the SEAL snap a salute and blurt, "Sir!"

"You know him?" I tried to pull my hand free, but Elliot kept a firm hold on me.

"He's a VIP, sir."

VIP could mean many things, from upper government official to someone like Vice Admiral Haney. "VIP or not, I'm about five seconds from tossing him in the snow."

Elliot didn't let me go.

I counted to five. When he kept holding on, me and my wolf had enough. I shifted my weight, grabbed hold of the front of his pristine suit, and tossed the man directly on top of Nicole and Richard.

He released me and landed with a grunt.

Instead of the anger I expected, Elliot burst into laughter. The man bumped fists with Richard. "Glad to see you in one piece, Richard."

"Get off me, both of you," the werewolf replied.

Nicole pouted. "But I like you where I have you."

I doubted I would ever understand werewolves or their human friends. "Lane, you're fresh. Pull an op together, set a watch, and dispose of the electronics. We'll stick to the short-range comms from this point forward."

"Yes, sir!"

Sleep would soothe my nerves more than anything, and I had a feeling things would be rough once I got back up—if the tail didn't locate us first. If the tail did, Lane could handle it. If my guess was correct, so could Richard. Add in Desmond, Nicole, Amber, and eight other werewolves, and I had hope they could handle things without my intervention.

I was halfway to the larger cabin before Dante intercepted me. I tensed, but the man kept out of arm's reach, twisting to face Richard and Nicole, who were still lying in the snow. "Don't give Amber or Nicole any trouble, Richard. I'll take care of Declan."

Richard saluted from his prone position beneath Nicole.

"I wasn't aware I needed to be taken care of," I grumbled, narrowing my eyes. "Bob."

Grinning, Dante slapped his hand to my back and gave me a shove forward. "Damn Desmond anyway for ruining our perfectly good arrangement. How can anyone dislike the name Bob? It worked so well for us, Declan."

"I know, right?" I heaved a sigh. "Do you have to deal with them all the time?"

"Unfortunately."

"I could toss you off the side now. Put you out of your misery. It's the least I could do as your friend," I offered.

Dante laughed. "Richard would cry."

"Dante," the werewolf in question growled. "Do not make me come over there."

"You should. You can stand guard. It's the least you can do since I had to come to Europe to pull your ass out of the fire. Let Desmond and Nicole work with Lane, Sanders, and Amber on a plan. You can come join me and Declan."

"What about me?" Elliot demanded.

"Stand around and boss Desmond around. You know how much he likes that."

Elliot got to his feet and dusted the snow off his suit. "Why are you being an ass today, Dante?"

"Declan brings out the best in me. Desmond doesn't care. You know he needs supervision especially when weapons are involved. I saw the inventory they made off with. They need the supervision. Do not let them turn this into a large-scale international incident."

Desmond laughed. "He's probably right, Elliot. We need your unending wisdom. Otherwise, we *will* turn this into an international incident. Think about it. Amber has access to a lot of weaponry right now. If we leave her unsupervised, she'll start wars because she can. Oh, send that programmer over. I bet he has good ideas. That young man has a hell of a head on his shoulders."

"You all test my patience." Elliot flipped a rude gesture in Dante's direction. "Fine, run away. I see how it is. Leave me to do the heavy work as usual."

Dante sighed. "Amber, did you *really* have to kidnap him, too? Dealing with Desmond and Richard together is bad enough. But Elliot, too? What did I ever do to you?"

I nudged Dante with my elbow. "Are you sure you don't want me to toss you over the edge? It'll only hurt for a second."

"I'll be all right. I'm not sure about you, though. Maybe you should run and escape while you can. I'll slow them down for you."

"*Mine*," Desmond and Nicole yelled. Turning to each other, father and daughter glared, and with a snarl, Nicole lunged. The two rolled in the snow, leaving Richard to make a snow angel.

"What is wrong with you people?" Pinching my nose, I weighed my options, wondering if I could leave them to fend for themselves.

"I wouldn't wish them on anyone. I'm so sorry, Declan," Dante said, giving me a push in the direction of the cabin. "Richard, come protect us from your wife and father-in-law."

"Why me?"

Dante sighed and shook his head. "Because if I let you and Nicole stay in the same room right now, no one will get anything done for the next week, and we don't have a week to let her satisfy herself you're actually in one piece. Come on, Richard."

"I protest. You're not stealing him. He just got here." Nicole jammed her hand under her father's chin and grabbed a handful of snow. "Do not make me shoot you, Dante."

"You wouldn't shoot me."

"Just because I haven't shot you yet doesn't mean I won't."

Desmond took advantage of his daughter's distraction to roll over and pin her beneath him. "Just go, Richard."

With my chances of getting any sleep deteriorating by the second, I sighed, shook my head, and headed inside, already planning my escape. Anthony and Lane would manage without me, wouldn't they?

I had my doubts.

ANTHONY SEEMED eager to join the planning session, hesitating long enough to scrutinize Richard and Dante. My friend, co-worker, and conspirator narrowed his eyes, dismissed both men with a huff, and headed for the other cabin.

Richard stared at Anthony's back, his brown eyes streaked with wolf yellow. "Now *that* is a ballsy human. I want him, Dante."

"No," I snarled. "Mine."

Great. I was going to be as bad as Nicole and Desmond at the rate I was going.

The other werewolf turned to me, bared his teeth, and growled at me. "What are you going to do about it, puppy?"

My wolf wanted me to shift and deal with the male. The urge to grip Richard's throat in my teeth until he submitted conflicted with my habit of retreating and giving other werewolves a wide berth.

If I didn't, he'd take Anthony away from me. The thought of losing my friend to another werewolf frightened my wolf.

My wolf's fright infuriated me so much I

lunged for Richard's throat, embracing my wolf's shape.

Pink paws and glowing fur or not, I wouldn't let another werewolf steal Anthony from me. In my desperation to drive Richard out of my territory, I fought to rush the process. Pain blinded me, and the taste of my blood washed over my tongue.

I had no idea how long I hung in the space between seconds, fire burning through my body, but when I finished shifting, I slammed into the other werewolf. My teeth missed his neck, and my fangs sank into his clothes without digging into his flesh.

I was aware of the gold cuff wrapped around my foreleg, the only thing on me that hadn't shifted and become a part of my body.

Richard wrapped his arms around my neck and pinned my head to him, one hand wrapping around my muzzle. "And Nicole says *I* have a temper. Jesus! A little help here, Dante."

Snarling, I clawed at Richard and fought to free my head and neck from his grip. For his small size, he had muscles of steel, and the harder I fought, the tighter he held onto me until stabbing pain jolted through my muzzle. My growls dissolved into yips, and I thrashed.

"You pissed him off. You deal with him. I know you're edgy, but that's not how you thank him. Idiot. Don't threaten his partner. In case you didn't notice, you're hurting him.

Ease your grip. He was shot twice getting the bitches out. Desmond told me it was one round through the arm and a graze across the shoulder, and they were both healing slow."

While Richard growled, the vice-like hold on my muzzle eased. He held my upper body off the ground, forcing me to stand on my hind paws, which limited my range of motion.

I was strong, but Richard was stronger, and he acted like he didn't even notice me struggling in his arms. "That was a Normal. Not a witch. Not a wolf."

"And? Give me a break, Richard. You bonded with Alex back when you didn't have a pack. He was a Normal. He was also three. Desmond suspects he's probably bonded with Anthony at the very least, and it wouldn't surprise him if he's been warming up to Lane." Dante sighed, coming into my field of vision. The man reached out and seized the scruff of my neck. "Desmond said he refused to shift last night. Nicole calls him a stray. She likes him a lot. They've been fighting over who gets to keep him since she flew over."

I kept growling, but I was too intrigued by Richard and Dante's argument to put much effort into my attempt to sink my teeth into the rival werewolf's neck.

"All right."

"Apologize."

"He attacked me."

I snarled at Richard's incredulous tone of voice.

"He called himself a werewolf, Richard."

As the silence stretched on, and my wolf's discomfort grew until I whined, lifting my front paws in my effort to claw free of the pair's hold.

"And?"

"Desmond said he didn't know what a Fenerec was."

"All right."

"Apologize."

Richard huffed.

"Richard."

"He attacked me."

"I'm about to attack you, Richard. You deserved it. Pity he didn't get a hold on you because he rushed it. Damned good rush, too. Better than you. Stings, doesn't it? Found a wolf who can beat you on the draw. When Nicole and Desmond find out, they're going to brawl for the right to have him. Now apologize."

"You're siding with him?"

"Damned straight I'm siding with him. He found Patricia. You didn't. He did. *He* found her, *he* busted her out, and then *he* found *your* ass and led us right to you. *Apologize.*"

"Fine."

"That's not an apology."

"It's close enough."

Dante sighed. "I'm going to give you two choices. Choice one: put Declan down, lower your head, and apologize. Choice two: Get your ass kicked around this cabin by me. When I'm finished, I will march over to the other cabin, inform your father you were abusing Declan, and watch you get your ass kicked again. When he's done, I'm going to tell Nicole you threatened Declan. When she's done kicking your ass, I'll let the SEAL have a turn with you. What'll it be, punk?"

"You really are being an ass today, Dante."

"It has been a really, really long day. My day started thirty-six hours ago. So?"

"Fine."

Dante released his hold on the back of my neck and systematically cracked his knuckles. "I may have asked Evelyn for a favor before I left. She may have agreed."

"You wouldn't."

"I shift faster than you."

"Fucking witch!"

"One."

"Don't you *even*, Dante."

"Two."

"You wouldn't dare."

"Three."

"Dante!"

"Apologize."

"He attacked me!"

"Four."

Richard dropped me. Unprepared to land, I hit the floor hard enough I yelped. I scrambled away from the fighting pair. Dante towered over Richard, and he had his teeth bared in a snarl.

The werewolf growled back. "Come on. Give me a break here. I wasn't serious."

Dante pursued Richard across the sitting room to the couch. "I don't care. He has no way to know that. Apologize."

"No."

"Five."

Richard tensed. "What are you counting to, Dante?"

"Three."

"Oh shit."

Dante grinned.

Chapter Twenty

CLOTHES LITTERED the sitting room floor and, for the life of me, I couldn't figure out why Dante and Richard were stripping.

Dante attended to each button of his suit as though he had all of the time in the world. The werewolf tore his shirt in his effort to pull it over his head, snarling curses at the tall man.

I wasn't sure why Richard was pacing and keeping his distance from Dante, who laughed. The sock Richard flung across the room fell short, which only made Dante laugh harder.

"You could just apologize. Then I won't have to put so much effort into this. Thirty-six hours without sleep, Richard. I know you're cranky and you're tired, too, but you didn't get grabbed by Amber fresh off her beating the shit out of six SEALs. I put up with that to come out here and chase after your tail."

Richard hissed like a cat, and I twisted my ears back. Confusion kept me frozen in place when I should have been turning tail and making a run for the safety of the higher peaks.

"You're really going to make me do this, aren't you?"

Bolting to the kitchen, Richard put the island between him and Dante and howled, "I'm not making you do anything!"

With delicate care, Dante draped his suit jacket over the back of the couch, smoothing the material. "Really?"

"Damn it, Dante. I said fine."

"Fine is not an apology."

Richard spat curses, hissed again, and ducked behind the island. Sighing, Dante turned to me, working his way out of his shirt, which joined his jacket on the couch. "It's your first time seeing a Fenerec transform, isn't it? Go on. Have a look. Unlike him, I have dignity, so I will not be leaving my clothes scattered all over your floor."

I cast a longing stare at the closed front door.

"He'll be five or ten minutes. I cheat." With a soft laugh, the man tossed the rest of his couch. "Not as good as you do, though. That was damned impressive. I don't think I've ever seen anyone shift so fast, not even Richard, who is the only wolf I know crazy enough to risk his life to do it." Dante pointed to the kitchen. "Go have a look."

My wolf's curiosity goaded me into creeping to where the hardwood met the tiles. Hesitating at the island, I glanced over my shoulder at Dante.

"If I thought he was going to be stupid, I wouldn't suggest you watch. And if he does decide to do something stupid, I'll come over and kick him until he stops. He's not going to hurt you if he knows what's good for him."

On the other side of the island, Richard growled, and in the deep sound, I heard pain. Alarmed, I jerked in the direction of the other werewolf.

Richard was curled on the floor, his body shaking. Bone and muscle shifted under his skin. Fur replaced flesh in chunks, leaving bare muscle open to the air.

I shuddered. When I transformed, it felt like it took forever to force my body to accept another shape. In reality, it was only a few seconds.

For Richard, the seconds stretched into minutes, and the longer it took, the more it alarmed me and my wolf. Whining, I backed away, tucking my tail and flattening my ears.

"Desmond was right. You really haven't seen another Fenerec before, have you?" Dante crouched beside me to watch Richard. "Ah, he's being slow about it today. He's really worn out. Alas, I'm a man of my word. Nicole'll forgive me. Probably. Who the hell am I kidding? Once she finishes with Richard, she's going to beat me black and blue. I better shift, too. I don't know how you Fenerec deal with this all the time. It hurts like hell."

The scent of damp forest filled the air, and unlike Richard, who fought his way from man to wolf, Dante flowed like water over the ground. White fur blanketed him without exposing his muscle. He dropped to the floor on all fours, his body shrinking and condensing.

While the seconds ticked away into a minute, it wasn't long until a small canine regarded me with bright green eyes. No wolf I had ever seen had such a vibrant shade of eyes. Dante's paws were red, as were his chest, tail, and tips of his ears. Something about his body and coloration reminded me of a fox.

Shaking himself off, Dante stood on his hind paws to bump my muzzle with the top of his head. The difference in our size astounded me. On all fours, he barely came to the bottom of my belly.

While my eyes told me fox, my nose informed me the tiny canine was a wolf.

Richard huffed in front of me. Startled by the noise, I yipped and bolted across the room, hopping up on the couch with my hackles raised and my teeth showing.

Silver fur gleamed with a metallic shine over a body far larger than mine. Like Dante, the werewolf shook himself, making huffing noises. Dante barked once and lunged for Richard.

The wolf masquerading as a fox closed his teeth around Richard's throat and dangled, his paws at least a foot off the ground. With a long-suffering sigh, Richard stood still.

I lifted my nose and snuffled to breath in scents.

All I could detect was the cinnamon and spice of wolves and the sweet undertones of pleasure. Puzzled, I stared at the two. Dante paddled his hind paws and growled without releasing Richard's throat.

If Richard wanted to dislodge Dante, all it would take was a full body shake. Yet he stood with infinite patience until the smaller canine dropped back to the floor.

Warbling so loud I flinched at the sound, Richard dipped into a play bow, lifted a paw, and batted Dante across the room. Rolling to a halt, the tiny canine surged to his feet, tossed his head up, and howled.

The two howled and warbled at each other before tearing around the cabin. I winced at the crash from the other room. With my ability to cope with the absurd crumbling, I curled on the couch, grabbed hold of Dante's jacket and shirt with my teeth, and hid under them.

"What is going on in here?" Desmond bellowed.

There was an art to peeking out from beneath a pile of another man's clothing without revealing myself, and I pulled it off with as much dignity as pink, glowing wolf could.

The two insane canines running around my cabin helped to distract from my presence.

Desmond stood in the doorway with his daughter hovering behind him. Behind them, Amber and the other werewolf male, Sanders, waited.

A thud down the hallway made me wince. Judging from the volume of the noise, Richard had come to an unexpected halt with the help of a wall and a fox far less than a quarter his size.

Twin warbling howls answered Desmond.

"It seems you were correct in your assessment, Amber. As such, you—"

Anthony laughed. "Were you aware there is an overgrown wolf being attacked by a… is that a fox? I think it's a fox. Foxes are a lot smaller than I thought they would be. Huh."

"Do I need to shoot them?" Lane asked.

SEALs. At least I could trust them to come up with direct solutions to obstacles.

"I already told them, Dad. They didn't believe me."

"You told them."

"I told them I would disembowel them if they did something stupid like tell anyone. When they told me I was lying and Fenerec didn't exist, I may have zapped them both, transformed, and sat on them. They took it really well. You were sleeping in the hotel. I didn't think I needed to bother you about it, and they've been doing a great job pretending they don't know anything."

"You assaulted a pair of Normals?"

"I didn't want them panicking if Declan shifted during the full moon."

"I told her he doesn't. She didn't believe me. I mean, I knew he was weird, but I figured he was superstitious. If he's in New York, he's always underfoot once a month. I only noticed it was around the full moon because he's always been a bit superstitious. But, he was usually cooking so I didn't really think anything of it. I don't mind. I get fed and it makes him happy." Anthony chuckled. "Where *is* Declan anyway? And which one is Richard? Where's Dante?"

Nicole shoved her way past her father and pointed at the large silver wolf. "That's Richard. The fox is Snowflake. Sorry, Dante. The fox is Dante. Sorry!"

Richard and Dante sighed.

"What about Declan?"

"I'm going to guess he's the lump under Dante's clothes," Nicole replied.

Laughing, Amber eased her way past Desmond and into the cabin. "To be fair, I'd hide, too. Richard and Dante playing are enough to fray anyone's nerves. It's damned embarrassing watching a seventeen-pound fox beat the shit out of a three-hundred-and-fifty-pound wolf."

"He doesn't want to hurt Snowflake."

Amber glared at Nicole. "Woman, that is a man who survived a high-caliber round to the chest at point-blank range. Richard could probably toss him off a cliff without giving him more than a couple of scrapes and bruises. I swear, he's tougher than a Fenerec. Just admit it. When it comes to Dante, your mate's a pussy cat."

"Excuse me?"

"Pussy cat."

Warbling a complaint, Richard grabbed Dante by his tail and carried the fox over to Nicole, sat on his haunches, and waited. Dante howled complaints back at Richard, paddling his hind paws at the wolf's jaw.

"You win this time, Amber. Just this once." Securing a grip on Dante's scruff, Nicole glared at the large silver wolf and hissed, "Let him go."

Richard growled.

"I will zap you."

"She really will," Desmond muttered. "You should know that by now."

"Richard, let him go."

Heaving a sigh, Richard obeyed, turned tail, and headed towards me. He grunted, leaped over the coffee table, and landed on the couch. Two circles later, and he shoved his nose under me and shoved me to the far cushion before taking over the rest of the space.

I yipped and scrambled to stay hidden under Dante's jacket.

"Dad?"

"Yes, Nicolina?"

"He's pink."

"I do believe I saw that."

"And glowing."

"Yes, I do believe I saw that, too."

"Mine!" the woman roared, dropping Dante so she could lunge at her father, reaching for his throat. Lifting my head in alarm, I watched the pair tussle, but before I could move, Richard reached out and pinned me in place with his front paws and his chest. He propped his muzzle on the top of my head.

I froze, my attention focusing on the werewolf using me as a pillow.

"You all disgust me." Sanders pushed his way into the room, shook his head, and approached the couch, grabbing hold of Dante's clothing. "Richard, remove your paws from your witch's clothes. You know how he gets about your fur on his suits."

Richard huffed, shifting his paws enough Sanders could free Dante's jacket and shirt. The entire process, the wolf kept me pinned beneath him.

After tossing the clothes on the floor,

Sanders crouched in front of me. "Hello, Declan."

I twisted my ears back and stared at the wall.

"Dad. *Dad.*" I wasn't sure how Desmond pulled it off, but he had tossed his daughter over his shoulder, and she drummed her hands on his back. "I need him. I *need* him. He's pink. He's pink and he glows. He's *perfect.*"

I was either dead or hallucinating. There was nothing perfect about being pink or having glowing fur. Why couldn't anyone mention the frosted golden parts of my fur? I *liked* those parts.

How could anyone like my pink fur?

Bowing his head, Sanders sighed. "Amber?"

"Yes?"

"Could you ask Julie to come over, please?"

"Sure." Amber leaned out of the door and shouted, "Julie! Sanders wants you."

Amber's call brought all seven of the werewolf females to the cabin with Elliot trailing in their wake. They filed into the room, their attention focusing on Nicole and Desmond.

Setting his daughter on her feet, Desmond held her by the shoulders to keep her in place. "I found him first."

"Dad, come *on.*"

"You wanted me?" The hard edge in Julie's voice captured my attention, and I faced her.

"Want him?"

The woman's eyes narrowed. "Him? Him who?"

Sanders pointed at me. "Declan. Cliff diving chef wolf. The one who made the cookies and brownies you bitches were snarling over."

"Is this a trick question?"

"Yes."

Desmond barked a laugh, relaxing and pulling his daughter against him. "What on Earth are you doing, Sanders?"

"I'd ask the same of you, Desmond. You're playing with fire. Your firecracker daughter is going to get tired of your affection and floor you if you're not careful."

"I won't if he gives me Declan."

"You have a mate," Julie snarled, whirling to face Nicole.

"This is why I'm holding my puppy," Desmond said, wrapping his arms around Nicole's waist to keep her from reaching Julie. "She's an Alpha female, Julie. She doesn't want to *mate* with him, she wants him for her pack. I think she's hoping Richard will claim him. Why she's not doing it herself, I'm not sure."

Nicole struggled in Desmond's arms. "Because you're an asshole, Dad. Let me go, and I will."

"And that's why I'm not letting you go. Bad girl."

Julie's eyes widened, and her lips parted. "He's not claimed?"

"I hate Alphas," Elliot snarled, turning to the wall to bang his head into the wood.

Desmond laughed. "You're mated to one, Elliot. Give it up. You know you love us."

"All you do is cause me problems. I hate you all."

I considered making an escape, but before I could do more than shift my weight, Richard growled, and Sanders grabbed hold of the scruff of my neck. "You're not going anywhere. I've heard you're a slick wolf when you decide to make your getaway."

"So, decide for us. Who gets him? We can't let him run loose. He's pink. He's pink, and he glows. My daughter will turn the world upside down if he isn't safely in a pack, preferably hers. It's for the world, Elliot. You don't want the entire world to suffer through my daughter hunting for a new pack mate, do you?"

Elliot slumped against the wall. Dante sat on his brother's feet and yipped. "What do you want from me, Desmond?"

"The pink, glowing wolf and his two Normals. I'll take Julie, too. Her Alpha keeps annoying me, and he didn't work hard enough to find her. He doesn't deserve her."

"Dad! I want him. Why do you always have to get in the way? That's not fair."

"Wait, what?" Lane blurted.

Anthony fidgeted, eyeing the door like he was seriously considering making a run for it. "I think we're being auctioned off to werewolves, Lane."

"Fenerec, not werewolves. Calling a Fenerec a werewolf is a good way to have your face eaten. Good thing for you, I'm not the wrong werewolf." Desmond snickered pausing to drop a kiss on his daughter's brow. "Okay, I'm lying. I *am* the wrong Fenerec to push on that issue. It's fine this time, boys. Don't worry yourselves. You'll be under pack protection once we figure out which pack gets Declan. I really hope it's me. Go into the kitchen and see what Declan made for lunch while we sort this out."

Lane grabbed hold of Anthony's elbow and pulled him to the kitchen. Sliding around the island, the pair stopped and watched, whispering to each other.

"Why are you doing this, Desmond?" Elliot crouched, picked his brother up, and buried his nose in the white fur. "Go change and give your mate her wolf back, Dante."

Dante licked Elliot's chin before squirming free and leaping to the floor, trotting to the couch to grab his clothes up in his teeth before disappearing down the hallway.

"I'm not getting involved in this," Sanders announced, turning to perch on the arm of the couch without releasing my scruff. "Richard, get your heavy ass off the poor guy before you break his back. We don't know how old he is. Go sit with your devil dad and wait for Elliot to make a decision."

Baring his fangs, Richard growled and snapped at Sanders. Sanders stared until the silver wolf huffed, got up, and stretched out at Nicole's feet. The woman made a happy noise.

"I'm not letting you go, devil daughter. You'll try to claim Declan. I want him."

"But Daddy, I want him."

"I found him first."

"Actually, I did," Dante said, stepping down the hall wearing only his pants. His voice was husky with pain. "How do you damned wolves deal with that? It hurts like hell."

"You don't get a say in this, witch," Desmond hissed.

"You want a pack, and the person who can authorize you forming a pack is *my* twin. Watch it, fluffy."

Desmond scowled. "I hate when you do that."

"And that's exactly why I do it. That's for trying to bust into *my* rings."

"I love your witch, Richard. He's such a breath of fresh air. Daddy snarls at him and he doesn't care at all."

"Welcome to the family," Sanders muttered, shaking his head. Sliding down the arm, the werewolf worked his way under my shoulder and front paws. I tensed, but when I couldn't scent anything from Sanders beyond amusement and resignation, I relaxed. "There. That's not so bad, right? Despite appearances, Desmond's really good with puppies, even stubborn ones like Richard. He'll take good care of you."

"He's not a puppy," Julie said, crossing her arms over her chest. "He has his adult coat."

Sanders laughed. "Everyone is a puppy to Desmond except his mate, Julie. He slipped and called Wendy a puppy once. She didn't let him back in their den for over a week."

"I don't like it. Don't call him a puppy."

Everyone laughed, but it was Elliot who approached the woman and rested his hand on her shoulder. "Let it go, Miss Montgomery. Desmond—"

Baring her teeth, Julie lashed her arm at Elliot. The acrid bite of fury hung in the air. Before I could do more than tense, Desmond let go of his daughter, took several steps, and whipped his arm out, catching Julie across the chest. He flipped her to the floor so hard I felt the thump through the couch. "You forget your place. Be respectful in the presence of the Shadow Pope."

I filed the title away as something to ask someone about later.

Before Julie could get up, Desmond was on her, flipping her to her stomach before he braced a knee against her back, pinning her to the hardwood, one hand on the back of her neck. "What do you want me to do with her, sir?"

I flattened my ears and bared my fangs, but I didn't growl or snarl. Calculating the distance between me and Desmond, I tensed to lunge off the couch. Sanders's grip on my neck tightened. "Desmond."

"What?"

"Hunting wolves make no noise."

Desmond adjusted his hold on Julie so he could turn to face Sanders. The man's dark eyes focused on me, and gold gleamed around his pupils. My wolf snarled in my head and wanted me to lunge across the room in defense of the bitch, but I remained quiet, waiting.

"Is he fighting you?"

"No. That said, if you hurt her, I'm letting go of his scruff."

Snorting, Desmond shook his head. "Elliot?"

Elliot's mouth twitched, he sighed, and stared up at the ceiling. "For fuck's sake. Fine. Sanders, are you going to get in a pissing contest with Desmond if he has a small pack to make him happy?"

Slumping back against the couch, Sanders closed his eyes and dug his fingers into my fur. "I'm too tired for this. Why are you asking me, Elliot? Shouldn't you be asking your Alpha?"

"He's a dog right now." Richard growled,

and Elliot turned and kicked the wolf's ribs. "Well, you are."

"Elliot," Nicole warned.

The man sighed and threw his hands up in the air. "Last thing I need is to get mauled by a bitch that isn't my mate. I have a hard enough time keeping Vicky in line. It's like she lives to test my patience."

"We all do," Dante said, clapping his brother's shoulder. "You made a mistake. You let Desmond figure out you have a sense of humor."

"I've always had a sense of humor."

"It's true, he has." Desmond snickered, shaking his head. "I'll ask really nicely. Can I please have Declan? He puts up such a good fight. He doesn't back down. He's not afraid to look me in the eyes. He's smart, he's friendly, and he's damned good at his job. Best of all, he's pink, and he glows."

Had Desmond hit his head without me being aware of it? I watched the man for signs of a concussion, although he seemed stable on his feet, his eyes clear, and his mouth curved in a wide grin.

Elliot groaned. "What is it with your family and the color pink?"

"Richard started it. Richard and his pink Porsche, which he used to steal my daughter. His tie matched his car, too. It takes a real man to wear that shade of pink so well. Pink is the color of confidence and true masculinity."

I stared longingly at the door. Over the years, I had lived in fear of other werewolves. My gut instinct had been correct.

Werewolves were psychotic lunatics.

Sanders snorted. "I thought it was his baking skills that got under your skin, girl. A family-wide fetish with the color pink explains everything."

"He pissed me off the instant I saw him. Had to either kill him or keep him. Since he insisted on surviving my attempts to kill him, I kept him."

Julie drummed her fingers on the hardwood. "Could you let me up?"

Elliot narrowed his eyes as he considered her. "No, Miss Montgomery. I'm thinking about whether or not I'm going to allow Desmond to subjugate you."

"What?" the woman shrieked, struggling beneath Desmond. "You're not serious!"

"Oh, I'm serious." Elliot pointed at me. "Rogue unmated male wolf." He turned his finger to Julie. "Unmated bitch, part of a small to moderate sized pack with an absolutely terrible puppy survival rate." When Elliot gestured to Desmond, the werewolf growled. "Mated male with a young puppy, no pack except his mate, and lives next door to an Omega mated to an Alpha male with a stellar puppy survival rate."

Richard snapped his teeth.

Elliot didn't look very impressed or threatened by the massive wolf. "Pack balance, Richard. Yellowknife and Seattle are balanced. You have me and Dante, our mates, and some of the best wolves on the continent. I can't let you have another exotic."

Scowling, Nicole crossed her arms over her chest. "Just who are you calling an exotic?"

"You."

When Nicole lunged for Elliot's throat, Dante caught her by her waist and held her under his arm. She spat curses, clawing for the man who had stirred her wrath.

I whimpered and covered my eyes with my paws, although I peeked to keep an eye on the other werewolves.

Amber sighed and pinched the bridge of her nose. "Please don't make me have to start shooting. I don't have unlimited ammo today. Just accept it, Nicole. It's true. Yellowknife is a freak pack full of exotics. First, there is Richard, who needs the world's sexiest witch to keep him under control. It doesn't hurt he's a strong earth witch, either."

Grinning, Dante dipped into a bow. "Why thank you, Amber."

"His equally sexy witch twin is mated to an out-of-control witch who also happens to be a wolf. In case you've forgotten, he's the one who authorizes our paychecks."

Elliot smirked. "Amber thinks we're sexy, Dante."

"It's because we know how to handle firearms. Actually, I think it's more to do with the fact we encourage her to take us to the firing range to abuse us whenever she wants. It has absolutely nothing to do with our looks. In your case, you pay her to like you," Dante replied.

"Shut up," Amber ordered. The twins obeyed, although they grinned at each other. "As I was saying. Yellowknife is strong enough. Sanders, your pack is good, and since you have an Omega who can single-handedly set Desmond on his ass whenever she feels like it, you're not doing too bad in the exotic department, either."

Sanders laughed. "I don't suppose I can hire you to be my bodyguard, can I? You're about the only living thing who might be able to convince Sara not to kill me when I get home."

"You're on your own there, Sanders. If you convince Elliot to give Declan and the bitch to Desmond to form a pack, he'll probably stop making so many forays onto your property to annoy you."

"I really don't care, Amber. I don't have a horse in this race. I'm not getting in the way of a starry-eyed Desmond. I'm crazy, but I'm not *that* crazy. That said, I do want to know why he's so set on having Declan. I've never seen him so riled up since he was determined to adopt Richard and Alex. I mean, I can understand Julie. She's way too good for that pack she's in."

"Hey!" Julie squirmed beneath Desmond. "That's my pack you're talking about."

"Your Alpha is incompetent. Just accept it, Julie. If it weren't for the rules, I'd be making a road trip to drown his worthless ass." Sanders growled, drew a deep breath, and forced himself to relax.

I trembled at the rage in the werewolf's scent.

"Sorry, Declan. Julie's Alpha keeps trying to get his bitches to mate and he's too damned prideful to ask for help. Julie's the only unmated bitch in his pack, and next moon is the start of the winter rut. Without fail, his bitches transform during their pregnancies. The puppies die. I've wanted to kill him for years. Damn it, Elliot. He has fifteen bitches, and he convinces them to try to mate every year. It's wrong."

The room fell silent.

"And that's why I may permit Desmond to subjugate her. You know I try to work with the packs to ensure as many puppies survive as possible. You know I make every arrangement I can, including temporary pack transfers, to give bitches the best chance to keep their puppies alive. You know I have purposefully thrown Yellowknife and Seattle together to help share the load. It's the entire reason we have a Fenerec like Desmond on call." Elliot paced, spat a few curses, and kicked the wall. "I can't just put out a kill order for no damned reason. Without proof, I can't do anything."

Sanders sighed. "It's not your fault, Anderson."

"Like fucking hell it isn't my fault! It's my job."

"Not to interrupt or anything, but..." Lane leaned against the kitchen counter. "What, exactly, do you mean by subjugate?"

"Right. Normals." Elliot turned, leaned against the wall, and slid to the floor. "Nicole, your punishment for initiating a pair of Normals without permission is to be your father's gopher for a month."

Nicole screamed a wordless cry of frustration and stomped her foot. "You wouldn't."

Desmond made a sound similar to a cat's purr. "You shouldn't have done that, daughter. I find it a very suitable punishment. Your mother is going to be so happy with me. Where you go, our son follows, and I get you both for a month. This is better than Christmas."

"Lane, subjugation is the process of transferring a Fenerec from one pack to another," Sanders explained. "In Declan's case, we'll have to do a full dominance contest, so it'll be a bit rough, but Julie won't give Desmond a problem. Will you, Julie?"

"Damn it," Julie pounded her fist against the floor.

"I'm not sure I understand," the SEAL admitted.

"All right, Desmond. I'll give you Declan and permit you to form a sanctioned pack within Seattle's territory, but under one condition."

Desmond tensed. "What condition?"

"Answer a question for me. Where the hell did you find a glowing pink Fenerec?"

Chapter Twenty-One

I CONTEMPLATED MAKING a run for it, but Sanders kept a firm hold on my scruff, warning me I'd have to fight my way to freedom. Instead of running like I wanted, I waited, watched, and sighed my longing.

"Why don't you shift back to human?" Sanders suggested. "Go to wherever you stashed your clothes, get changed, and talk to us. We won't bite. Well, I make no promises about Desmond, but I won't bite. I won't make promises about Richard, either. I definitely won't make promises about the ladies, especially Julie."

The only one to react to Sanders's suggestion was Dante, and he stared at me, arching his brow in questioning. Did it have to do with the fact my clothes shifted with me?

Probably. Richard and Dante had removed their clothing before they had shifted.

"You just want him to explain how he got pink fur," Desmond accused.

"Maybe. He's softer than Richard." Sanders's statement drew everyone's attention.

Nicolina straightened, scowling at me before turning her glare on her husband. "Impossible. First, he bakes the absolute best brownies I have ever tasted in my life. Don't get me started on the cookies. Now his fur is softer?"

While I would have stayed safely hidden in the kitchen like a sane man, Anthony gave the group a wide berth, came to the couch, sat, and stared at me. I knew that look, and I turned my ears back.

That look landed me in trouble far too often. Anthony's sense of curiosity always got me into trouble. Sometimes when I was working a job, he'd notice a door somewhere and suggest I check it out. Those doors always led to interesting places for me to explore—or find even more interesting things within.

Without fail, those interesting things would find their way into my pockets, and a simple job became a complex job, and Anthony ended up having a lot more fun than me. It was a little like how I had managed to get a golden Egyptian wrist cuff stuck to me.

I still needed to figure out how to get it off. The wretched thing was still wrapped around my foreleg, although my fur did a reasonable job of hiding it. The werewolves were more interested in the fact I was pink and glowed than they were about my odd choice of jewelry.

Anthony reached over and touched his finger to the tip of my nose.

While I expected Sanders to maintain his death grip on my scruff, he released me. Given the choice of Anthony, Sanders, or Desmond and the other werewolves, I lunged across the couch and took over Anthony's lap, baring my teeth at the werewolf male.

"Some Fenerec hate attention. Actually, most of us hate being petted or otherwise treated as a house pet. Richard loves attention. Desmond does, too, when he thinks he can get away with it. Dignity is important to Desmond despite him rarely having any. He's happiest when someone is showing him affection. Don't tell anyone that since he's supposed to be an enforcer. Nicolina adores attention from the Anderson twins, Richard, and her close family and merely tolerates it from anyone else. I don't care either way. I suggest you ask before you touch." Sanders grinned, propped his feet up on the coffee table, and stretched out. "As a general rule, Alpha males will tolerate a lot from their pack; we're attention whores."

Anthony held his hands up. "Okay. What does that mean for me? Is he supposed to be this heavy?"

"What do you think he weighs in at, Sanders?" Elliot asked.

"One fifty? Maybe two hundred? Actually,

I might say lower. He's pretty scrawny under that fur." Sanders shrugged. "If he gets too heavy, Anthony, I'll remove him. You're not going to lose a hand if you pet him, so relax. If he didn't want you touching him, he wouldn't be on your lap."

I barked once, a warning call, and Sanders laughed. "I'm not going to do anything to your Normal, Declan. Relax already. Anyway, you don't have anything to worry about right now, Anthony. How long have you two been friends?

"A while. Six or seven years." Anthony sighed and shrugged. "Wouldn't be the first time I've woken up on the couch with Declan using me as a pillow. He was always human, though. I had no idea he…"

Desmond chuckled. "He can become a wolf? We try to avoid letting Normals know we actually exist. Were the times he used you as a pillow following one of his cooking binges?"

"It was."

Sanders chuckled. "Doesn't surprise me. I get the feeling he doesn't eat nearly enough, so sleeping after a large meal would be the norm. Fenerec feel safer sleeping near someone they trust. It's an instinct of ours. Good wolves hide their base instincts, but we slip when we feel comfortable and safe—and around people we trust."

Following Anthony's lead, Lane circled the island and leaned against it, crossing his arms over his chest. "His briefing file mentioned higher than normal metabolic requirements. There were specific instructions for doubled rations plus protein supplements. Medical note seemed to imply a hyper metabolism disorder of some sort."

Desmond and Sanders exchanged a long, silent look, and both men frowned. When they remained silent, Nicole growled, crossing her arms over her chest. The three finally turned their attention to Elliot, who held his hands up in surrender.

Like them, he remained silent.

As one, all four faced Amber and waited.

The woman sighed. "Why me?"

Elliot snorted. "Because you're damned good at your job, know Fenerec better than most, and know the requirements of an active duty Fenerec?"

"Now you're just sweet talking me, Elliot."

"I could bribe you."

Ambers eyes widened and sparkled, and she grinned. "You bribe me with guns. Always. You *always* bribe me with guns."

"Modified Glock 18. Matched set; one for you, one for Sara. Modified by Glock, specific for you two." Elliot smirked, leaning towards the woman. "Your choice of color."

"How modified are we talking?"

"Modified enough."

"It better be good, Your Eminence. You know I hate initiating Alpha-traited Fenerec.

I *hate* it. They're always trouble. Nicole gives me enough trouble."

"Only until he bonds with a sanctioned witch of his own," Elliot replied. "Glock 18. Modified."

"Was that English?" Anthony asked. "I'm pretty sure, individually, all of those words were in English, but when you string them together, they make zero sense."

"Amber?"

"Fine. I'll do it. First, Declan needs to become a human again." Amber's gaze focused on me. "Please don't make me force you, sir."

I flattened my ears at the challenge in her voice.

"Richard should go shift, too." Dante nudged the large wolf with his foot. "In the bathroom, preferably. Nicole, you may want to go with him. It took him a bit longer than I like, although he may have slowed it down so Declan could watch. Richard's shift alarmed him quite a bit."

Desmond crossed the room to me, crouching close without being in easy biting range. "I was worried about that. Go in the other room and change, Declan. If you need help with it, give a howl. Where are your clothes? I'll bring them for you."

"I'm fairly certain his clothes shifted with him," Dante said, pointing at me. "He's wearing an armband of some sort."

"Egyptian," Lane supplied. "The real deal, apparently. Yes, that's his. He said the hinges were damaged or something like that, so he couldn't get it off."

Grabbing hold of my paw, Desmond examined the cuff. "And he was wearing it when he shifted?"

I whined at the strength of the man's grip.

"Oh, be quiet. I'm not hurting you. I just want a look at the armband."

"He can probably give you a history lesson on it, do an appraisal, and talk your ear off for a few hours if you let him." Anthony set his hand on the top of my head. After a moment of hesitation, he stroked my fur. "He *is* soft."

I was torn between embarrassment and enjoyment. My wolf's contentment spread through me. While he wanted me to roll over and expose my belly, I restrained him.

Desmond released my paw and gave my shoulder a firm pat. "Go shift, Declan. Amber will go with you and stay on the other side of the door. If you need any help, she's your woman."

"Excuse me?" Julie demanded.

Sighing, Desmond shook his head. "Sanders, how long has she been fixated on the poor pup?"

"From my understanding, the moment he jumped off a cliff for them."

"Maybe you should run while you can, Declan," Desmond suggested. "Amber, keep an eye on him, please."

The other women laughed until Julie

turned on them snarling and snapping her teeth. It took Elliot, Dante, and Sanders working together to hold her back. While everyone was distracted, I slid off the couch and padded down the hallway, torn between shifting and making my escape out a window or sticking around and watching the fireworks.

AMBER STARED AT ME, her dark blue eyes as cold and hard as sapphires. Instead of waiting in the hall as I expected, she followed me into the cabin's master bedroom, locked on me with the same intensity of a hunting predator.

"My job is to make sure there are no problems. I can help if there are." Crossing her arms over her chest, she watched me without even blinking. "So, go on. Change. It's not like I haven't seen a naked man before."

Two could play the staring game, but within five minutes, I came to the conclusion she was a lot better at it. My wolf bristled at the woman's determination to force me to submit to her silent challenge.

I bristled at the thought of putting myself on display again. When I backed into the adjacent bathroom, she tailed me. Before I could nose the door close, she slapped her hand against the wood and held it open.

"No, sir. When Desmond gives an order, it's

wise to listen. He even said please. Just change." Amber frowned and paused. "Unless you don't know how to change back? Do you need help?"

I shook my head so hard I made myself dizzy.

"Then what's the problem?"

"He's probably shy," Richard said, his voice hoarse. Peering around the corner, he flashed a wide grin. "I'll watch him. You might need to help with Julie. It sounds like she's ready to maul someone out there."

"Seriously? What is wrong with that girl?" Amber huffed, sighed, and flexed her hands. "Is there anything more temperamental than an unmated bitch?"

"A pregnant one." Richard stepped out of Amber's way, his dark eyes twinkling. As the woman passed him, he kissed her cheek. "Thanks for coming."

"Of course. I wasn't going to leave Nicolina to conquer Europe on her own. I would've gone with her to Seattle to visit Wendy, but it took me a bit of time to bust Dante and Elliot out of house arrest."

"You didn't hurt those SEALs, did you?"

"Just their pride."

"You're terrible, Amber."

"I try. You sure you can handle him?"

"If I need help, I'll give a shout. Don't worry. I'll have a talk with him before we head back out. I'd rather not throw him to the wolves." Richard patted Amber's back before giving her shove towards the hallway. "Go help leash Julie."

"Try not to get mauled. I'd hate to explain to your daddy what happened to you."

Scowling, Richard flipped his middle finger at Amber. "Now you're just being mean."

Amber laughed and left the room. Flopping on the floor between the bedroom and the bathroom, Richard propped his chin in his hands. "Amber has absolutely no care for male pride or dignity. I think she lives to make us men uncomfortable. Let's clear the air a bit while you get around to deciding to shift. First, I'm not going to steal your Anthony. I appreciate Normals with backbone, and your Anthony is gutsy enough to handle Alphas. He's relaxed even around Desmond."

I turned an ear forward to indicate I was listening to Richard.

"It's easier to talk when you're a human. If you swear you won't try to dive out the bathroom window, I'll turn around if you're that embarrassed."

I bared my fangs and growled my irritation at his assumption I was embarrassed. I was, but that wasn't the real reason I hesitated. It was bad enough I was pink, but the fact I didn't shift in the same way other werewolves bothered me.

Wasn't I enough of a freak?

"Would it help if I apologized for worrying you? I really wasn't going to try to take him."

I huffed.

"Stubborn." Richard grinned at me. "I understand stubborn. That said, if I don't trot you out as a human, Amber will come back here and force you—or worse, Desmond will come and force you. It's not pleasant. I get you're edgy and nervous. One Alpha is bad enough, but there are a lot of us under the same roof right now, including Dante and Elliot; they're as close to Alphas as witches get. Go on and change. I'll protect you from the big bad wolves and witches out there."

I sighed, placed my paw on the door, and shoved. Laughing, Richard shuffled out of the way, giving me the illusion of privacy. I remained aware of the man waiting. The wood didn't feel like much of a barrier. Was Richard as strong as I was?

Probably.

I sighed, but my wolf was eager enough to return to the human form we so often frequented. While I regretted having shifted to a wolf in the first place, there was nothing I could do to hide my nature. As always, the pain of shifting seemed to last far longer than it did. Without the excuse of needing to change my clothes like Richard and Dante, I stood and stared at the door in a numb daze, gathering the courage to face the man.

Richard solved the problem for me, pulling open the door and looking me over head to toe. "That was *maybe* three seconds. Maybe. That's unbelievable."

"Unbelievable in a good or a bad way?" Like him, my voice was hoarse, although I blamed exhaustion more than the lingering pain of transformation.

"Good. I average five to ten minutes. Minute to a minute and a half if I want to risk bleeding out."

"How could you tell?"

"Your scent changed. More human, less wolf." Richard reached out and pressed his fingers to my throat to check my pulse. "You look like you're at least thirty pounds underweight. While there are a lot of lean Fenerec, you're rail thin. You need to eat."

"I ate," I replied, stiffening at Richard's disapproving tone.

"Double rations with protein supplements? That's not nearly enough to sustain one of our kind, Declan."

Part of me wanted to argue with him, but I realized I had no way of knowing. He did. I swallowed. "Then what is enough?"

Richard grinned. "Good. You're smart. We tend to eat five or six oversized meals a day to help hide our increased metabolism. The smart wolves go to multiple grocery stores and butchers to help hide the quantity of food being consumed."

"Just how oversized are we talking about?"

"Think a holiday meal without the risk of gaining those ten extra pounds afterwards."

I didn't come close to eating that much on a daily basis. "I've been okay."

"How long have you been this thin?" Richard poked me in the ribs.

Snorting, I shrugged. "When haven't I been this thin? Okay, I'm a little thinner than normal; it was a rough week after the extraction."

"Let me see the wounds."

I bristled at the command in his voice, but I unbuttoned my shirt and showed him the healing gunshot wounds.

"They are healing slowly. Is this normal for you?"

"No."

"Stress, probably. Slows all of us down. No sign of infection I can tell, no bleeding. Good enough for me. So. You have to have questions. Ask them."

I stared longingly at the bed, wondering if I could just flop without bothering. "You said you'd explain things." Instead of indulging in sleep, I buttoned my shirt. Once done, I rolled up my sleeve to check the gold cuff. It looked the same as it had before, and I still couldn't get it off.

While Richard watched me, he didn't comment on the Egyptian jewelry. "I need to know what you know first. What were you taught when you became a Fenerec?"

I blinked. "Pardon?"

Both of Richard's eyebrows rose. "Okay. I

obviously underestimated your ignorance. You really know nothing?"

"Probably a safe assumption."

"So, I guess you don't know why you're pink and your fur glows?"

The disappointment in Richard's voice had me gaping at him. "What is wrong with you?"

"Are you serious? I'd give half my tail for pink fur."

"Dye it, then," I snapped, sliding past him.

"Maybe I will!"

Chapter Twenty-Two

When I walked down the hallway, my hands stuffed in my pockets and muttering curses under my breath, the snarls of bickering wolves stopped, leaving an awkward silence in its wake. Richard nudged me with his elbow, herding me to the kitchen island until I sat on one of the stools.

"More escape routes if you're sitting here. You shouldn't feel as cornered," Richard murmured in my ear before leaning against the counter to regard the other werewolves. "We're going to have a few ground rules for this."

"This is going to be good," Desmond predicted, flopping on the couch and kicking his feet up on the coffee table. "Let's hear it, pup."

"Keep your aggression leashed. Declan doesn't know how to deal with it yet. You're liable to get your throat ripped out if you threaten him right now. He's tired, he's cranky, and he's territorial. Desmond, you'll want to treat him like you do any other Alpha you're handling."

"Alpha, eh?"

"Dad, your Canadian is showing."

Desmond grimaced. "This is your fault, Richard."

Most of the werewolves laughed. Julie crossed her arms over her chest, regarding me with narrowed eyes. "Why?"

Richard sighed. "Why what, Julie?"

"Is Desmond treating him like an Alpha."

"Because if he isn't one already, he will be."

Desmond straightened. "You're sure?"

"Pretty sure. He's an older, more aggressive version of me before I took over Yellowknife."

Desmond flinched, as did Dante, Amber, and Nicole. Patricia sighed.

When silence fell, Richard finally broke it with a sigh of his own. "We're going to take this at Declan's pace. No interrogations. I'm going to explain things to him, Anthony, and Lane, get them brought up to speed with the basics, and then let Amber take over from there."

Instead of saying a word, Desmond hopped to his feet and strode to the refrigerator. "Okay. We'll do it your way, pup. Everyone may as well make themselves comfortable. I'll take care of breakfast while you all talk. Hopefully you made enough to feed the hordes, Declan."

"I filled two refrigerators and freezers. There better be enough," I muttered.

"Plus enough baked goods for a wedding reception," Nicole added. "I need more of your brownies, Declan. I need them." The woman's grin was infectious, and I smiled back at her.

Julie's growl intrigued my wolf.

"Get your head in the game. I'm not tossing a puppy to an enthusiastic bitch." Richard bared his teeth at the werewolf woman. "Relax. Otherwise, I'm going to come over there and nip you myself."

She squeaked and backed away until she bumped into the wall.

"Damn, pup. You really don't hold back when you cook, do you?" Desmond pulled out half of the contents of the refrigerator, counted werewolf heads, and pulled out even more. "All right. He's probably a rogue Alpha. Won't be the first time we've come across one of those. Right, Elliot?"

"Leave my mate out of this."

"Mine, too," Dante added.

I sighed, wishing I knew what the werewolves were talking about. The only way I'd find out anything was if I'd ask. "What, exactly, is an Alpha?"

Everyone stared at me.

"I told you," Richard said, his tone smug. "Fenerec come in four different varieties. Alphas are dominant Fenerec who have a few extra instincts meant to defend their pack and nurture others of our kind. We're like regular wolves in many regards. Dominant Fenerec want to prove their place and are driven to protect weaker members of the pack. Submissive Fenerec are a lot less aggressive and rely on others to protect them. Omegas are special. They're like Alphas in some ways. They have a different set of instincts from other Fenerec. They have no problems controlling their wolves, and unlike other Fenerec, they do not have a set rank within a pack."

"I think I follow." I wasn't so certain about packs, but my wolf was interested. "What do you mean by having problems controlling their wolves?"

Richard stared at me, his mouth hanging open. "Okay, I was not expecting that question."

"Neither was I," Desmond admitted. "Are you aware of your wolf?"

"Yes."

"And your wolf doesn't try to control you?"

"Not really?" I shrugged. "We tend to agree on things, I guess."

Richard sat on the stool beside me. "You guess?"

"I've never had a problem."

Sanders stood in front of me, leaning towards me so his nose almost touched mine. "That sounds a lot like Sara. An Omega could easily go rogue and not have problems avoiding transformations. You sure he's Alpha, Richard?"

"I refuse to accept he is an Omega," Richard grumbled.

"Why?"

"Because that'll mean Seattle will have *two* Omegas. That's not fair."

Desmond snorted. "I'm with Richard on this. He's not an Omega."

"How do you figure?" Sanders demanded.

"Sara tries to *fix* problems. Declan *causes* them for fun."

"Can I ask a question?" Lane asked, holding up his hand like he was in school.

"Of course."

"What's the big deal with Omegas? You sound like an Omega is pretty important."

Richard sighed, turning his full attention to the SEAL. "There are currently seven Omegas around the entire world, Lane. They're rare. A pack with an Omega has a higher survival rate for puppies. We have fewer Fenerec who have to be put down if they go wild."

"Go wild?"

"That means the wolf side has totally taken over and there's nothing human left about the Fenerec. It's usually a death sentence."

"Unless you're Richard," Nicole said. "Richard is one of the few Fenerec who can go wild and come back after he's calmed down."

Letting out a heavy breath, Richard nodded his agreement. "Most rogues run wild and have to be put down. Fenerec require packs for stability. When I was a rogue, I had my little brother keeping me stable. I believe you and Anthony have been serving that function for Declan."

"Me?" Lane blurted.

With a shrug, Richard replied, "I have a feeling he has been leaning on his teammates. Alpha-traited males require a *lot* of support, especially if they do not have a witch. What do you think, Amber? Can you confirm it?"

"I'm pretty sure you're correct, Richard," the woman replied. "I think he's more attuned to Anthony of the two, but yes. I'm pretty sure he's bonding with them both. Not quite a pack bond, but not a witch bond, either. It's different. I'd guess he's trying to form a pack for himself without knowing how to do it and feeling his way through it."

Richard turned his full attention to me. "Declan, I do have one question for you. You were taken surprise by the mention of Fenerec. You've never met one of us before now. You haven't seemed at all surprised by the mention of witches. Why?"

I flinched, realizing the other werewolf was correct. If I lied, he'd probably be able to smell it; while I could lie without it altering my scent, I doubted I'd be able to get away with discussing my mother without betraying myself.

The truth was far too important to me.

"My mother was a witch, and she was killed because she murdered a human."

No one said a word, but the stench of dismay and horror hung in the air.

THE LONG SILENCE left me itching to escape. Everyone refused to look at me, which agitated me almost as much as the myriad of unpleasant scents assaulting my nose. Anger had a hot bite to it, and there was a sour undertone to the smells.

"It was a long time ago," I offered. "About two decades. I was recruited for government work shortly after."

Three years counted as shortly to me. Maybe if I changed the subject, they'd forget about my mother, what she had done, and the price she had paid for it.

"Who killed your mother?" Desmond asked, sliding a plate of reheated food to me.

"I wasn't there. I found her when she was dying."

"Wasn't us, then," Amber announced. "We don't leave people to die like that."

I reached for a fork, blinked as Amber's words sank in, and twisted towards the woman. "What?"

"You have no idea what the Inquisition is, do you?" she replied, her tone wry.

Instead of replying, I leveled my best blank stare at her.

"I'm going to take that as a no. The Inquisition is an organization dedicated to protecting Normal humans from anyone with supernatural talents, although the focus is typically Fenerec and witches. I won't lie. We can be a brutal group. Fenerec who run wild or kill Normal humans are put down. We kill them so they don't hurt others. The same applies to witches. I'm one of the enforcers, primarily for witches and other magic users, although I hunt Fenerec sometimes. Desmond works with the packs, but he will hunt rogue Fenerec, too. None of us like it, but it's better this way. The alternative is a lot worse."

The government had hit teams for dangerous people, so the concept wasn't new to me. If I hadn't been so good at finding things, I probably would have been assigned to one of those groups.

My skills with a sniper rifle had drawn a lot of unwanted attention.

"I understand."

"You're okay with it?"

"Marine," Lane reminded the group. "A covert ops Marine. You've heard about black ops before, right? Well, you're looking at a legend in black ops. He's been the subject of an international manhunt for almost a decade, and we only caught up with him because he made a single mistake."

I grunted at the pride in Lane's voice. "Legend is a bit much, Lane."

"Not really. Your track record is unmatched."

Grabbing my fork, I stabbed at the leftover roasted chicken Desmond had given me. "Bullshit."

"You've survived more S missions than anyone else in the armed forces. You have a Medal of Honor. You have earned how many Purple Hearts?"

"Can we not talk about this?"

Lane snorted, joined Desmond in the kitchen, and plundered the leftovers. "It's important they know what they're dealing with. If they could have ever convinced you to take your sniper skills to the field, you would've easily been the best."

"What do you mean by that, Lane?" Richard asked.

"I mean just what I said. He won't go on missions for the kill shot. His handler could never convince him to do it."

Desmond made a satisfied noise. "Who was his handler?"

"His handler was Vice Admiral Haney, and his code name is the Bard. After turning up from so many S-level missions alive, Declan was saddled with the Man the Bard Couldn't Kill."

Nicole's growl drew my full attention to her. "S stands for suicide, doesn't it?"

"There's a reason I got out when an opportunity presented itself." Shrugging, I turned back to my food and ate, trying to ignore the feel of so many eyes on me.

"This Haney is going to be a problem, isn't he?" Desmond's growl echoed his daughter's, and I tensed as the acrid bite of anger intensified. "How many of these missions are we talking about, Lane?"

"The number wasn't revealed in my briefing. I only found out the type when Declan told me."

"Declan?"

I shrugged. "I stopped counting after twenty."

"In how many years?"

"A decade, give or take. Most were in the last three or so years I was in, though. Prior, I was the one they brought in to find information or things fast."

"Were you a Fenerec the entire time, or was the ritual performed during your tour of duty?"

I met Desmond's gaze. "What ritual?"

The man choked on his own spit.

"I forgot to mention that part. I asked him already." Hopping up on a stool, Richard reached for a jar of cookies and dug one out. "Damn. Your cookies *are* better than mine. I'm going to have to step up my game."

"You don't remember a ritual?"

"He could be like Sara. Attacked?" Sanders stared at me, cocking his head to the side. "Were you?"

"No, I don't think so." Puzzled, I turned to Richard. "Could you tell me what you're talking about, please?"

"There are three ways someone can become a Fenerec. First, you undergo a ritual performed by another Fenerec. If you survive, you become a Fenerec. Second, you're attacked by a Fenerec during a full blood moon. Sanders's mate, Sara, was changed into a Fenerec that way. It's extremely rare; we try to avoid performing rituals during a blood moon. The unexpected happens. Third, you're born that way. I was. Desmond was. Nicole was. Most become Fenerec through the ritual."

"Okay."

"So?"

"So what?"

"Which is it?"

I stared at Richard until the man chuckled and bit into another cookie.

"Obviously, Declan's response to someone asking a dumb question is the silent treatment."

"I don't remember any ritual, and I think I'd remember if a werewolf attacked me."

The other werewolves sighed in unison.

"Fenerec, please," Richard muttered. "Werewolf is such a derogatory term."

"We turn into wolves during a full moon. Werewolf seems pretty accurate to me."

"Was your father a Fenerec? Or your mother?"

I kept staring at Richard. "I told you my mother was a witch."

"I'm a wizard *and* a Fenerec," Nicole chirped, waving her hand. "I'm so badass I'm surprised they haven't microchipped me yet so they can keep track of me."

"You'd just fry the chips, beautiful," Richard replied, shaking his head and rolling his eyes.

Elliot chuckled. "My mate's a witch and a Fenerec. Terrible witch, amazing Fenerec. Well, she's an amazing witch when she's doing her one trick, otherwise, forget it. When I'm honest about it, she's not the greatest Fenerec either. She needs a push to shift way too often. Damn it. Who am I kidding? She's a mess."

I bet I'd fit right in with Elliot's mate, but instead of saying so, I turned to Nicole. "Wizard?"

"Don't ask that question yet, Declan," Amber advised. "It's complicated, it'll probably make you uncomfortable, and her demonstrations of her powers usually involve pain and suffering for someone."

"Okay. No, my mother didn't smell like a Fenerec. I've only scented a few others before I met you folks."

"Your father?"

"Never met him, but no. I don't think so." The questions dug up a lot of uncomfortable things about my past, but she had never mentioned my father having been a werewolf; she would have.

She had often muttered about wishing he had been. Things would have been easier—and he wouldn't have left. That was the only thing she had known for certain about werewolves. Males didn't leave their mates, not if they still lived.

"Damn," Desmond breathed. "A random True-born."

It was difficult to keep the frustration out of my voice. "I have no idea what that means."

Elliot cleared his throat. "True-borns are wolves born to a human mother. Reverse True-borns are humans born to wolf mothers. My mate is a Reverse True-born. Random True-borns are when neither of the parents are a Fenerec. The odds of a True-born birth are pretty low even when one or both parents are Fenerec. I'll look into the last time it happened when we're home. Hasn't happened during my time as the Shadow Pope, though. You would have been born during my predecessor's reign, and I have no recollection of a known instance happening during his, either. Actually, I can't think of a single instance of a Normal or witch couple having one since the invention of the ultrasound. Desmond?"

"I've met one, and that was before the United States was a country."

I felt my brows rise. "You look like you're in your mid-twenties or early thirties."

"So do you. And?"

"How old *are* you?" I blurted.

"Old enough, puppy."

Julie growled.

"Quiet, puppy," Desmond snapped.

The woman obeyed, but she bared her teeth, although she refused to meet Desmond's yellow-tinged eyes.

"Why don't you ladies head back to the other cabin for a while? Julie, you can stay if you sit on the couch and stay quiet."

"No," Patricia hissed. "Richard gets in trouble without adult supervision."

Everyone faced the woman from Richard's pack.

"What? It's true. If I leave, he'll get in trouble."

"She has a point," Dante said, shrugging.

Desmond sighed. "He has adult supervision."

"Who?" the woman replied, arching a brow. "Not you. You antagonize him because you think it's fun to have your daughter try to kill you. Dante and Elliot? They're instigators, too."

"Fine, you can stay. Rest of you, go get some sleep." Desmond pointed to the door and waited until the grumbling women filed out the front door. "Eat something, too, ladies!"

Sliding up to me, Amber leaned against the counter, holding her hand out to Richard.

The man gave her a cookie. "When was the first time you shifted into a wolf?"

When had been the first time I had shifted? My wolf didn't care for the passage of time like I did, but we had been young. Not yet an adult, not yet capable of protecting our mother.

My mother hadn't allowed us to transform for many years, I remembered that much. Every time my wolf had wanted to run free, she had scolded us. We had listened, because we had scented her fear.

How old had I been? The years had slid into one another, and I hadn't cared too much about them until my mother had died.

"Ten? Thirteen? Not really sure. Mother was pretty strict about shifting."

"What was the color of your puppy coat?" Amber asked, reaching over to steal a cookie out of Richard's hand.

"Sorry, what?"

"Your puppy coat color. Before you shed out to your adult coat."

A silent stare worked on Amber as well as it had on Richard.

"You've always been pink? You've always glowed?" Amber leaned towards me, narrowing her eyes as she looked me over. "You're a pretty man, Declan. I'm thinking I'm starting to regret declining your proposal."

Julie hissed like a cat, and I couldn't help but laugh at her antics. "What is it with you?"

"You're completely oblivious, aren't you?" Richard sighed. "Poor Julie."

"Oblivious?"

Amber snickered. "She wants to drag you to the nearest bedroom and have her way with you, Declan. She's rutting early. Use your nose."

I fell back on my silent stare and used it on Amber, so I wouldn't have to ask an embarrassing question.

"Surely you've had certain urges in the winter, Declan," Desmond said. "Right?"

"I purposefully avoid civilization for the entirety of winter. I go to my cabin. Oh, Dante. Cabin. You owe me a cabin."

"I already said I'd get you a line on one. Part of your fee. Richard would probably be glad to host you at his lodge this rut, though. We've got a few unmated bitches in our pack. Some Fenerec-born, too. How many is it, Richard? Ten or fifteen? How about you, Sanders?"

"Twelve," Richard supplied.

"Five in Seattle."

"Seventeen candidates. Eighteen if we count Julie."

"You better be counting me," the woman in question snarled.

I turned to Richard, my eyes wide. "I'm up for sale, aren't I?"

"Like a stallion. Welcome to life as a Fenerec. Until a lady successfully forms a mating bond with you, you're a prime piece of real estate. There are a lot more males than females, and females either want really submissive wolves or really dominant males for their mates. They'll fight to the death over an Alpha-traited male. Fortunately, many bitches will go for a one and done; if the bond doesn't stick right away, they'll turn their hunt elsewhere. Some, however, will hunt you until they're satisfied their failed first few attempts to bond weren't due to some fluke. Some hunt without making the formal attempt at mating for years. Right, Patricia?"

"The chase was almost as nice as our bonding. I want to be home *now* in case that wasn't obvious."

"We have to deal with the tail first," Richard replied, smiling at the woman. "I promised I'd get you home safe and sound to your mate."

"Should've brought him with you."

"His mother would kill me. You want me dead, don't you? Sophie would murder me if I took her precious baby boy to Europe. That didn't stop him from wanting to come, but I made him stay with Lisa and Alex to help protect the rest of the pack." Sighing, Richard picked up the cookie jar and set it on the coffee table. "Both of you ladies sit and eat cookies."

"He's not up for sale if I've already decided no other bitch will have him," Julie pointed out. "You should let me have him now, Mr. Desmond."

"Why are you bringing me into this? I'm not your Alpha yet."

"You will be."

"Accepting me as your Alpha so you can sink your teeth into him?"

"Yes."

I stared at Julie, wondering just what I had gotten myself into when I had quietly let her keep me pinned to the floor in Scallywag's castle. She was a pretty woman, and my wolf really liked her stubborn pride and aggression.

I had to admit my wolf was right; there was little sexier than a confident, headstrong woman.

Laughing, Richard slid towards me and nudged me with his elbow. "She's pretty and interested. Very interested."

Lane cleared his throat. "If you're not interested in her, Declan, I am."

There was something satisfying about hissing at the SEAL like a cat.

Chapter Twenty-Three

Exhaustion weighed me down, but with so many werewolves in close proximity, neither me nor my wolf could relax enough to sleep. To make matters worse, I was unwilling to leave Anthony and Lane even with Desmond and Richard on guard.

The presence of three male werewolves should have bothered me more. My wolf wasn't sure what to make of them, but they were so relaxed around each other I was able to lower my guard a little. I didn't even mind the presence of the Anderson twins, although something about Elliot made me tense.

I might've even enjoyed myself if it weren't for the fact Julie tracked my every movement, her posture tense and alert. The yellow gleam in her eyes unnerved me more than it did my wolf, although I was aware of his resentment.

We were not prey. In winter, we were the hunter, and we took care with prospective mates. I wanted a woman who could stand with me on equal footing, one who could withstand my wolf's aggression without fear, and one who challenged me on all levels.

During my days working for the government, it had been easy enough to suppress my wolf's desire for a mate. To mate, we needed a den. Neither one of us was willing to abandon our future mate or our puppies.

My life didn't allow for a mate nor puppies. I understood that, as did my wolf.

I had taken to retreating to a cabin in the winter for many reasons. The most important of them was something my wolf and I agreed on: our mate deserved better than frenzied lust, and so did I.

When we mated, it would be with the right woman, and I'd know her long before the winter moons rose. She would like me for who I was, not because of what I was. I would want her for more than being the same species during the mating season.

Resisting the urge to bare my teeth and warn the woman away with a snarl, I retreated to the kitchen. Unlike in the United States, eggs weren't refrigerated, and there were enough in the basket left for me to work with. If I couldn't sleep, I'd eat. Eating helped me control my growing unease at the attention of a woman who didn't know me and showed no interest in learning who I was under the surface.

After a check in the refrigerator and in the

cupboards, I decided I had enough leftover ingredients for another batch of cookies. If I couldn't sleep, I'd bake.

I grabbed the basket of eggs and went on a hunt for the measuring cups.

"Declan, what are you doing with those eggs?" Desmond joined me in the kitchen, perching on one of the stools.

"Using them."

"Why?"

Instead of answering, I measured ingredients and focused my attention on remaining silent. Maybe the witches and Fenerec knew what I was, but I hadn't gone undetected for so long growling my displeasure when things didn't go my way.

"He's annoyed," Anthony stated.

I cracked an egg a little too hard and had to fish out shells with a fork. Once again, I ignored Desmond's questioning stare and opted for silence.

"Enlighten me, please."

"I already told you."

It took every bit of my self-control to avoid smirking at my friend's reply. While I didn't like repeating myself, either, Anthony sometimes took his dislike of it a little too far. I kept an eye on him, where he was seated safely away from the Fenerec and witches on the other side of the kitchen with Lane.

If he offended someone, I was close enough to intervene.

"Declan?"

Anthony chuckled. "I wouldn't if I were you."

"What do you mean by that?"

"I mean I wouldn't push him right now if I were you. He's baking. If he's baking this time of day without a reason, he's annoyed. When he's annoyed enough he's fishing out shells from his eggs, it's really not a good idea to bother him."

"I'd like to know why."

"Why do you want to know?"

"There are a lot of us in an enclosed space. Let's keep the peace."

"Then tell that lady over there to stop treating him like a piece of meat. I told you, he doesn't like women, okay? He especially doesn't like pushy, entitled women who think they deserve to get their way because she's the opposite gender. If you want him to relax, get rid of the broad."

Julie rose to her feet, and every muscle in my body tensed. The growl slipped out before I could stop it, and my wolf's instinct to defend what was ours surged.

Desmond rose, too, and he stared at the woman, showing his teeth. "Sit."

One moment slipped into the next, and when the woman didn't obey, Desmond's posture changed. Sanders and Richard burst into motion. With a curse, Sanders smacked his arm into Julie's midriff and shoved her down.

Richard collided with Desmond halfway

across the sitting room. Despite his small size, Richard got a hold of his father-in-law and held his ground. The two men snarled and growled at each other without words.

"I think I'm going to rethink my approach on which pack gets Julie," Elliot announced, watching the scuffle from his perch on the arm of the couch beside his twin. "What do you think, Dante?"

"Why are you asking me? Amber?"

"Don't look at me. I'm not getting between those two."

Dante sighed. "Nicole?"

With a heavy sigh, Nicole shrugged and held her hands up. "Don't look at me. If you want me dealing with it, you tell your twin to give Declan to my pack. Let Dad deal with her as he sees fit. I get she's rutting early and she's under a lot of stress, but she's being a bit of a bitch, Dante. Look at him. He's not comfortable. She's acting like he's a piece of meat and it's time for her to have dinner. She's behaving like she owns him when she does not."

"Fucking slut," Julie snarled, struggling against Sanders's hold on her. "Who do you think you are?"

I felt my brows rise, and I turned, leaned against the counter, and stared at the woman I had helped rescue from Scallywag's castle in France. Rage and her wolf's influence had turned her eyes bright yellow, and her teeth were bared.

Nicole's expression smoothed to a neutral

mask, which worried me far more than Julie's open anger. The promise of violence hung between the two women with Sanders caught in the line of fire.

Without any guarantees the Fenerec wouldn't turn on Anthony or Lane, I slid my way across the kitchen until I stood beside the SEAL, watching Sanders struggle to keep Julie pinned to the couch.

I wasn't sure how Richard did it, but he forced Desmond back to the kitchen. "Let them sort it out."

Desmond growled but jerked his head in a nod.

"Sanders," Richard called, and I found it interesting the small man was confident enough to turn his attention away from his father-in-law for even a moment.

Releasing Julie, Sanders stepped out of the way. The instant he lost his hold on her, the woman lunged across the coffee table at Nicole.

"You can't buy this sort of entertainment," Lane commented, leaning back to rest his elbows on the counter. "What have you gotten us into, Declan?"

"Why does everyone blame me?" I sighed, hooked a stool with my foot, and dragged it over so I could sit.

I had no idea how Richard's short wife managed to floor a woman who was far larger than her and itching for a fight, but Julie fell with a thump. In the time it took me to suck in a surprised breath, Nicole was on top of her opponent. The crack of a slap cut over the sounds of the two women snarling at each other.

Maybe Julie was far larger than Nicole, but Nicole wanted to win far more and knew no boundaries. Anything within the woman's reach was a fair target. When slapping didn't subdue her opponent, Nicole clawed, punched, kneed, and bit without any mercy.

A slash of her nails down Julie's face secured Nicole's victory, followed by an application of teeth on the woman's throat. Nicole flexed her hands, growling until Julie went limp beneath her.

"Remind me never to say anything about fighting like a girl ever again," Lane whispered to me.

"You can go back to baking, Declan," Richard said, gesturing to where I had been measuring out ingredients. "Nicole can handle things from here."

"I'm also armed," Lane said, patting his holster.

While I had my doubts, I returned to my cookies, keeping an eye on the two women lying on the floor warily. Neither spoke in words, but when Nicole finally let Julie up from the floor, the pair headed for the door.

"Richard?"

I had forgotten about Patricia's presence, and I flinched at the sound of the woman's voice.

Richard shook his head. "Keep her from killing Julie, please. That said, don't interfere unless you must. It's better if Nicole puts Julie in her place. If Dad has to do it, it'll get ugly."

"You'll be okay?"

With a dismissive wave of his hand, Richard replied, "I'll be fine. Amber, keep an eye on Nicole, would you?"

Patricia and Amber grumbled but followed after the snarling Fenerec females. When they were gone, I sighed my relief.

THE COOKIES WERE SO terrible I refused to inflict them on anyone else. Unable to accept defeat, I choked them down and growled at anyone who tried to steal one from the tray.

"He fucked them up," Anthony declared after I had worked my way halfway through the batch.

"Shut up, Tony," I grumbled.

"He never allows anyone to eat his failures, and he refuses to waste ingredients."

I slumped over the counter, hung my head, and groaned. "Why are you doing this, Anthony?"

"I'm just helping them understand your special brand of psychosis, Declan."

"Why don't you explain the deal with Julie?" Desmond asked, relaxing on the couch.

"I already told you. He's not comfortable

around women. He doesn't like when they crowd him, and he appreciates his personal space. He values his privacy, and he doesn't enjoy when people get too close without his invitation." Anthony hopped off his stool, slid along the counter until he was within reach of the ruined cookies, looked me in the eyes, and took one. "I don't like that broad, either. She's too pushy."

"You're going to lose your taste buds if you eat that. It's that bad."

The way Anthony smiled warned me my friend had no intention of listening to me, which he confirmed several moments later by taking a chomp out of the cookie. "You should use these as weapons, Declan. Did I just break a tooth?"

While the programmer complained, the cookie disappeared with several loud crunches, and I twitched at every sound. "Yet you ate it anyway."

"I'll eat more unless you throw them out—or crush them and turn them into pie crust."

I blinked, stared at the cookie tray, eyeballed the remaining ingredients, and dumped the remaining cookies onto the cutting board so I could go to work crushing them. "Sugar or apple?"

"Apple." Anthony thumped my shoulder and headed for the couch. "Managing Declan is very simple, gentlemen. Respect his space, give him an outlet for his anxiety, and let him bake in peace. You'll want to keep that broad away from him, though, or we're going to have to find another market to get sufficient ingredients—and run the risk of adding a lot of extra pounds when he feeds us. I'd be particularly wary if the broad goes after someone he likes when he's armed. Declan doesn't like shooting people, but if someone threatens someone he likes, shots will be fired, and he prefers to maim rather than kill."

I grimaced at the reminder Anthony had seen me do just that not long after I had recruited him.

In reality, I didn't just fire for people I liked. I had no idea who the woman had been, but she hadn't done anything to deserve being attacked. I'd been working a dangerous enough heist I'd gone in armed. Her would-be rapist lost a kneecap and an elbow before I'd been done with him. Calling the cops to report the shooting—and save the man from bleeding to death on the street—had caused me a lot of trouble, although I had managed to drop off the radar.

To hide the evidence, I melted down a perfectly good gun and buried it deep in the woods.

"I'll keep that in mind. Listen up, pup. If she—or any other Fenerec—makes a run at Lane or Anthony, go for the kill and aim for between the eyes or for the temple. We have rules on how we interact with Normals. Our job is to protect them first and foremost. I'd rather not lose a bitch, but if you have to choose, you choose Lane and Anthony. She should know better than to even think about making a run at anyone."

I froze in mid preparations, staring at Desmond out of the corner of my eye. "I don't find that at all comforting."

"Good. That means you're smart. We'll do our best to straighten her out. For now, just stick with me, Richard, or Sanders; we're more than capable of keeping Julie under control. I'll make arrangements to help introduce you to the rut—and potential suitors—once we're back in the United States. Your terms." Desmond turned his attention to Elliot. "Right, Your Eminence?"

"He's your responsibility. You did a fine job with Sanders and Sara, so I trust you can handle any potential courtships with Declan. Dante, it might be ideal if you get him set up with a cabin in both the US and Canada. That'll let him go back and forth between Yellowknife and Seattle easily. I think there's a lot near Desmond's place up for sale. You arrange for the cabin, I'll deal with the land. Deal?"

"Consider it done."

"Two cabins are a bit excessive, don't you think? One's enough." I forced my attention back to baking, doubted the crushed cookies would make for edible crust, but at least a terrible pie went down a bit easier than rock-hard cookies.

"We'll discuss it when we return to the

United States," Elliot promised in a tone warning me there'd be no discussing it at all. "Our first order of business is to get situated and get out of here as soon as everyone's rested enough for the trip."

I handled it the same way I did whenever I got an order I didn't like. I sighed and replied, "Yes, sir."

Chapter Twenty-Four

IF WE HAD BEEN WISE, we would have left the cabins within minutes of bringing Richard, Sanders, and the ladies out from the hot zone. I would also never make the mistake of underestimating how persistent a group capable of tracking werewolves could be.

Gunfire echoed over the mountains, and the rumble underfoot warned me the noise had triggered an avalanche somewhere. Desmond, Richard, and Sanders bolted out the door, and they took weapons from the stash with them, leaving me with Anthony and Lane.

"Guard him," I ordered the SEAL, and with a slow, purposeful stride, I retrieved my sniper rifle, checked it over, and grabbed its ammunition box. On second thought, I grabbed a pair of binoculars, ones with night vision should I need them.

Unlike the others, I needed time to get into place with a good view and a few minutes to set up shop, but no one would be getting close to the cabins without my consent. With my weapon ready, I grabbed someone's jacket, slipped outside, circled the large cabin, and headed for the cliffs. Unless a rockfall had changed things, I'd find a goat track up the side to an outcropping, a spot offering unparalleled visibility over the cabins and all ways to them.

Unless someone came down the cliff from above, happened to be at just the right angle, and knew exactly where to stand, no one would spot me on my perch. I used the jacket to obscure my path, checked its pockets for anything of value, and when I found nothing, I slung it over my shoulder to serve as a blanket once I was in position.

It took me longer than I liked to work my way up the cliff, pressing as close to the rock as possible so I wouldn't ruin my day with a long and potentially fatal fall to the ground far below. The ledge offered enough room for me to stretch out, and I used the jacket to keep the worst of the ice and snow off me while I set up my sniper rifle.

It didn't take me long to get the gun into position, the scope set up, and begin my job of monitoring the cabins. I'd measured the distance as a hair over a thousand meters between my ledge and the yard, which would make for a long shot I couldn't afford to miss.

My wolf quieted in my head, and I recognized his behavior as him settling in for the hunt. *My* preference limited my targets to knees and elbows as often as possible. If I gave him his way, I'd make a head shot every time, something I'd regret later.

If anyone went after Anthony or Lane, I'd be forced to squeeze the trigger, and when I did, my victim wouldn't be getting back up again. A chill far more intense than the mountain air sank into my bones. Clenching my teeth, I checked my gun one more time and locked my attention on my cabin.

Ideally, my two friends would stay inside where it was safe, leaving the werewolves to prowl the grounds in search of the source of gunfire. I worried it came from the top of the mountain where the old couple lived far from prying eyes. A road weaved up the mountain directly to their home, something that set the cabins apart from everywhere else in the area.

Only those who were invited knew how to access the cliffside trail large enough for a single vehicle with little room to spare.

The werewolves, Amber, and the Anderson twins scattered, heading up the mountain. A quick head count reassured me all of them meant to go, leaving Lane behind to protect Anthony. I relaxed.

Then I tensed when one of the women veered off from the hunting pack, backtracked, and slinked behind a tree, waiting for the others to continue without her. My anxiety strengthened. I could only think of one woman who'd have any reason to return to the undefended cabins.

Julie.

I grabbed the binoculars and checked to confirm my suspicions. The woman scowled, peeking from behind the tree to confirm no one had noticed she'd fallen behind.

What was she after? Why?

My wolf had an idea on what she wanted: me. Unfortunately, to get me, she'd have to get around Anthony, who already disliked her for being so pushy. I knew myself well enough to understand what my wolf's base instinct was to do with a problem.

It'd end in bloodshed, be it hers, Lane's, or Anthony's. If things went south, all of them would be hurt or killed. It didn't take me long to come to the conclusion I didn't give a shit what happened to Julie.

I couldn't allow anything to happen to Lane, who'd been saddled with me because of my mistake, and Anthony, who had been by my side for so many years, tolerating me and my wolf better than anyone else. I set aside the binoculars and tracked Julie's movement with the scope of my sniper rifle.

She headed for the cabin, and the glint of metal at her hip warned me she was armed. Step by step, she drew closer to the two people I needed to protect. I hoped she'd return to Desmond's cabin and hide, but she angled towards mine without a single sign of hesitation.

Lane noticed her coming long before she reached the door, and he stood on the front step, his hand on his Beretta. Behind him, Anthony hovered.

Neither man looked happy to see her. I couldn't tell what they were saying, but Lane's expression darkened, and he shook his head. I guessed she was asking about me, probably hoping to pursue her plans to nip at my neck so she could attempt to mate.

My wolf growled in my head, and I aimed for her head. With less than ten feet between her and Lane, if she moved, I'd have only one good shot.

"Walk away," I begged in a whisper despite knowing she couldn't hear me.

I didn't want to hurt her.

She took a step forward, and her expression twisted. She said something, and her entire body tensed. Lane snapped something back, and he secured his grip on his gun.

They both moved at the same time, but I was faster. I locked my target, and with my wolf's insistent howls ringing in my head, I firmed my grip on the rifle and pulled the trigger. Like when I shifted, time slowed. Even as I squeezed, I made adjustments to my aim, the way I rested on the rock, and even how I glared through the scope at Julie's hair-covered temple.

If I had had a better chance to prepare, I would have used a suppressor on the rifle. The weapon discharged with a deafening bang. The muzzle flash and haze of heat stung my eyes along with the cold wind and hint of gunpowder.

It felt like an eternity before the bullet blasted free of the barrel towards its mark. The seconds stretched into one another, and one thought alone ran through my head: don't miss, don't miss, don't miss.

If I missed, I ran a high chance of hitting Lane or Anthony—or of Julie hurting one of them before I had a chance to get a second shot off.

The woman never reached either man, and she crumpled to the ground. I closed my eyes, so I wouldn't have to watch the rest.

A second gunshot rang out, close enough to leave me no doubt the SEAL confirmed my kill the safest way possible. My wolf fell into shocked silence.

After finally meeting an unmated female of our kind, to protect others, I had killed her.

SNOW FELL and covered me and my rifle, but I remained on my ledge, staring in a numb daze at the cabins far below. More gunfire echoed over the mountain. I should have moved. I should have done something other than stare without really seeing anything at all.

The sun set, and it wasn't until it rose that

the others returned. A quick check through my scope revealed one of the Anderson twins was limping although I couldn't tell which one and couldn't force myself to check for which one was taller.

Lane had left Julie's body where it had fallen, and while the snow blanketed her, there was no mistaking the shape of a corpse. The SEAL stepped out of the cabin with Anthony following behind them.

My wolf wanted me to slink down from my ledge and rejoin the pack below, convinced we had done nothing wrong by obeying Desmond's orders.

I had killed before, but not like I'd killed her. I had put my hand to my rifle understanding I would end her life if she went after Lane or Anthony. It hadn't been in the heat of battle.

Her death came with intent. I had had time to think it through.

I had still pulled the trigger.

The snow kept falling, and I ignored its chill, waiting for the other werewolves and their human friends to leave. When they did, shortly before sunset, they took Anthony and Lane with them.

While I hadn't trusted Julie, I believed Desmond would remain true to his word. The SEAL and my friend would be safe enough with him. I waited for the lights of both SUVs to fade away and darkness to smother the land before I rose from my spot, gathered my sniper rifle, and shifted.

With my fur illuminating my path, I picked my way down from the ledge.

I found where they had buried Julie's body behind the cabins, and as hers was a shallow grave, I took the time to gather rocks, building a cairn so she wouldn't be disturbed. The scent of the other werewolves lingered, but instead of the grief I expected, the bite of anger stung my nose. Anger at who?

Julie for going after Lane and Anthony, or me for defending them as was my duty? I doubted I'd ever know.

It'd be better for everyone if I disappeared without a trace. Deep in the Swiss Alps, I could remain as a wolf without anyone being the wiser for my presence. I could head north and east. With so much land in Poland or Russia, and so few people, I could disappear. Siberia might work, too.

My wolf didn't argue with me, and I headed higher up the mountain. I feared the worst; Bodwin and his wife would fight back against anyone who encroached on their territory. Those who had followed Richard had worried him enough, even with the help of another Alpha and the females. If so many couldn't fight off the tail, what could two hope to accomplish?

I smelled their blood long before I reached their cabin home on the peak. With it, the too sweet stench of death hung in the air and choked off my breath. Bullet holes riddled the wood, and someone had broken out all the glass in their windows.

Tossing back my head, I howled, and my grief bled into the sound—for Julie, for Bodwin, and for the bent old woman who'd wanted my pies and cookies even more than her cantankerous husband had. After they'd shot me, they had welcomed me into their home, and I'd cooked for them. Their prickly friendship had been exactly what I needed.

They hadn't let me get too close, which made leaving again easier.

Their words had implied rejection, but their outstretched hands had welcomed me—and taken every last one of my bribes to allow me close to them.

The front door hung off one hinge, and I pushed my way through. Every step deeper inside their home, the scent of their blood intensified. I checked the entire cabin, but while I found where they'd been killed, their bodies were gone.

Red-brown paw prints marked where one—or both—of their dogs had returned and searched for the old couple. I followed the trail.

I found the first dog in the back yard, dead for long enough I suspected he'd been killed with his owners.

The second wasn't a dog at all, but a wolf, and with a start, I realized the blood spread through the cabin belonged to her, where a bullet had torn through her shoulder. The disturbed snow revealed where someone had dug a grave, and after a closer look, I realized someone had taken the time to build a cairn over their bodies.

The wolf protected them, and her growls deepened to tooth-bared snarls when I drew too close.

I should have known Bodwin would've done something like keep a wolf as a pet and call her a dog. If I left her out in the cold and injured, she'd die.

I shifted, and my transformation startled a yip from the animal, and she cowered, tucking her tail and struggling to rise so she could escape me.

How had triumph turned to tragedy so fast?

"I'm so sorry," I whispered.

If I had been smarter, if I hadn't trusted in the seclusion of Bodwin's mountain, him and his wife would still be alive. Julie would still be alive, too, because we would have gone our different ways, and I would've escaped from her with Lane and Anthony.

The wolf cringed and kept snarling at me, and I didn't blame her in the slightest. I was grateful I'd kept the jacket; it'd make a good bandage for the wolf's shoulder until I could figure out a better way to care for her—if she let me get close enough to help her.

It took me several hours to get near her, and I only succeeded in the end because she grew too weak to fight me. I inspected her shoulder to discover a bullet still lodged in her shoulder. She stared at me with dull eyes while I poked and prodded the injury. In the end, I had to return to Bodwin's cabin to retrieve a knife and bandages, so I could cut the round out and wrap the injury.

While it took a little work, I tied the jacket around her to help keep her warm until she healed enough to hunt on her own. I carried her closer to Bodwin's cabin, and with a heavy heart, I raided it for supplies, several prepaid credit cards, and everything I'd need to make a run for it with an injured wolf. I located enough meat in their refrigerator and freezer to feed their animals for several weeks and delayed long enough to feed her. While suspicious, she accepted my offerings.

Caring for an injured wolf would complicate my plans, but I'd make do. There was plenty of room for two far to the north. If I couldn't return her to the wilds, I'd care for her myself.

That was the least I could do after my failure.

I found ten bodies on the way down Bodwin's mountain, Americans if I judged from their gear and choice of weapons, probable mercenaries but possible military; I'd seen their functional, durable setup before. All of them had been mauled by wolves, even the ones who'd been shot. I left their bodies to rot and cursed them for having caused so much trouble and misery.

WITH AN INJURED WOLF TO FEED, it took far longer than I liked to work my way north and east through the Swiss Alps and crossed the border into Austria. I located a used car dealership and even felt a little guilty for stealing one of the oldest trucks I could find off the lot, an antique I could hot-wire without too much difficulty.

I had the US military to thank for that skill. At least I'd emerged with one victory: Haney hadn't kept me long. Desmond and the other werewolves had let me go, and maybe when the guilt no longer bit so deep or hurt so much, I'd give Bob—no, Dante—a call.

At the very least, I'd apologize and make sure Anthony and Lane were safe.

I packed the wolf into the truck's cab, hid my sniper rifle under the seat, and drove until I approached the Slovakia border. Waiting until deep at night, I ditched the vehicle in a used car lot and carried the wolf across the border through a section of forest far enough north of Bratislava to avoid detection. In Slovakia, I repeated my tactic until I reached where its borders bumped against Poland and Ukraine.

Upon my arrival, I shifted, and I herded Bodwin's wolf along with me, matching my pace to her limp. My wolf disapproved, but I ignored his wishes. Slow or not, I wouldn't abandon her. As though she understood why she was stuck with me, her scent seemed marred with grief, and beneath the musk marking her as a lesser cousin, I detected a faint hint of spice, something neither my wolf nor I could make sense of.

Later, I would have time to think about it.

But first, I would go north and east to the end of civilization and to the rugged fringes of Russia, where I would carve a place for myself and Bodwin's wolf, a place I could call home, where I might one day find peace.

To be continued in Wild Wolf.

www.ingramcontent.com/pod-product-compliance
Lightning Source LLC
LaVergne TN
LVHW041814070325
805396LV00002B/229
9781649641021